THE
FIRST
CASUALTY

THE
FIRST
CASUALTY

By William Powell

LYLE STUART INC.
Secaucus, N.J.

First edition

Copyright © 1979 by William Powell
All rights reserved. No part of this book may
be reproduced in any form except by a newspaper
or magazine reviewer who wants to quote brief
passages in connection with a review.

Queries regarding rights and permissions
should be addressed to Lyle Stuart Inc.
120 Enterprise Ave., Secaucus, N.J. 07094

Published by Lyle Stuart Inc. Published simultaneously
in Canada by George J. McLeod Limited
Don Mills, Ontario

Manufactured in the United States of America

Library of Congress Cataloging in Publication Data

Powell, William, 1949-
   The first casualty.

   1. Franz Ferdinand, Archduke of Austria, 1763-1914—
Fiction.   I. Title.
PZ4.P8868Fi   [PS3566.0835]   813'.5'4   79-17454
ISBN 0-8184-0291-1

Contents

THE
FIRST
CASUALTY

Prologue

It was June 28, 1914.

It was hot.

Dr. Rudloph Cistler perspired. He had a secret theory that old people perspired more than the young. He was old—the oldest practicing lawyer in Sarajevo.

He was also the poorest. The office in which he sat chronicled the decline of his career. The paint peeled and the plaster crumbled. Cracked window panes had not been replaced. The desk at which he sat was old and rickety.

Life had not been kind to Dr. Rudolph Cistler, but then he had never expected it to be. Life was rarely kind to a southern Slav.

The old man rose from the desk and joined his daughter at the window overlooking the quay. The sides of the wide cobblestone avenue were already crowded with Muslims and Magyars. Across the river he could see the skyline of the souk, a pincushion of painted minarets. Cistler pursed his lips. Uniformed officers attempted to keep the crowds out of the road.

"Everyone's out to see the Crown Prince," Stega murmured. "I suppose he'll be pleased."

Cistler heard the bitterness in his daughter's voice and shared it. The old man shook his head angrily.

"An insult. An insult to every Slav. Why did he pick today? Of all days to make a state visit, why Vidovdan?"

"Perhaps he didn't know what Vidovdan was?" Stega replied.

"There are a lot of hot-headed young men who do."

"Papa . . ."

"Look at that crowd! Not a Slav face in it. All Muslims and Magyars. Landowners. They can afford to wave those little Austrian flags!"

"Papa, you mustn't get upset."

"I'm too old to be upset by obscenities!" Cistler brushed his flowing gray hair out of his eyes. "Vidovdan. A memorial to five centuries of Turkish occupation. A day on which Slav passions boil. And Crown Prince Ferdinand comes to pay us a visit. To remind us of a more recent occupation."

"You mustn't get excited. You know what the doctor—"

"Damn the doctor! Damn Crown Prince Ferdinand!" Cistler turned away from the window. The sight of the crowds milling around on Appel Quay angered him. But Stega was right. He mustn't allow himself to get upset.

He leaned on the corner of his desk.

"If I were a younger man . . ."

"Papa," Stega said sternly.

"I can say what I like. A senile old man like myself has liberties not granted to the young. I would be honored if anyone took me seriously enough to have me arrested."

"You're speaking like a fool."

"Perhaps in this crazy world only fools speak the truth."

Cistler turned his back to the window and walked to the far side of his desk. Once again the temptation was there. It wasn't strong, but it was there. Stega was right. The doctor had been right. He must not allow himself to become upset. He took a deep breath and tried to forget the hunger deep within him.

It had been over a year since Cistler had had a drink. He

had almost dried out completely. His hands no longer trembled. But now and then, when he was upset, the cravings came. They were not nearly as strong as they used to be. He could handle them now. He would never, he resolved, go through the sickness again.

"I can see the motorcars," Stega called from the window.

Cistler reached for his pipe. Stega was more than just a daughter. Without her, he would never have made it through the sickness. She was like her mother. Strong. She should have been married by now. But Cistler knew why his daughter wasn't married. She had shared his disgrace.

"That must be his car," Stega said. "There's a woman beside him. He must have brought his wife."

Cistler filled his pipe and lit it. If only there was a way to lift the cloud of shame. A way to prove himself. Not only to the other lawyers, but to Stega and, perhaps most importantly, to himself. He was competent now. He had the experience. All he needed was one case. One case to prove himself to himself.

He puffed on his pipe and sent a cloud of blue tobacco smoke swirling toward the ceiling.

Old Dr. Cistler was not prepared to have his prayers answered as suddenly and violently as they were.

An explosion roared in the street below. Stega's eyes grew wide. She gasped. "Oh my God!"

Cistler ran to the window.

PART ONE

The Union or Death

The man who kills a tyrant pleases God.

—BALKAN PROVERB

No government can have a right to obedience from a people who have not freely consented to it.

—JOHN LOCKE

CHAPTER ONE

The Training of a Terrorist

During the spring of 1913, there was very little rain on the Balkans. But no one seemed to mind, not even the farmers. Everyone was preoccupied with the war—the war that would drive the Turks out of Europe forever.

There was one man, however, who made it his business to think beyond the immediate conflict. He had no doubt that the Slavs would be victorious. He was concerned about what would happen after the victory. His name was Colonel Dragutin Dimitrievitch, better known by the men he commanded as Apis, the fly.

Even though he had passed fifty, Colonel Apis was lean and muscular. His features were aquiline. His faintly hooked nose and thin scultpured lips gave the impression of cruelty. The glare in his sharp eyes produced unquestioned obedience.

On the morning of June 2, 1913, Colonel Apis sat in his Belgrade office reading the morning newspaper. A white-

and-brown mongrel lay panting before his desk. The morning paper contained the details of the Treaty of London, signed only days before. Colonel Apis did not share the public jubilation over Turkey's expulsion from Europe. He had expected it. In fact, he would have settled for nothing less.

Colonel Apis was the most powerful and feared man in the Balkans. His nickname was already almost legendary among the military. A great many of the stories that surrounded Apis were either false or exaggerated. There was nothing false, however, in the story that he had cut King Alexander's throat ten years before. And there was nothing exaggerated about the reports that he had personally supervised the dismemberment of Queen Draga.

After Austria had annexed Bosnia into the empire in 1908, Colonel Apis had formed a clandestine paramilitary organization dedicated to liberating Bosnia and uniting all the Southern Slavs. He had developed within the Serbian army a secret network of highly skilled and fanatically dedicated commandos, *komitadji*, as they called themselves. Apis used the war against the Turks as a training ground for *komitadji*. They learned quickly. They stockpiled weapons and explosives. The network grew larger and stronger.

The organization of *komitadji* was called The Union or Death.

Apis whistled softly and the white-and-brown mongrel trotted to his side. He was preoccupied. Unconsciously his left hand patted the dog's head. A week before, he had been promoted to chief of Serbian military intelligence. That pleased him. It was an ideal position for the leader of The Union or Death to be in. It also indicated that the politicians were beginning to appreciate how strong the Union really was.

Two of the candidates had sought his support for the upcoming election. But elections were for public consumption. This one had already been decided. Pastich would be the next prime minister. Apis had thrown his support behind

Pastich only after he had received his promotion. Such were the ways and means of real power.

A knock came at his office door.

"*Napred!*"

Obediently his staff sergeant opened the door and ushered in a frail young man who promptly attempted a clumsy salute.

"You're not a solider," Apis barked. "Stop pretending to be." Apis folded the newspaper and casually tossed it to one side of his desk. The white-and-brown mongrel growled at the slender young man.

"I would like to be a soldier, sir."

"Then you're in the wrong office. There's a recruiting station by the Sava, in Kalemegdan Park. I suggest you go there."

"I've been there, sir."

"And?"

"I was rejected on medical grounds."

"And you want me to overrule the doctors?"

"No, sir. I want to be a *komitadji.*"

Apis registered the word calmly. The young man's face was sharp and possibly intelligent. "How old are you?"

"Nineteen, sir."

"And you want to be a *komitadji?*" Apis lit a cigarette and leaned back in his chair. The sun from the open window caught his gold-capped teeth and flashed at the young man.

Apis watched the young man closely.

"Why do you want to be a *komitadji?*"

"It is the duty of every true Slav to drive foreign invaders from our soil."

The young man did not avoid Apis's cold stare. There might be strength in that, Apis thought. He wondered how the young man would respond under pressure.

"Are you nervous?"

"No, sir."

"You bite your fingernails." Apis pointed to the young man's left hand.

"A bad habit, sir."

"A sign of weakness in a man!" Apis snapped.

The young man showed no emotion.

"Have you ever ignored a Slav in trouble?"

"I don't understand, sir."

"Have you ever watched an Austrian policeman arresting a Slav peasant and failed to do anything about it?"

"Yes, sir." There was a slight hesitation in the young man's reply.

"Did you think you were helpless to prevent it?"

"Yes, sir."

"Is that an appropriate attitude for a *komitadji*?"

"No sir. But *komitadji* are armed. I was not."

"Had you been armed you would have done something?"

"I'm not sure, sir."

"Not sure?"

"It would depend upon . . ."

"Have you ever been frightened of the Austrians?" The young man hesitated again. Apis repeated his question.

"Yes, sir. When I was young, my village refused to pay its taxes. The harvest had been bad. Austrian soldiers came."

"And you were frightened?"

"Yes, sir."

"Is fear acceptable in a *komitadji*?"

"Without fear there can be no courage—only madness."

"A good answer," Apis replied. The young man took pressure fairly well. There was strength in him. "You have been recommended?"

"Captain Ciganovitch said that you would have my file, sir."

Apis looked down at his cluttered desk.

"Your name?"

"Gavrilo Princip, sir."

Apis picked up a folder from the desk and scanned the contents. "Consumptive?"

"It will not interfere with my work, sir."

"Ciganovitch has given you an excellent recommendation. He is usually fairly critical of new recruits. He says you have courage. But courage without skill is like a bomb without a fuse. Useless." Apis turned back to the folder. Finally he looked up. "How much do you want to be a *komitadji?*"

"More than anything else, sir."

"More than your own life?"

"It is my duty to serve my people. If that duty requires my life, I will give it."

"Have you ever seen a dead body, Princip?"

"Yes, sir, my sister in Grahovo."

"Does the idea of pain frighten you?"

"Yes, sir."

Apis nodded thoughtfully. He was not displeased with the young man's answers. There was none of the weakness of bravado. There was a honesty that suggested real strength.

"Have you ever killed a man?"

"No, sir."

"You would do so if ordered?"

"Yes, sir."

"You may just have that chance." Apis grimaced at his private joke. "Naturally you will say nothing to anyone about this meeting. We will be in touch with you. Goodbye, Gavrilo Princip."

§   §   §

Three days after Gavrilo Princip had met with Apis, the Union did get in touch with him.

Gavrilo had just returned from work at the state printing office. He entered the small attic room he had rented and began to prepare his supper—a thin turnip gruel laced with goat meat.

A knock came at the door. Without waiting for Gavrilo to answer, three men entered. Gavrilo did not know them.

"Princip?" the tallest of the three demanded. Gavrilo nodded. "You're to come with us."

"Who are you?"

"Friends of the Slav people." It was the standard reply of a *komitadji*. "Apis wants you." Gavrilo nodded.

"Turn around," the second man ordered. Gavrilo did as he was told. A blindfold was placed over his eyes and tied at the back of his neck. "Can you see?"

Gavrilo shook his head.

The three men did not speak as they led him down the rickety staircase. They paused at the foot of the stairs.

"We're going to pick you up and put you in the back of a wagon. Remain silent."

Gavrilo felt one of the men grab his legs and another seize his armpits. He was lifted from the ground. Gavrilo felt the cool of the evening air against his face, and then felt himself being lowered into the back of a wagon. A burlap sack was thrown over him.

"Remain absolutely still," ordered the first man after jumping into the back of the wagon. The wagon started over the cobblestones. It was bumpy but not painful. Gavrilo knew it would have been useless to protest the blindfold. The union had its methods, and these men had their orders.

Gavrilo had heard rumors about what happened to *komitadji* who failed to follow orders.

A bullet in the kneecap was usual.

Gavrilo could not be sure where or how long they traveled. It felt like something over an hour, but it might have been less. His body was stiff from the ride and his muscles were cramped from remaining so still.

When the wagon stopped the burlap sack was pulled off him, and he was carried from the back of the wagon. Finally he was placed upon the ground. It was soft, moist with dew. He wondered if they had taken him out of the city.

One of the men helped him to his feet and then led him forward over a door step and into a house. The blindfold was removed and Gavrilo could see that he was standing in a sparsely furnished room on the ground floor. There was a bare wooden table in the center of the room with two chairs. An oil lamp flickered in the corner.

"Sit," the tallest of the three men instructed him. The other two men disappeared through a low archway. Gavrilo sat at the table.

Within a few moments a fourth man appeared in the doorway. He exchanged glances with the tall man. There was something in the exchange that was more than just a greeting. It worried Gavrilo.

"Won't be long now."

"Guilty?" the tall man asked.

The other man nodded. He appeared tired and impatient. "If Apis wasn't such a stickler for details the tribunal would have been over an hour ago. There wasn't any question about the evidence."

"Much damage?"

"Two good men will have to disappear for a while." The fourth man shrugged and reached inside his military jacket for a cigarette. He placed the cigarette between his lips and looked down at Gavrilo.

"You're the one who wants to be a *komitadji?*"

Gavrilo nodded.

"You'll have your chance tonight."

Gavrilo remained silent. He didn't understand. What chance would he have? What was this tribunal that they were talking about? Why would two good men have to disappear? Where did he come into all this business?

One of the men who had come to Gavrilo's attic room stepped into the archway.

"They're ready."

The tall man gestured for Gavrilo to stand up and follow him. They walked down a short hallway and came to a flight of steps that led down to a brightly lit cellar.

"If you want my advice," the tall man whispered. "You'll keep your mouth shut and do exactly as you're told."

The cellar was large. The center of the room was occupied with a large table. Around the table sat six men.

Gavrilo recognized two of them. At the head of the table sat Apis. The lean colonel stared grimly off into space. To the right of Apis, sat Captain Milan Ciganovitch, officer in charge of student recruiting in Belgrade. Ciganovitch smiled at Gavrilo.

The tall man led Gavrilo to a chair by the left wall. Against the right wall was a man tied to a chair. There was a cloth sack tied over his head. Gavrilo guessed that a trial of some sort had taken place.

"Let's get this over and done with," said a bearded man sitting halfway down the table.

"Any other business, before I pass sentence?" Apis asked. The table was silent. Apis rose to his feet. His thin lips were drawn tight against his teeth. Apis turned to face the prisoner.

"Zoni Simic, you have been found guilty by this court of passing information about the union to the Pastich government." All eyes were upon Apis. Gavrilo was frightened. He suddenly understood why he was there.

"When you took your oath as a *komitadji*," Apis continued, "you understood what the penalty would be if you ever broke the *gluvonem*. You have broken your oath of silence. In the name of almighty God, this court sentences you to death. The sentence will be carried out immediately. May God have mercy upon your soul."

Captain Milan Ciganovitch rose to his feet and turned his scarred face to where Gavrilo sat. He drew his service revolver from his hip holster and held it out to Gavrilo.

"You know how to use it?" Ciganovitch asked.

Gavrilo's palms were moist. He recognized that he was being tested. All eyes at the table were upon him, inspecting his every reaction. There must be no hesitation. He must not appear weak. His heart pounded and his pulse raced.

"It's single action," Ciganovitch continued. "Stand no more than three feet in front of the prisoner. Cock the hammer. Aim for the middle of the face and squeeze the trigger."

Gavrilo looked down at the service revolver and then back up into the face of Ciganovitch. Ciganovitch's eyes told him not to hesitate. Be quick, they told him. Show no weakness.

From the corner of his eyes, Gavrilo saw the bearded man at the table slip his right hand to his own revolver. It was then that Gavrilo understood what failure would mean. Perspiration formed on his upper lip.

Apis was expressionless as he watched the young man walk toward the prisoner. The lean colonel had executed many men himself. The sight produced no emotion for him.

Gavrilo positioned himself three feet in front of the man. The prisoner seemed to sense Gavrilo's closeness. He struggled. Muffled sounds came from within the cloth sack tied over his head.

Gavrilo leveled the revolver at the center of the cloth sack. He bit his lip. *Dear God,* he prayed, *author of all justice, grant that what I am about to do may be according to your eternal will.*

He cocked the hammer and squeezed the trigger. The revolver exploded. The prisoner jerked like a puppet whose strings had been pulled too suddenly. The prisoner's head fell forward and rested on his shoulder.

Gavrilo fainted.

The next thing Gavrilo was aware of was Ciganovitch holding a damp towel against his forehead.

"Neko and I had a bet. I said you'd be sick. Neko said you'd faint."

Gavrilo looked over to the table. There was only one man left sitting there. The others had left. It was the bearded *komitadji* who had kept his hand on his revolver during the execution. The bearded man smiled.

"First time you've killed a man?"

Gavrilo nodded.

"Enjoy it?" the bearded man asked.

"Not very much."

"That's good. There's only one thing more dangerous

than a coward, and that's a *komitadji* who enjoys killing."
The bearded man rose from the table and crossed to where
Gavrilo lay. "My name's Neko Tankosic. Major Tankosic.
I'm in charge of training new *komitadji*. We'll be seeing
quite a bit of each other."

§   §   §

In the months that followed Gavrilo did see a great deal
of Major Tankosic, and the more the young man saw of the
major the more impressed he became.

Tankosic had learned to be a *komitadji* in the Serbian
army. He was a professional, highly skilled and extremely
tough with the young men he trained.

On August 19, 1913, Gavrilo was ordered to report to a
small village seven miles south of Skoplje. When Gavrilo
arrived at the deserted farmhouse, he was met by Tankosic
and fourteen other young men. His training had started in
earnest.

"Even if you forget everything I have told you, you must
remember two things," Tankosic bellowed at the young men
seated at the table. "Speed and secrecy. When you attack,
you do it like lightning. When you retreat, you do it like
lightning. Everything you do must be done with speed.
The Austrians are stronger than us. They have greater numbers, more arms, better communications. But we have speed.
Before they even realize that they have been attacked, you
will have disappeared. Quickness must become second
nature to you. You will eat quickly, sleep quickly, even take
a shit quickly."

Several young men chuckled. Tankosic stared angrily at
them.

"You think I'm joking? There is nothing easier than killing
a man squatting over a latrine. Don't forget that." Tankosic
paused and stared at the fifteen young men. All the smiles
had disappeared. On the whole he was pleased with them.
In the five short weeks he had had them, they had become
familiar with weapons handling, learned a healthy respect

for various explosives, and most importantly they had learned discipline.

"Gabrez," Major Tankosic bellowed. "What's the most valuable weapon a *komitadji* has?"

"His rifle," Trifun Gabrez replied tentatively. Gabrez had great physical strength but little mental ability.

"Speed and surprise, Gabrez. Speed and surprise. There are times when you will not have a rifle. There are times when you will have only a knife or a stick. There are times when you will only have your bare hands. But Gabrez, you will always have speed. You will always have the element of surprise. They are valuable weapons."

"Cabrinovitch," Tankosic barked, "You are alone and unarmed. You have been ordered to kill the chief of police in a certain town. You recognize that silence is essential. How do you go about it?"

Nedelijko Cabrinovitch, the youngest of the men at the table, snapped his reply: "Set his house on fire, sir."

"Without observing his movements? You will probably end up roasting his wife and children. Think before you act. Your most valuable tool is your brain. Use it!"

§ § §

Gavrilo stood on the edge of a small stream. Through the woods he could hear the others. Even though it was only a practice, Gavrilo's stomach was on fire with adrenaline.

His orders were simple. He was to return to the house and kill Tankosic. The other recruits were out looking for him. He listened again to the sounds of the forest. They were a little closer.

Tankosic's words came to him: *Do the unexpected! Do it suddenly!*

He turned and headed toward the sounds. Three hundred meters later, he had Trifun Gabrez in sight. He crept closer to the young man who was hunting him. He had changed the nature of the game. He would hunt those who hunted him.

He waited for Gabrez to come closer. It would be no use to struggle with the larger man. It would have to be a clean, silent kill. Gabrez was now within striking distance. Still Gavrilo waited.

Gavrilo inched around the tree that separated him from his target. He watched Gabrez wipe the perspiration from his forehead. Gavrilo sprang.

Gabrez felt his hair grabbed and his head jerked back. There was the prick of a razor-sharp knife between his collar bone and shoulder blade.

"I have just severed your subclavian artery. You will lose consciousness within seconds. Death will follow rapidly."

Gavrilo withdrew the commando knife. Trifun smiled a little sheepishly and shrugged.

Rapidly Gavrilo searched Trifun Gabrez, removed his jacket, his rifle, and his belt. Just as rapidly he disappeared back into the woods. He now made his way back to the farmhouse. He had completed the first phase of his orders. He had secured a firearm.

Again Tankosic's words came to him: *Know your terrain! Never stand and fight in an unfavorable position!*

He knew the house would be guarded, but he was not sure how many of the recruits had remained behind. He decided to approach the house from the rear.

In the rear of the farmhouse were two sheds originally designed to hold farm animals. Gavrilo had already decided upon a tentative plan. He would do the unexpected. "Never let the enemy rest," Tankosic had said.

Gavrilo slipped from the edge of the woods to the rear of the first shed. He could see Nedelijko Cabrinovitch leaning against the outside of the farmhouse. To the left of Nedelijko was a window through which he could see the outline of Major Tankosic sitting at his desk.

Gavrilo slid toward the shed door. He watched Nedelijko carefully. Silently he inched the wooden door open and squeezed inside. The interior of the shed was cluttered with rusted farm equipment. He waited for his eyes to adjust to the darkness.

In the corner of the shed was what he sought. Two large cans of kerosene. He made for them quickly, soaking Trifun's jacket and cloth belt. He carried the dripping jacket and belt back to the door. He now had an incendiary bomb and fuse.

Just as he reached the door of the shed he heard a movement behind him.

"Halt," Tankosic's voice whispered. The major appeared from behind a pile of broken farm equipment. He held a machine pistol in his hand. "You were doing very well until you decided to use the kerosene. That was expected."

"But I saw you through the window. . . ."

"That was Ilic wearing my jacket. Why were you in such a hurry? Why didn't you wait for the cover of darkness? Who did you take the rifle from?"

"Trifun."

Tankosic nodded. He was not displeased with Princip. If it had been a real operation, the chances were good that Princip would have succeeded.

§   §   §

The training had continued for another two weeks. Tankosic had them up before dawn. He ran them ten kilometers before breakfast. He taught them map reading and simple coding. He taught them how to make a landmine out of an ordinary grenade. He taught them escape and evasion, how to kill silently, how to withstand pain, how to sabotage train tracks, how to recognize the moment to attack and how to recognize the moment to retreat. But foremost he taught them discipline.

As the weeks passed, Gavrilo grew friendly with Nedelijko Cabrinovitch and Trifun Gabrez. All three were Bosnian, and all three shared the common goal of liberating their homeland from the Austrian invaders.

Gavrilo had learned his hatred early. It had grown within him almost as if it was part of his body. It had become a reflex, something he did not question or think about, something conditioned like blinking when dust settled near his eyes.

It was easy for a Slav to learn hatred in Bosnia. Slavs were not second-class citizens; they were nonpeople. For the most part they were ignored. They performed menial labor in the towns and cities, and in the country they tended the land owned by the Muslims and Magyars. Usually they were born in wattle huts and lived in those same huts until they died.

Gavrilo had been born and brought up in Grahovo, a particularly poor mountain village just south of Travnik. His father was a tenant farmer and, like most Slav men of the village, worked Magyar land. But unlike many Slav men, Kari Princip did not hide his fury.

Gavrilo remembered back to that morning in the winter when his father had left the wattle cottage. Gavrilo had followed. They passed the Magyar houses. Neither father nor son turned toward them. He remembered that the sun had not quite risen above the snow-capped mountains. A goat bleated, and then the chapel bell tolled.

It was a lonely and frightening sound to the young boy, who ran to keep up with the large strides of his father.

Behind him, his mother and aunt walked, black-veiled and silent. The Magyar houses looked cold and sinister to the young boy, like hungry predators poised on their haunches.

Gavrilo remembered the cold wind; the way it curled about the mountains before it struck down upon his village. He looked up into his father's face. The old gnarled face looked straight ahead. Gavrilo had seen his father's fury earlier that morning. Not even his mother had been able to calm him.

The Slav neighbors left their houses and walked behind his mother. The women began to moan. The sound of their mourning stuck in the boy's mind. Why had the doctor failed to come? Because he was a Magyar.

Even when they took his sister to the doctor, he had refused to see them. Why? Because the doctor was a Magyar and they were Slavs.

Even after his father had sold their pig and borrowed money, the doctor had refused to see them. Why? Because Slav life was cheap.

And his sister had died. Whether the doctor could have saved her, no one knew. All Gavrilo knew was that the doctor hadn't tried.

The old Orthodox priest stood in front of the whitewashed chapel. He laid his old hand on Gavrilo's father's shoulder. "Now is not the time for anger," the old priest whispered.

His father glared back at the priest. "It was not your daughter the Magyars murdered."

The old priest led the mourners around the chapel to a small overgrown burying ground. The wind had frozen the tall grass that grew by the side of the graves so that it crunched underfoot.

He stood at the graveside and watched his father and the other men carry the coffin from the chapel. Father Petrovitch began to recite the prayer for the dead, but his voice was muffled by the wind. Again Gavrilo remembered looking into the face of his father. Beneath the coarse beard, his father's lips were drawn white against his yellow teeth.

The coffin was lowered into the ground. The mourners, who had stood silently during the priest's prayer, now moaned loudly. Beneath the sound of their wailing, Gavrilo heard the bump as the coffin came to a rest against the rocky, frost-encrusted earth.

"Learn from what you see, Gavrilo. Watch them bury another Slav." His father's voice quivered with emotion. "Never forget how easy it is to bury a Slav. Learn that."

§ § §

Two years after the funeral of his sister, Gavrilo learned another lesson.

It had been February, but that was by the old calendar. He remembered that winter had come to the village sooner than expected. The first snow had fallen in October and had destroyed most of the harvest.

February was always a hard month for the villages in the mountains. It was when the grain from the previous autumn either ran out or became too rotten to eat. Only the Magyars knew the taste of red meat during February. But there was Lent, and Lent was a good thing. It was much easier to fast for God than it was to go hungry because there was no food.

That February had been a particularly difficult one. The chickens had been eaten to the point where his mother dared not behead another. The eggs were needed.

It was after two hours of Latin grammar that Gavrilo had first realized that something was very wrong.

A Slav neighbor had interrupted the lesson. He had spoken with Father Petrovitch in private. When the old priest returned to the table at which Gavrilo worked, he had appeared puzzled. And then, for no apparent reason, the old priest had slammed his fist against the table. Gavrilo was startled. He had never seen the old priest lose his temper.

Father Petrovitch had sent Gavrilo home.

"Your mother will need you now."

Although his mother had stopped crying by the time Gavrilo had arrived home, the stains from her tears were visible on her wrinkled cheeks. He had rushed to his mother's side. After a few moments, she had told him to sit down.

She told him that the Austrian tax collector had come to their village that morning. The villagers had been expecting him for several weeks. According to his mother, the men of the village had had a meeting three weeks before and had decided not to pay their winter taxes.

Gavrilo's father had been among those men.

That morning the tax collector had arrived and had demanded payment. The men of the village had assembled in front of Benic's house to explain the problem of the ruined harvest. They had told the Austrian tax collector of the early winter and that they would make up their winter taxes in the summer when the first harvest was in.

The tax collector, however, was not interested in the problems of farming in the mountains. He had responded by calling the villagers lying Slav dogs. One of the village men had lost his temper and had knocked out three of the tax collector's front teeth.

An hour passed before the tax collector returned to Grahovo, accompanied by nine Austrian policemen. They arrested six men trom the village and confiscated all the chickens and potatoes and half the grain. Gavrilo's mother, like most of the other village women, had hidden her salt pork and her barley.

But Gavrilo's father had been among those arrested.

In the afternoon Gavrilo did his father's chores. Not until nearly sunset did he have a chance to get away from the cottage, and make his way up the road to the chapel. He entered and found Father Petrovitch kneeling within the iconostasis. Gavrilo knelt and crossed himself. He waited for the old priest to finish his evening prayers.

Finally Father Petrovitch rose to his feet and turned around. He saw Gavrilo and waved the boy to his side.

"I thought you might come to see me," the old priest said, laying his rough hand on Gavrilo's shoulder. "Come, sit down—we can talk for a minute."

Gavrilo followed the black-robed priest to the first row of wooden benches.

"You are disturbed about your father?"

Gavrilo nodded.

"You must understand that as a servant of the Almighty, I do not agree with violence. . . ."

"It was my father who hit the tax collector?"

"It was your father. I cannot condone his action, but I won't condemn it either. Does one just lie down and starve without lifting a finger to save oneself? How long can the meek continue to be meek? How long can suffering be endured before a man tears the cross from his shoulders and wields it as a club? I don't know the answers, Gavrilo."

"What will happen to my father?"

"He'll be tried for assaulting an official of the Austrian government."

"And then?"

"He'll probably go to jail."

"For how long?" Gavrilo demanded.

"I don't know, my son. We shall find out next week. The tax collector was not badly hurt. It should not be very long." For the first time the old priest saw the fear in Gavrilo's expression. "Perhaps only two or three months. Your father will be home before you know it."

But Gavrilo's father never came home. He was sentenced to two year's hard labor. He died in prison after only six months.

§   §   §

The orders from Belgrade did not come until the second week in October. Tankosic called them together and gave them instructions. Gavrilo, Nedelijko, and Trifun were to proceed immediately to Belgrade. Ciganovitch would have their housing arrangements.

They arrived in Belgrade on October 24. Ciganovitch had secured them a rented room in the section of Belgrade that borders the Sava River. They were given identity cards and told that if they saw a certain man in the Ministry of Information, he would find them jobs.

Despite their initial disappointment about not being ordered to Bosnia, they followed the orders carefully. There would come a time when they were needed.

During the winter of 1913 Gavrilo, Nedelijko, and Trifun became friends. They shared the rented room and worked together in the Ministry of Information. More than that they shared the knowledge that they were *komitadji*, sworn by death to drive foreign invaders from their homeland.

Spring comes slowly in the Balkans. It comes especially slowly to those who are impatient.

And Gavrilo, Nedelijko, and Trifun were impatient. Their impatience was caused by a small news article that appeared on the front page of the Belgrade paper:

> VIENNA, MAY 4—A spokesman for the Imperial Court announced today that Archduke Franz Ferdinand, Crown Prince of the Empire, will make a state visit to Bosnia in June. After attending a week of military maneuvers at Mostar, the Crown Prince will meet with Governor Potiorek for an official reception in Sarajevo.
>
> The last visit to Bosnia by Austrian royalty was in 1910, when the Emperor . . .

"Something should be done about that," Nedelijko had snapped.

"It says down here," Gavrilo continued reading, "that Ferdinand will parade through Sarajevo on June 28."

There was a moment of shocked silence. Trifun was the first to speak.

"Vidovdan!"

"Something must be done!" Nedelijko cried.

The idea of doing something sank into Gavrilo's mind the way a pebble sinks into a still pond. What was the point of their training if they were just going to sit around Belgrade? What was the point of being *komitadjis* if the Austrian Crown Prince could parade through Bosnia on the most sacred of days, Vidovdan.

The more Gavrilo thought of Archduke Ferdinand's planned visit, the more important doing something became. It was almost as if there were no alternative, as if doing something had become a necessity, something conditioned like removing one's fingers from the heat of a flame.

Perhaps a lesser man would have felt fear, and perhaps a greater man would have questioned the necessity he felt. But Gavrilo was neither a coward nor a philosopher. He was a dedicated and impatient *komitadji*.

On May 7, 1914, Gavrilo and Nedelijko approached Captain Milan Ciganovitch with their plan.

"We cannot allow it to pass unnoticed," Nedelijko said.

"His visit reasserts Austrian domination over Bosnia," Gavrilo added. "We have a plan."

Ciganovitch chuckled at the young men's enthusiasm. He laid his hand on Nedelijko's shoulder. His grip was soft, almost feminine.

"You two actually want to try for the Austrian Crown Prince?" Ciganovitch's voice was filled with incredulity.

"It's Vidovdan!"

Ciganovitch laughed out loud. He slipped his arm about Nedelijo's shoulders and squeezed the younger man gently.

"You crazy Bosnians! It's madness, you know. But it just may be a kind of madness Apis will like. I can't make you any promises. But I'll talk to Apis. I'll tell him what you've told me."

§ § §

Not until the following day did Captain Milan Ciganovitch have an opportunity to see Apis. His scarred face twitched nervously as he told Apis about his visit from the young men. Apis remained silent throughout the telling.

"The young Bosnians want a chance at the Crown Prince," Apis repeated almost to himself. "It's mad, of course. But it may be mad in just the right way. Ferdinand's a royal nuisance. You know about this land reform of his?"

Ciganovitch shook his head.

"Ferdinand's put forth a proposal to change the land policy in Bosnia. Instead of only allowing Muslims and Magyars to own land, Slavs would be allowed to own land."

"It's about time," Ciganovitch murmured.

"Idiot! Have you dung for brains!" Apis barked and

Ciganovitch's scarred face twitched more furiously. "Of course Slavs should be allowed to own land. It's their land in the first place. But if this land reform goes through, our plans, the plans of the union, will be set back for years. Don't you see? Ferdinand will become a hero to the Bosnian Slavs. The discontent that so many years have cultivated will disappear instantly."

Apis reached for a cigarette. He did not like Ciganovitch and made few attempts to hide his feelings.

"If something were to happen to the Archduke during his trip to Bosnia there would probably be a backlash in Vienna against the Bosnian Slavs. Quite probably the land reform proposal would be defeated."

Apis lit the cigarette. Ciganovitch's scarred face annoyed him. There was something about the mouth. Or was it the eyes? . . . Apis couldn't put his finger on it.

"What should I tell the young Bosnians?"

"Tell them Apis is interested. Tell them I'm thinking about the possibilities. Get hold of Tankosic. I want to talk to him. I want to find out how well trained these young men really are."

§   §   §

Captain Milan Ciganovitch did not betray the Union because he wanted to. He did so because of fear. A fear that was even greater than his fear of the punishment the Union meted out to informers.

The Union merely shot informers. But they castrated homosexuals and choked them to death with their own sexual organs.

The source of Ciganovitch's fear was something that had happened nine years before. He had been a young lieutenant at the time, stationed in Volim. There had been a young Muslim boy. There was no question that Ciganovitch had had too much to drink, but the boy had provoked him. The boy had teased him. Ciganovitch hadn't meant to hurt anyone.

Ciganovitch had taken the boy to the flat roof of his building and had made love to him. When it was over the boy had demanded money. Ciganovitch had refused. The boy had threatened to expose him. There had been unbridled contempt and disgust on the boy's face. Ciganovitch had had too much to drink. And the boy was standing too close to the edge of the roof. Perhaps it was the disgust on the boy's face that provoked Ciganovitch to act. A slight, almost insignificant little shove. The boy had tumbled off the roof and fallen two stories to the street below.

Unfortunately for Ciganovitch the boy did not die. Both of his legs were broken, and there was a strong possibility that he would never walk again. But this did not hamper the boy from telling the police all about Captain Milan Ciganovitch.

Ciganovitch was arrested and charged with homosexual rape and attempted murder. The case was self-evident. Ciganovitch did not have a chance. The boy's father was a wealthy and influential merchant. Ciganovitch resigned himself to public disgrace and lengthy imprisonment.

But then Jovo Moyen came into his life, and with him came a glimmer of hope.

Moyen worked for the government in Belgrade. Ciganovitch had never been able to discover what exactly Moyen did in the government, but he was certainly not connected with the military. Moyen visited Ciganovitch in jail just before the trial.

He suggested to Ciganovitch that there were ways to avoid the trial. The government needed information on The Union or Death. Ciganovitch was a member. Perhaps there could be cooperation. Ciganovitch was fully aware of the Union's punishment for informing, but the prospect of public disgrace and imprisonment was grim enough for him to agree to cooperate.

The charges against Ciganovitch were mysteriously dropped. A large sum of money was paid to the boy's family. Ciganovitch was transferred back to Belgrade. And, at long last, the government had cracked the *gluvonem,* the code of silence.

The evening after Ciganovitch had spoken with Apis, he put a small classified advertisement in the Belgrade paper: "LOST: A LARGE WHITE CAT. ANSWERS TO THE NAME JOVO. REWARD OFFERED. PLEASE CONTACT MR. TOKNIK AT 135 GOTOV STREET."

It was the signal to Moyen that Ciganovitch wanted to see him. The meeting was set for the Toknik Café at 1:35 the following day.

Moyen was late, and Ciganovitch was bad tempered. They sat at a small table in the rear of the café.

"You'll excuse me if I order—I haven't had lunch yet," Moyen said with a grin.

"You'll excuse me if I don't join you. Every minute I'm with you is another nail in my coffin."

"Something going on?"

"Might be. Nothing definite yet. Three young Bosnians want to take a crack at the Austrian Crown Prince."

"Ferdinand?"

"During his visit to Bosnia. I think Apis liked the idea. He's thinking it over. He said something about Ferdinand's land-reform proposal."

Moyen nodded thoughtfully.

"When, how, and who's involved?"

"When and how haven't been decided yet. Three young Bosnians are involved. Tankosic trained them last autumn."

Moyen's eyes widened slightly.

"Tankosic trained them?" Moyen asked. Ciganovitch nodded. Moyen grunted. He had learned to have a healthy respect for anyone Tankosic had trained.

"When's Apis going to make a decision?"

"He wants to talk it over with Tankosic But it can't be too long. Ferdinand's due in Bosnia in June."

Again Moyen nodded thoughtfully.

Ciganovitch rose to his feet. His scarred face twitched nervously. "I'll be in touch when I know more."

Days passed into weeks, and still nothing was heard from Ciganovitch. It was taking too long. Nedelijko felt sure their plan would never be approved. Trifun held out some hope. Gavrilo waited as impatiently as the rest, but in silence.

Even while Gavrilo, Nedelijko, and Trifun waited impatiently in Belgrade, students in Sarajevo were not idle. They, too, were aware of the grotesque insult that was being planned for Vidovdan.

There was Bogdan Zerajic, a Slav student, who became a hero. After three hours of waiting by the Kaiser Bridge, the governor's carriage finally appeared. Bogdan acted quickly. He pulled a revolver from beneath his shirt and fired five shots into the carriage. After the shots had been fired, Governor Potiorek stepped from the carriage, unhurt but frowning.

Bogdan Zerajic lifted the revolver to his mouth and blew the top of his own head off.

He was buried secretly. Colonel Smyra, chief of the Bosnian security police, feared Zerajic's grave might become a Mecca for other young fanatics. As it happened, two students followed the burial detail and made a map of the spot. Within a week the maps started to appear on the sides of public buildings, on lamp posts; one was even pasted on the front of the police station.

Gavrilo and Nedelijko read about Bogdan Zerajic in the Belgrade papers. For the first time the two friends realized that they were really part of something much larger than a single conspiracy. There was a movement, a rebellion, even an insurrection brewing.

Their impatience reached fever pitch.

The rains came and turned the rock fields into marshland. But still nothing was heard from Ciganovitch.

The warm spring sun settled in the sky. The thaw began. Insects appeared from nowhere. The frozen rubbish that had lain in the gutters all winter began to decompose. Gavrilo watched the Balkan sparrows pluck maggots from the rotting turnip heads, gobbling them down quickly and then pecking for more. He watched and wondered if the birds would not become their own victims, eaten from the inside out, as he was being eaten from the inside out.

§   §   §

It was raining the morning that Ciganovitch contacted them. Thick gray clouds lay across the Balkan peninsula like a winding sheet. Ciganovitch opened his door and, without a word, motioned for the three young men to enter.

"You've heard?" Nedelikjo asked.

"Apis has approved your plan."

"Weapons," Gavrilo said. "We'll need weapons."

"Everything has been taken care of," Ciganovitch replied sharply. The young men's enthusiasm began to annoy him. His scarred face twitched nervously.

"Now listen carefully." Ciganovitch proceeded to outline the plan that Apis had approved. He gave them instructions for crossing the border and finally pushed a suitcase toward Gavrilo.

"There're three pistols in there, one hundred rounds of ammunition, three grenades, and thee vials of cyanide. You are to have the cyanide on your person at all times. If you are arrested, you are to drink it. Do you understand? That is a direct order from Apis!"

The three young men nodded. Gavrilo rose to his feet. The other two followed him.

"Go with God," Ciganovitch said.

"Repent ye invaders and despair, for God rides with us!" Gavrilo quoted the Vidovdan banner the Slavs carried into battle.

Ciganovitch nodded, but remembered that the Slavs had lost that battle of Kossovo Polje.

In the rear of the Crven Vrag Café two men sat huddled together.

"Why didn't you get this to me sooner?"

"Apis had me out at Zauzet picking up the weapons."

"Oh Christ," Moyen said with exhaustion. "Pastich will be furious."

"He can't afford to be too furious."

"You would be surprised."

Ciganovitch edged himself to the side of the chair. He wanted to leave.

"Did you follow my instructions about the weapons?"

"I didn't have time."

"You mean they have live ammunition?"

Ciganovitch nodded.

§   §   §

Jovo Moyen, special adviser to Prime Minister Pastich, did not get to bed until late that night. There was much to do.

He visited Pastich at home. As predicted Pastich was furious.

"That crazy bastard should have been behind bars years ago."

"Much of the army is loyal to Apis."

"But if these three students are successful, the Austrian government is going to point the guilty finger right at us. They're just waiting for an excuse to invade Serbia. You think that's too farfetched. You probably thought the way Austria annexed Bosnia was farfetched too. Oh Christ almighty!"

"You want to try to arrest Apis?" Moyen asked softly. Pastich calmed down and slowly shook his head. Even though he was prime minister, he knew he did not have that power. It would be civil war.

"But we've got to warn Vienna. Draft a telegram to Berchtold. No, not to Berchtold. Send it to Hotzendorf. Don't mention Apis or the Union. If we mention that bastard we'll have to arrest him. Tell them that we have information about a plot against Archduke Ferdinand's life while he's on this trip to Bosnia. Tell them to keep that lunatic Crown Prince at home."

Moyen nodded and turned toward the door.

"One more thing, Moyen." Pastich was grave. Moyen saw a faint look of fear in the prime minister's eyes. "Close the border to those young Bosnians. Arrest them. Send out the order to all border stations. Armed and dangerous. Use whatever force is necessary."

Moyen nodded. He knew that by sending out such an order he was signing Ciganovitch's death warrant, but he had no choice. Before long the *gluvonem,* the code of silence, would be repaired.

CHAPTER TWO

A Warning Is Ignored

In a plush office in Vienna, General Conrad von Hotzendorf sat smoking his pipe. He was in his mid-fifties but looked older. The crow's-feet at the corners of his eyes had already extended back to his graying temples.

He waited impatiently. He was always impatient. As Austrian chief of staff it was his business to be impatient.

Hotzendorf sucked on his pipe. There had been a time when Austria had really been great. When Austrians had held the Turks at the very gates of Vienna. But those days were gone. The appeasers had the ear of the emperor.

How was the process of decay going to end? Hotzendorf knew only too well. The appeasers would dominate the political situation until they had pushed the empire into a position where war was unavoidable. Then they would quietly disappear. The generals would then take over, but lacking the well-trained army that was vital for victory.

Hotzendorf never for a moment doubted that there would

be war. He had wanted to invade Italy. But the Piedmont was a forgotten issue. He had wanted to invade Serbia when Austria had annexed Bosnia. It would have taken three days and would have solved the Slav problem once and for all.

He had wanted to invade Russia. Everyone knew that a general mobilization in Russia would take six weeks. With the Kaiser's help, he would have been dining in St. Petersburg within three.

But Archduke Francis Ferdinand had been horrified by the suggestion. "There is little point in even considering such a lunatic idea," Ferdinand had said in front of the entire cabinet. "Ignoring for a moment the unhappy event of a Russian victory, let us examine what would happen were Austria victorious. In order for Austria to maintain control over a land mass the size of Russia it would be necessary to weaken the present Russian government. We would have to exile the czar and set up a republican government. Do you gentlemen have any idea what effect republicanism on that scale would mean? We'd be playing into the hands of the revolutionaries. It would be the death knell not only for the Romanovs, but also for the Hohenzollerns and the Hapsburgs."

Ferdinand had embarrassed him. Ferdinand had a habit of embarrassing people.

Hotzendorf rose from his seat when the others arrived. He greeted them formally. After they were seated he spoke. "I have received a telegram from Belgrade, signed by Prime Minister Pastich. It states that he has knowledge of a plot against the life of Archduke Ferdinand. This plot is to be carried out while the Crown Prince is visiting Bosnia. Pastich continues to advise us that it would be unwise for the archduke to make such a journey."

Hotzendorf paused and cast his eyes about the room.

Count Berchtold, foreign minister and one of the cleverest men in Vienna, cradled his chin. He was slender, and all his features seemed compressed into a desire to be inconspicuous.

Count Harrach sat next to Berchtold. Hotzendorf knew very little about the young count, except that he was an excellent military commander, had won several medals for personal bravery, and most important, was one of the very few men that Archduke Ferdinand trusted.

The other member of the group was the imperial chamberlain, Prince Montenuovo. He was short, fat, and balding. Hotzendorf, like everyone else in Vienna, was well aware of the feud between Montenuovo and Ferdinand. It had begun over Ferdinand's desire to marry a commoner but had become self-perpetuating thereafter.

"Do you think Pastich is telling the truth?" Berchtold asked. "He may be lying in order to cause Austria to lose face."

There was silence for a moment while the rest of them digested what the foreign minister had said. The silence was broken by the imperial chamberlain.

"Why isn't Ferdinand here?" Montenuovo demanded.

"He was busy. He sent me instead," Count Harrach replied. Harrach knew the real reason Ferdinand had not come to Vienna was that Montenuovo would be present.

"Busy?" Montenuovo repeated. "Too busy to attend a meeting about his own welfare? But then there is an old saying that one's manners are a product of the circles one moves in."

Harrach tensed. Montenuovo's last remark had been directed at Ferdinand's wife, Duchess Sophie.

"I think Pastich is lying," Montenuovo continued. "He wants Ferdinand to appear a coward."

"If the archduke is killed," Harrach snapped, "I imagine you will carry your grief well."

"Come now," Montenuovo said with thinly veiled amusement. "We are all concerned about any danger there might be to the Crown Prince. But we must also think of the empire. Too often people in important positions think only of themselves."

"Archduke Ferdinand is not a coward."

"You misunderstand, young man. I was not implying that Ferdinand would deny his country. We all know that Ferdinand is not afraid of death or dishonor. We all know that Ferdinand would do anything within his power for the empire. But we have all learned that his carnal appetites are not within his power."

"You will apologize immediately!" Harrach roared.

"Gentlemen!" Hotzendorf shouted. "We have serious matters before us."

Harrach gripped the edge of his chair. He felt foolish. He had allowed Montenuovo to bait him.

"I suggest," the young count announced, "that we advise Ferdinand to cancel the trip. Our primary concern must be with his safety."

"What are the effects of losing face in Bosnia?" Berchtold asked.

"Bosnia," Hotenzdorf replied, "is· in turmoil. The last state visit was four years ago. The Bosnian students are influenced by Serbian propaganda. There is a small but fairly strong nationalist movement. One of the objectives of the Crown Prince's visit is to dilute the strength of the radical pan-Slavists. He would be going to announce his support of land reform."

"Can I take it," Harrach asked angrily, "that you are suggesting that we place Ferdinand's life in danger in order to mollify a handful of student radicals?"

"Of course not," Hotzendorf responded wearily. "I was merely answering Berchtold's question."

Hotzendorf realized that the telegram could not be discussed sensibly. The feud between Montenuovo and Ferdinand had rendered rational discussion impossible.

"All we can do," Hotzendorf concluded the meeting, "is to relay to Ferdinand the context of our discussion and let him make up his own mind. Of course, if he decides to continue with the trip, we will notify Potiorek and the security police in Bosnia."

Harrach was silent. Berchtold nodded. Montenuovo grinned.

"I hope," the imperial chamberlain said to Harrach, "that you will not forget to give my regards to Ferdinand˙ and the woman he married."

§ § §

Count Harrach rode south into the Bohemian mountains, away from Vienna and the indignities of the imperial chamberlain. Why was the feud still going on? Ferdinand had been married for fourteen years. It was lunacy and, in this case, dangerous.

His mind mulled over the meeting and the text of Pastich's telegram. He would try to convince Ferdinand not to go to Bosnia. He organized his arguments. He would be at Konopischt in just over an hour. He would have to have his arguments prepared.

While Count Harrach rode south to Konopischt bringing the news of Pastich's telegram, Archduke Francis Ferdinand strolled in his rose garden.

It was his custom to stroll in the rose garden in the early evening. It soothed his nerves. And at the present moment his nerves were sorely in need of soothing.

Fritz Gruber, timber merchant and owner of the hunting lodge at Konopischt, had threatened to raise the Archduke's rent. He'd made some comment about saplings being destroyed. But Ferdinand saw through the lies. It was greed.

Ferdinand was an imposing figure of a man; tall and heavy-set with glaring eyes and a waxed moustache that soared out like eagle wings. He had a reputation for being both unpredictable and bad tempered.

He liked being away from Vienna, away from the scorn of the imperial court. Konopischt was a quiet place, a place to relax, a place to regroup all of one's forces and wait for the next attack.

There had been very few moments of happiness in Francis Ferdinand's life. As a child, he had been frail and sickly. The doctors had diagnosed consumption. Terminal consumption. Swiss sanatoriums and trips to Egypt had helped a little. He remembered eavesdropping on a conversation. It had been many years before but still the words made his muscles tighten in fury.

"The child is weaker. . . . The doctors have been consulted. . . . We must cut expenses. . . . A sanatorium . . . It's a matter of months."

It had been then, when he was twelve, standing behind the great tapestry in the entrance hall at Belvedere, listening to the young Prince Montenuovo, that he had become determined to survive. All his twelve-year-old energy was thrust into survival. He exercised in private, building his body into something that looked like it might live more than just a few months.

But no matter how firm his biceps became, no matter how large his chest grew, no matter how many laps he could run around the garden at Belvedere, he was not invited to any royal functions.

It had been decided—decided by the young imperial chamberlain, Montenuovo—that he couldn't survive. For medical reasons the young archduke was expelled from the Hapsburg family, buried alive at Belvedere.

Even his mother accepted the chamberlain's decision. Ferdinand remembered her with vague distaste. He had not known her well enough to hate her. Sometimes when he lost his temper and could not locate the source of his anger nor find anything satisfying to vent it upon, he would secretly wish he had known his mother better so that he could hate her.

With bitterness so intense that it bordered on lunacy, he remembered his first invitation to the imperial court. It had been ironic. A balance between life and death. Only after Rudolph's suicide at Mayerling had Ferdinand been exhumed from his tomb at Belvedere. With Crown Prince

Rudolph dead, Ferdinand had become the Emperor's successor, the new heir apparent to the Austro-Hungarian empire.

It was there at Konopischt, among his prize roses, that Ferdinand remembered his first royal outing: Rudolph's funeral.

The black-draped carriage stood in front of him. Behind him the great Louis XIV mantle clock struck one. Ferdinand grimaced at the sound. He was determined to be late for his first public appearance as the Crown Prince. He had waited to survive; now Rudolph could wait to be buried.

Suicide! Ferdinand thought for the fifth time. It was incredible. More than incredible. It was disgusting.

He winced slightly as he entered the carriage. The horses started with a jerk. Ferdinand cursed.

Rudolph had been found with a woman. Both dead. A suicide pact! Ferdinand shook his head. It would be the best-kept secret. There had been confusion in the newspapers. One had attributed death to consumption, another to heart failure.

It was a good thing that Rudolph was dead. But suicide . . . ! Montenuovo had acted quickly. The coverup was well underway. Four foreign correspondents who had dared to print the truth had been expelled. Ferdinand smiled bitterly. Was the archfamily so fragile that it could be shattered by something so fundamental as the truth?

But it was a good thing that Rudolph was dead. He wondered if anyone would say that when he was dead. He was sure of it. He didn't have many friends. He didn't want friends. He didn't like people very much. He did, however, like his dogs. His hunting hounds were his closest friends.

"Slower," Ferdinand roared at the driver. "Drive those horses slower." As if in exaggerated obedience, the driver brought the three pairs of white horses to a halt.

"What are we stopping for?"

"To pick up General Conrad von Hotzendorf, if it please Your Highness."

It did not please Ferdinand, but he said nothing.

"Good afternoon, Your Highness," General Hotzendorf greeted Ferdinand formally.

"Get in, Conrad," Ferdinand barked, slamming the carriage door behind the general.

The carriage moved, and again Ferdinand was jerked back in his seat. His empty eyes stared at Hotzendorf. Ferdinand had known the general for a long time, perhaps too long. Hotzendorf's courage was well known, but unfortunately for the empire, his intelligence was not. He had all the qualities of excellent cannon fodder. Hotzendorf answered all political questions in terms of how many troops he could mobilize. A damned fool.

"A tragedy."

"Rudolph? Rudolph was an idiot to get mixed up with that bitch," Ferdinand snapped.

"Montenuovo's kept it out of the press."

"Hurrah for Montenuovo. Rudolph retains his public image, and the family lives happily ever after."

"You would have had them print the truth?" Conrad von Hotzendorf asked with disbelief.

"Why should the oldest family in Europe forge new habits at this late date?"

The two rode on in silence for a short while.

"We have joined the funeral procession," Hotzendorf commented. "We are entering the Kärtnerstrasse."

Ferdinand's eyes fluttered slightly but remained closed. The mental picture was too pleasant to be discarded by the general's comments. By the weekend he would be at Pressburg. He lived for his weekends at Pressburg. It was another case in which the truth could not be told. She appeared in his mind once more. Her auburn hair splashed from the disheveled bun to her soft white shoulders.

There was nothing common about her. Her stature was that of a queen, even if her rank was not. Her smile was regal. And Ferdinand was in love with her.

He wondered if the fragile Hapsburg family could stand that truth.

The carriage stopped too suddenly. The image of the woman he loved was shattered. Ferdinand cursed.

Ferdinand and Hotzendorf stepped from the carriage onto the steps of St. Stephen's.

A hushed buzz passed through the crowd. "That's him. The one to the right of General Hotzendorf. That's the new Crown Prince."

The steps of St. Stephen's were lined with three rows of honor guard. Ferdinand's gaze scanned the entranceway. His eyes fell upon a soldier's boot. There, beside the highly polished heel, was a clump of red mud. The archduke held the dirty boot in focus for a moment before turning to greet his uncle, the emperor.

"Your Imperial Highness," Ferdinand said, bowing from the waist.

"Ferdinand." The solemn voice of the Emperor hesitated. He laid his withered hand on Ferdinand's shoulder. "You are now the Crown Prince, the future of the empire."

"You have my sympathy," Ferdinand mumbled. He thought of his favorite hunting hound and felt real sorrow. He had shot the hound by accident.

"Thank you," the emperor replied, his gray eyes becoming cloudy, but he had much practice at holding emotion within himself. Private feelings were for private places.

The emperor turned and walked up the wide avenue of the cathedral. Ferdinand followed, unconscious of the thousands of curious eyes that watched his every movement. He was still upset over his favorite hound.

Just before the purple velvet of the altar was Rudolph's satin-lined coffin. His dead face had been rouged by a heavy-handed undertaker. His puffy cheeks were like red apples. He didn't look dead at all, but rather like some wealthy drunkard who had passed out in the imperial casket.

Members of the family backed away from the casket as the Emperor and the new Crown Prince approached. The emperor went directly to the side of the casket.

Ferdinand paused and whispered to an elderly archduchess at his right, "Did you know that suicide is a mortal sin?"

The elderly archduchess was shocked, not so much by the fact that Rudolph would spend eternity in hell, but rather that anyone would mention it.

Ferdinand left the cathedral disgusted with the family and disgusted with himself. The funeral had been a lie in the sight of God. The entire family had conspired to live the lie that Rudolph died of heart failure. They had desecrated the holy sacraments. Ferdinand despised them.

But he also despised himself. He, too, was living a lie. Would the truth be so damning? He didn't care. He would not continue to desecrate his love for Sophie. He had made his decision. If she was strong enough, they would declare war on the family.

As he had done every other weekend for the past seven months, Ferdinand traveled to Pressburg Castle. He had become a regular visitor and was expected. Archduchess Isabella assumed that the Crown Prince was interested in her daughter, Marie Christina, and Marie Christina was too vain to see otherwise. Actually Ferdinand came to Pressburg to see a lady-in-waiting, Sophie Chotek.

They had met at one of Archduchess Isabella's weekend parties. They had danced. They had talked. Ferdinand could not remember a person he was more at ease with. Over the months that passed they had continued to meet in secret. Ferdinand was bound by law to marry a Hapsburg.

He crossed the sweeping lawn that led up to the rear façade of Pressburg Castle. He was in love and he was determined. Everything was cheapened by secrecy. Everything was desecrated by living a lie. Something had to be done.

He turned to the path that led through the woods to the summer house. It was there, out of sight of the castle and prying eyes, that he had arranged to meet Sophie Chotek.

She was sitting in a rattan chair when he appeared.

"Good morning."

"Yes," Ferdinand said, returning her smile. "It is a good morning." They entered the summer house, and Ferdinand crossed to the large oak table in the solarium. On the table was a vase of flowers. He knew Sophie had put it there.

"From the greenhouse?"

She nodded.

It had been seven months of confusion for each of them. Ferdinand was ashamed of using Archduchess Isabella and Marie Christina. He was ashamed of his own shame. Sophie was frightened. She knew that if the family ever discovered that they were seeing each other they would move heaven and earth to destroy her. Ferdinand withdrew a primrose from the vase and smelled it.

"You like flowers?"

"I like the wildflowers," she replied, a mischievous smile flashing across her face. She was beautiful when she smiled. Vibrant and vital. "The ones that defy the imperial gardener and pop up in the middle of the imperial lawn."

Ferdinand chuckled.

"The weeds? You are the defender of the royal weeds?" Before Sophie could reply, he clasped her shoulders and kissed her. He could feel her muscles tense slightly as their lips met. It was the damned lie! The secrecy! It was destroying them.

"Is it unpleasant to kiss me?" Ferdinand pulled away from her. She cast her eyes down toward the floor and trembled.

"Perhaps you think it is your duty to make love to the Crown Prince?"

"Ferdinand, please . . ."

"Your duty. The duty of a lady-in-waiting?"

Sophie shook her head slowly, avoiding his eyes.

"And if I ordered you to my bed?"

"It is my duty to please you," Sophie whispered, her voicing trembling with emotion.

"Only your duty?" Ferdinand demanded angrily.

"Not only my duty."

"What else then?"

Sophie remained silent for a moment. Ferdinand cursed himself. Why was he angry with her? She had done nothing to make him angry. Sophie bit the inside of her lip to control the flood of tears welling up within her. *Oh, God,* she thought, *if I could . . . If I could only tell him . . .* She covered her face with her hands and allowed herself to weep.

Ferdinand turned away from her. The strain was too much. It consumed them. Everything that was decent became an obscenity because of the lie they lived. He finally plucked a small purple flower from the vase on the table and forced it into her hand.

"Would you like to see my flowers?" he asked softly. The question was not as casual as it sounded. Sophie grasped its meaning at once. Her mouth fell open. Ferdinand had just asked her to marry him. She caught her breath and turned away from him. His flowers were at Belvedere, and there was only one way she could visit Belvedere—as his wife.

But she wasn't a Hapsburg. She bowed her head. The law was sacred. The Crown Prince had to marry a Hapsburg. In her daydreams this same scene had appeared to her, but the reality of it was like a sharp kick in the abdomen.

"Goddamit!" Ferdinand roared at the sound of renewed sobbing. Any display of emotion angered him. She would have corrected his language had she not been so confused. "All I asked was whether you wanted to see my flowers. Stop crying. There's nothing to cry about."

"I wasn't crying."

"I could order you to Belvedere," he snapped furiously. The tone of Ferdinand's voice suddenly struck Sophie as funny, and she began to laugh.

Ferdinand was forced to smile. If she could laugh, then perhaps she was strong enough, and if she was strong enough then they could fight and win. There would be casualties on both sides. They would declare their own private war on the imperial court.

He tried again to put something into words, but all that came from his lips was a low groan. Sophie looked at him and waited. She was afraid of what he was trying to say. Her heart pounded.

"I want you to come to Belvedere. I want you to see my roses." He took hold of her hand. "I'll even have a weed or two planted for you."

Sophie's smile faded.

"And what, Ferdinand, would you tell your uncle? Would you tell the Emperor that you were entertaining an obscure Czech countess? Would you tell him that you have taken a lady-in-waiting as a mistress?"

"Damn the emperor!"

"But it's the law."

"Damn the law!"

Sophie smiled sadly at Ferdinand's fury. He took a deep breath and released a sigh.

"Sophie, you will come to Belvedere, and you will be treated as a queen. The queen. No one will dare to think of you as a lady-in-waiting. No one!"

She could not look into Ferdinand's face. His determination frightened her. She had seen him like this before, and didn't know how much of what he said was possible and how much was madness.

"Ferdinand," she began hesitantly, "please listen to me. You can't be serious. My coming to Belvedere is a wonderful dream, but it can't be anything more than a dream. You come to Pressburg each weekend. We meet in secret. Think of what would happen if Archduchess Isabella discovered we were seeing each other. We must remain friends. To be more than friends is impossible."

"To hell with possibility! You said you like the weeds that

pop up in the royal lawn. Well, Sophie Chotek, take a look at a weed that's about to smash through the foundations of the winter palace."

Sophie closed her eyes. She felt the strength of the Archduke flow into her. For a moment his wild eyes reassured her. She wanted to believe that it was possible. She wanted to believe that they could wage war on the imperial court and win.

Her reassurance was short-lived. There appeared on her face another smile, provoked, not by determination, but by resignation and defeat. Ferdinand read the change quickly. It angered him. He was impotent alone.

"I'll write to the holy father. And the czar. The Kaiser will give me support."

"Please, Ferdinand," she cried. "Please don't say any more!"

"Would you like to come to Belvedere?" he asked softly. It was a different question, and she did not reply at once. There was a long moment of silence before she turned and stared directly into Ferdinand's eyes.

"You would really plant a weed in your garden?" she asked.

§   §   §

It was a cold morning in March when Ferdinand arrived at the Hofburg. He had requested an audience with his uncle, the emperor.

Ferdinand remembered his uncle's eyes when he had told him his intention to marry Sophie Chotek. The gray irises clouded. The old man's body seemed to shiver slightly as if a draught had managed to find its way into the winter palace. That was all. There was no other sign of emotion or surprise. Ferdinand had expected none. There was silence after Ferdinand had made his announcement. And then came Franz Joseph's fatherly look—the one Ferdinand despised the most.

"Impossible. You know the law as well as I do. Hapsburgs must marry Hapsburgs. That is the law."

"I know the law," Ferdinand replied. "I was brought up with the law. It's engraved on me. But there's something else engraved on me. I love Sophie. I intend to marry her. You are the emperor. You make the laws. You can grant me permission. That is within your power."

"Within my power!" the emperor snapped. "The fate of Austria is in God's hands. And you, Archduke Francis Ferdinand, are the fate of Austria. You have been chosen by the Almighty. You will, upon my death, be anointed with the same sacred oils as all Hapsburg emperors have been. You will be responsible to God. Do I have it in my power to condone the desecration of something as holy as Hapsburg blood?"

"I seek your permission. It is within your power."

"You do need my permission, nephew!" the emperor snarled. The paternal tone had disappeared. Ruthlessness had replaced it. "If you marry that woman without my permission I'll banish you and your heirs forever."

Ferdinand heard the words ring in his ears. He had expected the threat. It was not a surprise, but the venom in his uncle's voice was.

Ferdinand left the Hofburg in a particularly bad temper. He cursed his uncle, the fragile royal family, and Vienna as a whole. He was not sure how to fight a man who held all the power. He remembered walking, not where he walked, just walking frantically through crowded streets, unaware of everything that surrounded him, conscious only of his impotence.

He had writen to the Kaiser, the czar, and the pope. But he had heard nothing from them. Why would they ignore his plea for help? Ferdinand knew that the pope looked upon him as the revitalizer of Catholicism in Austria. Why hadn't the holy father come to his aid? And the czar? Why was his friend Nicholas silent?

He walked on in anger. Vienna was a city of rumor and calumny. Vienna fed upon scandal. How Vienna would love to get its hands on the information that Ferdinand wanted to marry a commoner. Ferdinand stopped in his tracks. Perhaps there was a way to fight a man who held all the power! Why should Vienna go hungry? Suddenly he grinned. The emperor had forbidden him to marry Sophie, but he had said nothing about scandalizing Vienna!

It might seem bad form to members of the royal house, but there were no rules in war, and Ferdinand considered himself at war.

Ferdinand went ahead with his plan. Within a week, Sophie was moved into Belvedere. She was given a separate wing. The two of them attended the opera together in the imperial box. They allowed themselves to be seen strolling in the Hofburg Gardens.

Within a week the gossip columns in the Vienna papers were full of the story. Speculation was endless. Had the Crown Prince gone mad? Sophie Chotek was pregnant? Sophie's impoverished background was chewed over in the cafés and restaurants. The more conservative papers called it a national disgrace.

Within ten days a message arrived from the Hofburg: Emperor Franz Joseph wanted to see Ferdinand immediately.

Ferdinand remembered the second imperial audience with slightly more pleasure than the first. Franz Joseph was in a rage.

"Not only is your behavior lunatic, but you have written to Wilhelm, Nicholas, and the pope," his uncle announced without any other form of greeting. Ferdinand's heart leaped. His friends had not ignored his plea for help. "I have letters here from them." The emperor slapped the podium he stood behind. Franz Joseph always stood during imperial audiences. He claimed that people came to their business quicker if they were forced to stand.

Ferdinand took a step forward.

"No, you will not see them. But you may be satisfied to learn that they encourage me to allow you to marry this commoner."

"Sophie is not a commoner. She is a Czech countess."

"It's the same thing. She is not a Hapsburg. Every other woman in Czechoslovakia is a countess." Emperor Franz Joseph paused and glared at his nephew. "Don't look so pleased with yourself. I have not changed my mind. But I am willing to compromise."

"Compromise?"

"You must stop this disgraceful behavior. The papers are full of it. Move that woman out of Belvedere and refrain from seeing her for six months. Then, if you still want to marry her, I'll reconsider my decision."

Although the words had been the Emperor's, the sentiments could only have been one man's.

"Montenuovo suggested that?"

"As chamberlain he advised me. It is his business to be concerned about impropriety."

"A suitable concern for him."

"He is not responsible for the conditions of his birth."

"A bastard will always be accursed in the eyes of God."

"You should be more tolerant, nephew. Do you accept the compromise?"

"Do I have a choice?"

"Not if you want to marry that woman."

§ § §

The following six months of separation were for Ferdinand like six years or six centuries. Ferdinand lived only for the mail he received from Sophie. He lost his appetite and his doctors worried about a recurrence of consumption.

His interests failed him. Even his passion for hunting waned. His temper grew maniacally abrupt, and his servants grew more afraid of him than usual. The only time he found any peace was when the mail arrived and there was a letter from Sophie.

Montenuovo was not inactive during the separation. The possibility of Ferdinand's marriage to Sophie Chotek became an obsession with him. He instructed members of the royal house to visit Sophie and put pressure on her. If she really loved Ferdinand, they would say, she would not see him again. When this failed, Monenuovo used Sophie's own brothers. But Sophie had made a promise to Ferdinand which no amount of pressure could make her break.

The imperial chamberlain started sending visitors to Belvedere to see Ferdinand. The visitors were female, attractive, and all instructed well by Montenuovo. It infuriated Ferdinand. Montenuovo had turned Belvedere into a brothel.

If the Crown Prince had once given way to temptation, and had taken one of those well-paid young whores to bed, Montenuovo would have gone straight to Sophie with full details of his unfaithfulness.

It was war.

The six months finally passed, and Ferdinand requested an audience with the emperor. His request was lost. He repeated the request. Montenuovo sent the reply that due to ill health the emperor was not granting audienecs in the forseeable future.

Ferdinand replied that he was moving Sophie Chotek back into Belvedere.

Finally, after eight months of separation from Sophie, Ferdinand was granted an audience.

The emperor appeared old and sick and tired. He leaned wearily on the podium.

"I am convinced of your love for the woman," he said. "I do not want you to be unhappy. But I must uphold the law. You may marry the woman, the Czech countess, but it must be a *morganatic* marriage."

Ferdinand's mouth fell open. It was the unexpected. It was the final blow in the war.

"The woman can never be a Hapsburg; she can never become queen. If the marriage produces children they will never be considered Hapsburgs. They will never succeed you as emperor."

Sophie would remain a lady-in-waiting. His children would be commoners! When he spoke, Ferdinand's voice cracked with emotion. "I accept the conditions for marriage."

"You will publicly sign the morganatic oath, renouncing your wife-to-be and any children."

"I accept the conditions!"

The Emperor sighed. There was just a hint of pity in the old man's gray eyes.

"Although this Chotek woman can never be a Hapsburg, upon your marriage I will grant her the title of duchess."

"I accept the conditions!" Ferdinand shouted.

"Montenuovo will take care of the arrangements for the signing of the oath."

"Montenuovo will make bastards of my children!" Ferdinand roared.

"Your children will be legitimate, but they will not be Hapsburgs."

The old emperor closed his eyes. He was exhausted. The war was over. Both sides had been wounded.

But for Ferdinand the first real casualties had not yet been born. His children. He prayed that his children, and his children's children, would forgive him.

§ § §

Ferdinand stood in the official apartments of the Hofburg. Montenuvo had invited the entire royal house to witness Ferdinand's oath. The hall was crowded with royalty.

The emperor entered the hall but remained standing. The gathered crowd bowed from the waist. Franz Joseph nodded to Montenuovo, who read the morganatic oath. The expression on Ferdinand's face did not change.

When Montenuovo had finished reading, Ferdinand

stepped forward and knelt before a small table. Two large candlesticks stood on either side of the table. The cardinal prince–archbishop lifted a small crucifix from the table. Hapsburg emperors had sworn by this cross for three hundred years.

Ferdinand removed the white glove from his right hand took the crucifix. The cardinal prince–archbishop recited the oath. Ferdinand repeated it. Only the cardinal prince–archbishop saw the tears in Ferdinand's eyes.

Ferdinand and Sophie were married two days later in a small chapel in the Capuchins. He wore the Grand Order of St. Stephen on the full uniform of a cavalry general. Sophie wore a simple white satin gown and carried a bouquet of myrtles mixed with lilies of the valley.

The only member of the royal family to attend the wedding was Archduke Karl, Ferdinand's fifteen-year-old nephew.

Had the wedding not been morganatic, had Ferdinand fallen in love with a Hapsburg, had Montenuovo not been so obsessed with imperial protocol, had the actual wedding ceremony been postponed a day or two, the course of European history might have been quite different.

As it was, Ferdinand and Sophie were married on June 28, 1900. The day the Balkan Slavs call Vidovdan.

§　§　§

At just after six o'clock in the evening, under the still warm spring sun, Count Harrach rode up to the hunting lodge at Konopischt. The lodge, a mock castle by design, had been built ten years before by a timber merchant who, by clever reforestation, had managed to make the great lodge pay for itself. The sweeping driveway curled in front of the lodge, around the pointed turrets, to the castle's stables. Harrach did not use the great double doors at the end of the driveway. He was not a guest. He was a friend.

Harrach handed his horse over to the care of Herr Dobler,

the master of the archduke's hounds, and walked toward the castle.

"Count Harrach," Duchess Sophie cried. "I didn't hear your horse. Welcome." Harrach smiled at Sophie. She was no longer young, but she could still be called beautiful, and there was a gracefulness about her. "Have you ridden all the way from Vienna?" He nodded. "You must be exhausted."

Her once-firm figure had softened slightly. The indelible scar of three painful births had settled, like dust after a duel, on her middle-aged body.

Harrach smiled at Max and Ernst, who were playing soldiers on the carpet. He was proud to be Ernst's godfather.

"Is Ferdinand busy?"

"Not too busy to see you, I'm sure. He's sitting in the rose garden."

Harrach bowed from the waist as it was fitting to bow to a queen. If any other man had bowed in such a fashion she would have suspected mockery, but not with Harrach. He was a friend.

The young count left the room through the double French doors that led to the sloping lawn. He walked slowly around the castle, organizing his thoughts.

The rose garden was beyond the sculptured privet hedge. Ferdinand had hired an English gardener especially to carve the hedges. That was the type of place Konopischt was, a place where people had time to sculpture hedges.

Harrach entered the rose garden and saw Ferdinand standing with the English gardener.

"Harrach!" Ferdinand shouted. "I'm glad you're back. I need your advice." The frightened gardener took a step backward. Harrach crossed to where Ferdinand stood. He looked down at the object of Ferdinand's displeasure.

"Insects," Ferdinand muttered. "Insects eating my roses. I don't want to lose them. But the damned insects are eating every blessed rose bush here."

"Archduke," Harrach said softly, "I have heard that planting onions and garlic helps."

The English gardener nodded.

"Onions and garlic?"

"I've heard that insects are repelled by the smell."

Ferdinand scratched his throat. It was a matter of balance. It would be an indignity to plant onions and garlic among his prize roses, but he was forced to concede that it would be an even greater indignity if they were eaten alive by insects. Ferdinand shrugged his broad shoulders. All of life seemed a compromise between degrees of humiliation.

"Plant onions and garlic," he ordered the gardener. He then turned to Harrach. "Tell me, my friend, what was so urgent in Vienna?"

As Ferdinand and the young count walked toward the lodge, Harrach conveyed the gist of the discussion in Vienna, playing down Montenuovo's insults and emphasizing the dangers of the upcoming trip to Bosnia. But Ferdinand was too perceptive to be unaware of the imperial chamberlain's manners.

"Perhaps I should have gone to Vienna myself. One day you will be my second."

Harrach steered Ferdinand away from the subject of a duel by explaining the text of Pastich's telegram.

"Cancel the trip?" Ferdinand snorted, but then laughed. "Out of the question! I'm not a coward. Anyway, I don't believe Pastich. All politicians are born liars."

"But Ferdinand, if there's the slightest chance that what Pastich said is true, we must—"

"We must proceed as planned. I have made special arrangements. No matter, there are more important things to discuss."

"Ferdinand, listen to me!" Harrach knew it was dangerous to interrupt the Archduke, but counted on his friendship to grant him such a privilege. "I know you are not a coward. I also know you are not a fool. Reconsider. The telegram may mean nothing, but is it wise to risk your safety and the safety of Duchess Sophie?"

This was Harrach's trump card. Ferdinand might risk his own life, but the young count was certain that the archduke would think twice about the safety of his wife.

"You worry too much," Ferdinand replied with a grin. "Worry's the worse disease known to man. Anyway, the trip's for Sophie."

"Archduke?"

"Can you keep a sceret?" Ferdinand asked, and Harrach nodded. "I've planned it as an anniversary present for Sophie. I've made the arrangements through Governor Potiorek. It'll be a week away from Vienna and the insults of my family."

"But Ferdinand . . ."

"No buts. We will go to Bosnia. Sophie needs a holiday. And I order you not to worry Sophie by telling her about Pastich's telegram. My life is threatened as regularly as my bowels move. If I took the threats seriously I'd be a lunatic by now."

Harrach nodded. It was useless to pursue the subject. There would be another time when Ferdinand was in a more receptive mood.

"Now forget about that. There are more important things to consider. Do you know Fritz Gruber?" Harrach shook his head. "Gruber is the son of the man who built Konopischt. His father died, and now the son owns the hunting lodge and the forests. I pay him rent." Ferdinand gestured violently with his left hand. "He's in the timber business, and the bastard wants to raise my rent."

Harrach had been following the archduke up to a point.

"I signed a lease," Ferdinand roared. "He can't do it. It's against the law."

"Did this Gruber character give a reason for wanting to raise your rent?"

"He said something about my overstocking the forests

with deer. Damaging his saplings. Or so he claims. He said he would go to court."

"Has he?"

"I don't care a damn whether he goes to court or not! I won't be cheated, Harrach. I signed a lease. That's all I know. That's all I need to know. I won't be cheated. I'll burn this godforsaken castle to the ground before I'll be cheated."

"Ferdinand . . ."

"I'll burn it to the ground!"

"Yes, of course," Harrach said gently, attempting to calm Ferdinand. But Ferdinand would not be calmed.

"Harrach, you will stay at Konopischt for a few days."

"I will be pleased to."

"Then you can help me burn this damned castle to the ground."

Harrach took the liberty of smiling.

"I'm serious," Ferdinand barked.

"I know you are," Harrach replied, the smile rapidly disappearing.

§ § §

Count Harrach stood in the stableyard. Even though it was still early morning he was exhausted. For three hours the previous evening he had argued with Ferdinand.

Fritz Gruber had gone to court with a convincing case. The judge had ruled in his favor. It had taken Count Harrach and Sophie hours to calm Ferdinand.

"I want four groups!" Ferdinand roared at the thirty-odd village men assembled in the stableyard. "Dobler, you'll take your group to the western perimeter. Wubbenhorst, your group will come down from the north. Stein and Weber, you'll follow the stream from the east."

Harrach stood silently, but the irony of the situation was not lost on him. He had come to Konopischt to talk Ferdinand out of attending a military maneuver but had become part of one.

Ferdinand had decided to vacate the premises, but the game in the forests was his, and he intended to take it with him.

Harrach ran his hand over the carved walnut stock of the rifle he held in his arms. He had never hunted with Ferdinand. The young count watched Ferdinand complete his instructions to the beaters, and then mounted his horse.

"A nice morning for the hunt," Harrach said.

Ferdinand nodded from the back of his horse. The two rode out of the stableyard, across the driveway, and into the forest.

After they had ridden for about twenty minutes, Ferdinand pulled his horse to a halt and pointed to an old carcass laying some twenty feet off the trail.

"Poacher?" Harrach asked.

Ferdinand nodded slowly. It did not appear to anger the archduke. Perhaps poaching was one of the professional hazards of royalty. Harrach stared down at the long-dead deer. Its skin had dried black and brittle and had pulled away from the rack of rib bones, leaving a display not too unlike the ivory keyboard of a harpsichord.

Harrach seized the opportunity.

"Wouldn't it be possible to have a holiday with Duchess Sophie somewhere other than Bosnia?"

"We've been through this before."

"Duchess Sophie might enjoy it more if you were—"

"It's politically important that I make that trip to Bosnia."

This was the first time Harrach had heard of a political reason for the state visit.

"Politically important?"

"The day after tomorrow the cabinet will receive my proposal for land reform in Bosnia. As you know, only Magyars and Muslims can own land in Bosnia. My proposal opens up landownership to everyone, including the Slavs."

"That's not going to be very popular in Vienna."

"Of course it isn't. The cabinet is going to be appalled. But that's because they're idiots. Except for Berchtold. He'll go for it because he understands in the long run we don't have a choice. If we're not very careful, we'll have a civil war in Bosnia."

"But what has this to do with your trip?"

"The cabinet will table my proposal for land reform. They don't have the courage to reject it immediately. Several of them owe me favors. It will be tabled. While I'm in Bosnia, I will make a public announcement that I have proposed this land reform and that the cabinet is considering it. The popular Slav support created by such an announcement should be enough to get it passed through the cabinet."

"But would the emperor sign it?"

"If there's enough strength in the cabinet, and if he realizes that civil war is the alternative, he may sign it. But if we're going to hold this empire together, we don't have a choice."

"Couldn't your support for land reform be announced somewhere other than in Bosnia?"

"It wouldn't generate enough popular support to get the proposal through the cabinet."

The two men rode on in silence until they came to the top of a small rise from which they could see the open meadowland that stretched down to the banks of a narrow stream. The tall, uncut meadow grass was dotted with yellow and purple flowers. The still air was hung with the odor of pollen. Dried seed pods rattled in the lazy morning breeze. Insects buzzed unmercifully.

They tethered their horses on the south side of the meadow and walked to a large upthrust boulder that crowned the top of the rise. Ferdinand stood for a few moments in silence, running his hand over the jagged surface of the rock.

"Glacial rock," he murmured. "Think of the strength it took to roll this boulder. It might have started rolling in Prussia or perhaps as far north as Russia. The glacier kicked it, like a football."

Ferdinand chuckled and slapped the boulder in mock

camaraderie. "That's the sort of strength that Austria needs."

An insect landed on Harrach's arm. He brushed it off.

"Ferdinand," Harrach began, "even considering the political reasons for your trip to Bosnia, I don't think you should go."

"You're a persistent bastard, aren't you?" Ferdinand replied with a grin. "My friend, I have no choice. Even if I was absolutely certain there would be an assassination attempt, I would still go. Perhaps someone else could change his mind, but I am the Crown Prince. I am like this boulder. Neither of us can rebel against our fate or our duty. They are one in the same."

"Your trip may be suicidal."

Ferdinand frowned and again ran his hand over the face of the rock, fingering the chipped fissures and following the streaky mineral deposits.

"Suicidal?" Ferdinand repeated thoughtfully and then shook his head. "I doubt it. All we have are unsubstantiated threats. I get many of them. Sometimes I think all Vienna will dance on my grave. But look at this boulder, Harrach. The strength that rolled this boulder as though it were a marble is the same strength that made me Crown Prince. I am in God's hands. When it is time for me to die, I will die. Not before. One always dies at the proper time."

There was a moment of silence before Ferdinand nudged his friend. They listened intently, heads cocked on one side like hounds just before the chase. Slowly the faint sounds of the beaters crept across the embroidered meadow. Ferdinand snapped the rifle's bolt in place.

"As they break onto the meadow," Ferdinand said, "you take the right side of the herd. Get the stragglers first and then work toward the center of the herd. For God's sake be careful of the beaters!"

The stillness of the meadow. Insects buzzing. The faraway rattle of a woodpecker searching an old tree for grubs. The barely audible whistle of the breeze among the cypress and the myrtle. And then the growing sounds of the beaters as they combed the woods, driving the game before them. The two men leaned against the boulder, rifles braced against their shoulders.

The sounds of the beaters came closer. Harrach wiped the perspiration from his hands. A branch cracked and Ferdinand moved his hand to his friend's shoulder.

"Wait until half of them are in the open."

Another branch cracked and the first stag broke out of the western thicket. Harrach tightened his grip on the rifle but left his finger limp about the trigger. He caught the fleeing animal in the rifle's sight and followed it. Time passed intolerably slowly as what appeared to be a ten- or even twelve-point buck leaped gracefully across the meadow.

Finally the others followed, breaking panic-ridden into the tall grass of the meadow.

"*Now!*"

The archduke's finger squeezed the trigger. The gun exploded. Ferdinand felt the rifle leap backward into his armpit. The shot caught a small buck in the middle of a leap and threw it sideways to the ground.

Both rifles continued to fire. Harrach was unconscious of the acrid powder smoke that made his eyes water, just as he was oblivious of the pain of the rifle's recoil. His shots seemed to have no effect. He knew he was not as good a marksman as Ferdinand, but still . . . The deer continued their panicked dash across the meadow. The lead bullets from his rifle seemed useless. He fired again and again. Finally there was nothing but a dull click. Mechanically he reloaded and fired again, but this time into the center of the herd; forgetting or choosing to ignore Ferdinand's instructions.

The yellow and purple wildflowers seemed to have lost their color, as if in a moment of panic the blood had drained from their petals. Bigger insects drowned out the buzzing gnats and flies. The woodpecker had flown away.

The big buck had made its way across the meadow and

into the opposite woods, wounded. It was the largest of this herd and would go far before bleeding to death.

Suddenly the beaters from the north appeared and Ferdinand's nudge told Harrach to be ready. Another herd of deer, larger than the last, broke onto the meadow. Harrach again felt the recoil of his rifle. A doe jolted as if by electric shock, stumbled and fell, kicked wildly for a moment, and then attempted to scramble to her feet. Harrach finished off the stationary target.

Ferdinand was raining bullets across the meadow and bringing down beasts on all sides. The understanding that Harrach should have the right side of the herd had been forgotten in the excitement. Harrach contented himself with finishing off those deer Ferdinand had only wounded.

The first group of beaters, instead of going back into the forest, ringed the meadow, making it impossible for the deer to escape. Not until Harrach saw this did he question the hunt.

Ferdinand snapped another clip into his rifle and without pausing rained more deadly fire down on the meadow. A spring fawn was thrown to the ground. An antlerless stag tumbled and fell.

The hunters heard the beaters approach from the far side of the narrow stream. Harrach ceased firing and watched. Dobler and Wubbenhorst emerged from the brush, singing and shouting, driving the game before them. The game broke onto the meadow.

First into view were three bucks with small racks. Before the bucks were twenty meters onto the meadow, Ferdinand had brought them to the ground. Following the bucks were the does and fawns, but Harrach's attention was elsewhere.

At the same moment another group of beaters appeared from the far end of the meadow, driving deer and rabbits before them. Ferdinand seemed lost in delirium. He shot back and forth across the meadow, right and then left and then right again. The timing was off. The fourth group of beaters had arrived too soon. There was too much to kill.

The meadow turned into a bloody confusion of beasts and beaters.

The deer ran in circles, panic stricken, searching for a break in the line of beaters; jolting suddenly with the impact of a bullet, stumbling, and then being mercifully dispatched by Harrach.

The shouting of the beaters and the roar of the rifles added to the chaos. Deer tripped over already dead or dying deer. The meadow was becoming blanketed with carcasses. It was an extermination.

Harrach had lost his taste for the hunt.

The final party of beaters arrived, driving before them the largest herd of deer that Konopischt held. Nine stags broke from the edges of the forest like a cavalry charge. Ferdinand roared, his rifle firing independently from his mind. The first wave of the charge fell. The dull click of another empty magazine. Ferdinand shouted a curse. Eight deer neared the opposite side of the meadow. There was a break in the line of beaters. Ferdinand reloaded and turned his gun on the fleeing deer.

Harrach wondered if the break in the line of beaters was intentional. Perhaps the beaters were as sickened as he was.

Three of the deer made it into the safety of the forest. The other five twitched and jerked and waited for Harrach to finish them off.

A few terrified rabbits tore about the body-strewn field searching for a break in the line of beaters. Ferdinand continued to shoot at them until the last one had either managed to escape or had been thrown high in the air by a bullet too large to hunt rabbits with.

And then there was nothing left to shoot at. The entire hunt had taken less than seventeen minutes. The meadow was covered with bodies and blood. The beaters, their clubs in hand, walked out onto the meadow to administer mercy to those beasts still alive.

Ferdinand sighed, leaning heavily on his rifle. He wiped the smoke stains from his cheeks and crinkled his nostrils as if to rid himself of the rancid smell of burned powder.

"Gruber's precious saplings should be safe for a long time," Ferdinand announced.

Harrach said nothing.

"Shall we see what we have accomplished?" Ferdinand led the way down to the meadow. A few of the beaters were still in the process of putting some of the animals out of their misery.

"Fifty-three deer," Ferdinand murmured.

"I cannot talk you out of going to Bosnia?" Harrach asked.

"I thought we had finished with that."

"I would like your permission to accompany you to Bosnia."

"To protect me?"

"To oversee the security measures."

"It would be a pleasure to have you along, but not a word to Sophie about the threat on my life."

Harrach nodded and turned his face away from Ferdinand. The sight of the slaughter made him feel sick.

CHAPTER THREE

Bosnia

At exactly ten minutes after two in the afternoon, Gavrilo, Nedelijko, and Trifun entered Loznica. It was a fairly large market town on the Drina that had, owing to its position on the river, grown into a major Serbian center of trade and commerce. The main street, bordered on either side by merchants and traders, led up to the stone bridge over the Drina—the border between Serbia and Bosnia.

Gavrilo led them to a café. His brow was wrinkled in thought. Despite Ciganovitch's instructions, he was concerned about the border crossing. Even though Captain Minic, the commanding officer of the border patrol in Loznica, was a member of the Union, Gavrilo expected trouble.

He was a *komitadji*. It was his business to expect trouble.

After an unsatisfying meal, they made their way to the border-patrol offices. Gavrilo carried the suitcase full of revolvers and grenades. Each of them had his small bottle of cyanide taped in his groin in such a way that only the most thorough search would reveal it.

They entered the border-patrol offices just after three. Gavrilo asked a sergeant behind a desk for Captain Minic. The sergeant inspected the young men with undisguised disdain and then ordered them to wait. Gavrilo tucked the suitcase between his legs.

They were kept waiting only a few minutes. The sergeant returned and beckoned for them to follow him. They were led into a small office. Captain Minic stood to greet them. His pistol was drawn from its holster and lay within easy reach on the desk.

"Your papers," Captain Minic ordered. Gavrilo placed their identification cards on the desk. Minic scanned the cards carefully. "Be seated."

Gavrilo watched Minic's face closely. There was suspicion in the captain's expression. Finally Minic pointed to Trifun Gabrez and demanded: "Your mother's maiden name?"

"My mother's maiden name?" Trifun repeated.

Minic reached to the pistol.

"Tell him your mother's name before she was married to your father," Nedelijko ordered.

"Jarek, I think."

Minic slipped the pistol back into the holster.

"Who sent you?"

"Apis."

"*Who?*"

"Colonel Apis, sir," Nedelijko corrected himself.

"Did you have any trouble getting this far?"

Gavrilo shook his head.

"A farmer gave us a ride in his wagon as far as Sabac. We spent last night there. Today we followed the river down to Loznica. There was no trouble."

"No trouble," Minic snorted angrily. "There's been trouble. Lot's of goddamn trouble. About this time yesterday I received a telegrammed directive from the prime minister ordering me to arrest you three."

Gavrilo's eyes narrowed dangerously.

"Yes, that's right," Minic continued. "Prime Minister Pastich knows about you."

"How?" Nedelijko demanded.

"I was about to ask you that."

"There's been an informer," Trifun murmured.

Gavrilo sat silently. Only six men knew about their plan. The three of them who sat in Captain Minic's office, and Apis, Tankosic, and Ciganovitch. There was no question about the integrity of the last three. They were senior officers in the union. That left only those present. . . .

"Did you speak to anyone before you left Belgrade?" Minic demanded.

The three young men shook their heads.

"You didn't boast about what you planned to do?"

Again the three young men indicated that they hadn't.

"I imagine that you can guess how furious Apis was," Captain Minic went on.

Two concerns predominated in Gavrilo's mind. First and foremost was the leak of information. How had Pastich come to know about them? Who was the informer? How much had been given away? Gavrilo turned his gaze upon Nedelijko and Trifun. Was it possible that one of them had turned informer?

The second worry that emerged from the confusion of his mind centered on what was going to happen next. Would all the plans be canceled? Would Minic disarm them and send them back to Belgrade? Perhaps he would disarm them and then allow them to cross the border into Serbia. Without weapons, it made no difference where they went.

Perhaps Captain Minic sensed Gavrilo's questions.

"Apis must consider your mission important."

"Has the mission been canceled?"

"I sent a telegram to Pastich this morning. You supposedly crossed the border yesterday, before I received his directive. That was Apis's order. But your orders have been changed. Apis thinks it likely that Pastich has sent a telegram to Vienna warning them about your mission. The Austrian border guards are probably already in possession of your names and descriptions. You cannot use your own identity cards."

Minic seized the three identity cards from the desk. "And we have not had time to make you new ones."

"How do we cross the border?" Nedelijko asked.

"Follow the river south. About four miles downstream, you'll find a boathouse. The owner has been paid. Take the boat and cross the river."

Minic leaned back in his chair. It was obvious from his tone of voice that he considered the three men too young and inexperienced to do the kind of work they were doing.

"You will be traveling in Bosnia without any travel documents. You know what to do if you are arrested?"

"We have cyanide," Gavrilo replied.

"You must not hesitate to use it."

§ § §

The next morning, after an uncomfortable night in the barracks at Loznica, the three young men started their seven-kilometer walk south along the Drina.

The Drina's history is as old as the Balkans. It flows south from the Austrian Alps, becoming the Drina only after it branches from the Sava. The meandering Drina, unlike so many rivers, does not end. There is no point at which it flows into the sea. Rather, it branches into many smaller rivers, and those rivers in turn flow into thousands of riverlets. The water from these Drina-fed streams irrigates all of southern Serbia and Macedonia.

There is a legend about the river. It is said that an oath taken by the waters of the Drina is unbreakable. While the oath is remembered the Drina will flow and the southern Slavs will live at peace. When the oath is forgotten, the Drina will stop flowing. The cobalt-blue water will disappear, and blood will take its place. Oddly enough, when the drought of 1912 dried up the Drina, the Balkans had gone to war.

Gavrilo walked in silence. Nedelijko and Trifun talked softly to each other. The forest that came up to the edge of the gorge was full of birds—the gray and black Balkan crows, the larks, the graceful swallows, and the elusive falcon.

It was midmorning when they sighted the boathouse. The river had widened and the gorge walls sloped gently outward. Gavrilo carried the suitcase, which now seemed so much heavier than before.

The boathouse was small, built on the riverbank and extending a little way out into the water on stilts. Gavrilo paused, still within the cover of the woods. He remembered Tankosic's words: *The easiest objective is always the most dangerous.*

There had already been one informer. There was no guarantee there would not be another.

Again Tankosic's words came back to Gavrilo: *The ideal* komitadji *must be a combination of cat burglar, gunman, and poacher!*

Gavrilo opened the suitcase, extracted one of the three Brownings, and loaded the six chambers with shells. Trifun and Nedelijko watched silently. Although officially they were all of the same rank, Gavrilo's leadership was accepted and unquestioned.

"For me?" Trifun whispered.

"With your eyesight," Nedelijko chuckled softly, "you'd blow your own balls off!"

"I passed Tankosic's test," Trifun replied.

"Quiet," Gavrilo whispered. "Nedelijko, take the ridge above the boathouse. Stay out of sight." Gavrilo handed the suitcase to Nedelijko. "Trifun, count to ten slowly and then walk casually to the boathouse. We'll cover you. If anything looks wrong, get out of there as fast as you can."

Trifun nodded.

Gavrilo ducked down behind a low shrub. He watched Nedelijko run to the ridge. Trifun began to count.

Gavrilo inched his way forward to a shallow depression. The trail they had come down was also used by Serbian border patrols. They had seen none so far. Gavrilo watched Trifun begin to walk toward the boathouse. Gavrilo listened intently to the forest. Something had changed. Something was different. It took him several seconds to understand what was wrong. All the time they had walked along the river, he had heard birds. Suddenly there were no birds.

Something or someone had scared them away.

Nedelijko was in position on the ridge.

Trifun was halfway to the boathouse when Gavrilo first heard the sound of voices. It came from the trail they had taken. Trifun heard the voices at the same time as Gavrilo, and broke into a crouched run across the loose silt to the boathouse.

Gavrilo turned toward the trail and leveled the Browning revolver.

Five Serbian soldiers broke into the clearing. The first two were engaged in conversation. The fourth laughed loudly. Gavrilo held his breath. Trifun had made it to the boathouse but had left deep footprints in the silt at the river's edge.

The Serbian patrol walked down into the clearing. The first two paused some fifteen meters from the boathouse. There was a conversation that Gavrilo could not hear. Finally three of them walked back up the trail and began collecting kindling wood.

Damn! Gavrilo cursed them silently. They were going to cook their lunch. What could he do? Tankosic's words echoed silently in his mind: *The brain is the* komitadji's *most valuable tool. Use it!*

Even if Nedelijko had armed himself from the suitcase, forcing a conflict was lunacy. Each of the Serbian soldiers had a carbine slung over his shoulder. Trifun was unarmed, and Gavrilo's own revolver was next to useless at that range.

Use the brain, he ordered himself. Use the brain! What had Tankosic said about situations like this? *The closest friend a* komitadji *has is patience, for patience is the mother of cunning.*

Patience then, but a prepared patience.

Gavrilo crawled closer to the Serbian patrol, moving slowly and cautiously and soundlessly. He wanted to hear their conversation.

The largest of the Serbian soldiers untied an olive-green backpack and spread several tin pots on the ground. He gestured to a younger soldier to fill them from the river. A bearded soldier sat on a fallen tree trunk and began to unlace his boots.

"These damned boots don't fit."

"Don't complain to me," replied the largest of the soldiers, who was now blowing on the fire. "You just have big feet."

"At least we got transferred to days. Those night patrols were driving me crazy."

"The little woman," another soldier snorted with a laugh. "She kept wondering what you were patrolling for."

"You can laugh, you don't have eighty kilos of woman to bite your head off."

"All you ever do is complain," the largest of the soldiers snapped. "You deserve her. Now be quiet."

"Gerwig!" the youngest of the soldiers shouted from the river bank. "Come here and see what I've found."

The largest of the soldiers rose to his feet.

"What do you want now?"

"Footprints in the sand."

Gavrilo held his breath and leveled the revolver at the large chest of the man named Gerwig.

"Footprints," Gerwig repeated with undisguised sarcasm. "Our young friend has found footprints. Would you like another stripe for your arm? Captain Minic has been looking for those footprints for weeks."

The other soldiers chuckled. The young soldier filled the tin pots and returned to the camp fire.

Suddenly a twig snapped behind Gavrilo. He whirled into a crouch, the revolver steady in his hand.

"It's only me," Nedelijko whispered.

Gavrilo lowered the gun.

"What are we going to do?"

"Wait in silence," Gavrilo murmured.

And it was in silence that they waited, watching the soldiers eat, rest, repack their kit bags, and finally trudge off to complete their patrol.

Gavrilo was first at the boathouse. He swung open the river-warped door and peered into the dim interior. At first Gavrilo could see no sign of Trifun. Nedelijko read the confusion on Gavrilo's face and pointed to the small rowboat that rocked gently in the shallow water.

"The idiot fell asleep," Nedelijko whispered with a chuckle. "It's a damn good thing he didn't snore."

Nedelijko shook the big boy's shoulder and Trifun grunted into awareness.

"Have they gone?"

"What would you care? Did you have a nice sleep?" Nedelijko snapped.

"I thought they were never going to leave. It got so hot in here. I couldn't keep my eyes open."

"Dead men also have trouble staying awake!" Gavrilo snapped. "Don't let it happen again."

Gavrilo braced his feet against the wooden walkway and untied the small boat. Then they pushed the boat from the shadows of the boathouse out into the brilliant afternoon sun.

Trifun rowed unevenly and the boat zigzagged through the water. Gavrilo held the handgrip of the revolver and searched the shoreline for any sign of the patrol.

Nedelijko whispered instructions to Trifun. The big boy could not grasp that to go left he had to pull on the right oar, but compensated by making each stroke as deep and powerful as possible.

They could not land directly opposite the boathouse due to the rocky Bosnian shoreline, and so Gavrilo ordered Trifun to row downstream.

About a kilometer farther downstream there was a short stretch of pebble beach. Gavrilo ordered the boat beached. Once the three of them had climbed out of the boat, Gavrilo waded back into the water and pushed the boat out into the main current.

Later, when some peasant found it, he would assume it had broken its moorings.

Standing on the beach, Gavrilo felt a chill run through his frail body. The pebbles he stood upon were both familiar and foreign. It was Bosnia, his homeland, the land of his people. But it was a foreign land, owned, occupied, and abused by foreign invaders. For a moment he felt as if the soul of his people had crossed the river with him. He stared down at the rich blue water and silently swore never to forget his people.

Although it would have been shorter to walk due south in the direction of Sarajevo, Gavrilo started off almost due north. He had changed plans. If the Austrians had been warned, as Apis had thought, there would be patrols out looking for them. The roads to the south would be guarded. He led the other two north to Tuzla. They could catch a train from Tuzla to Sarajevo. There was a chance that the police would not search trains coming in from the north.

Gavrilo explained the change of plan to Nedelijko and Trifun. They did not argue.

In the late afternoon they managed to get a ride with a farmer and his goats. They would make Tuzla before dark. That was important. Gavrilo had heard of a man in Tuzla who might help them. Although he had never met the man, he had heard from Ciganovitch that the man was sympathetic to the Slav cause.

Gavrilo sought help from Donovitch of Tuzla, manager of the cinema, owner of the bank, and mayor of the town.

It was not common for so established a man to have any sympathies that did not lead directly to his own financial gain.

What made Donovitch's Slav sympathies even stranger was that he was a Magyar.

It was twilight when they reached the edge of Tuzla. They paused on the outskirts of the town. They was no question that they needed help. They had no identification papers— a criminal offense.

Gavrilo knew that the Austrian patrols would question anyone on the streets after dark. He decided not to take any unnecessary chances. "When you can't fight, retreat," Tankosic had said, "and when you can't retreat, coordinate!"

"We'll enter the town one at a time and meet at Donovitch's cinema." Gavrilo peeled off six banknotes and handed three to Nedelijko and three to Trifun. "For the tickets," he explained.

Picking up the suitcase, he began to walk into town. Nedelijko and Trifun would follow him at fifteen-minute intervals. The main street of Tuzla was dirt with large water-filled potholes. Gavrilo was aware of the rapidly falling darkness.

His first job was to find Donovitch. He headed toward the cinema.

As he rounded the corner of a frame cottage, he ran headlong into an Austrian patrol. Gavrilo's pulse beat angrily against the inside of his head. But he forced himself to remain calm and nodded casually to the Austrian soldiers.

"Your papers," ordered the closest soldier. Gavrilo's mind worked as fast as fear.

"They have been mailed to my uncle," Gavrilo replied in fluent German.

"Uncle?" the soldier repeated.

"Donovitch, the mayor," Gavrilo added. "I'm on my way to visit him."

"You have no identity papers?" the soldier demanded.

Gavrilo began to explain again but was silenced by a second soldier.

"No identity papers? Arrest him. I don't care a damn who his uncle is. No one is above the law."

The four soldiers seemed to take particular pleasure in arresting the mayor's nephew. But it was not the soldier's satisfaction that unnerved Gavrilo; it was the fear that they would search the suitcase he carried. He kept his hand from shaking by plunging it deep into his pocket until he felt the handgrip of the Browning revolver he had stuck beneath his shirt.

Two of the four soldiers took him to the police station. He carried the suitcase carefully so as not to strain under its weight. When they arrived, Gavrilo was ordered to sit on a wooden bench while one of the soldiers stood guard over him.

"What's going to happen?" Gavrilo murmured.

"We're going to eat you for dinner!"

"I've never been arrested before," Gavrilo continued with all the humility he could muster. Within him he felt fury, and he seriously calculated the odds of successfully shooting his way out of the police station.

"All Slavs should be arrested at least once," the soldier replied. "It teaches them respect."

Gavrilo remembered Apis's order about commiting suicide. He felt the cyanide vial taped in his groin. He slipped the suitcase beneath the bench. There might come a time for suicide, but that time had not yet arrived.

The door to the street was only twenty meters from where he sat. Darkness had fallen and the moon was still behind a blanket of clouds. If he could make it into the street, the police would have a hard time following him. He tried to assess his chances. If he made a break for the street there was no way that he could take the suitcase with him. It was much too heavy.

How long would it be before they searched him? All

prisoners were routinely searched. If he shot the soldier who guarded him and ran for the street, what were the chances that he could get out of Tuzla alive? Would Nedelijko and Trifun be picked up in the search for him?

Before Gavrilo had a chance to make up his mind whether to kill the man standing next to him, another soldier appeared and ordered Gavrilo into an inner office.

The room had three large oak desks. He was told to sit in a chair facing the center desk. Again, Gavrilo thrust the suitcase between his legs.

A sergeant, seated behind the center desk, spoke without looking up at Gavrilo.

"Name!"

"Louis Ranov," Gavrilo replied.

"Occupation?"

"I'm a student at the industrial school."

"You're a Slav."

"Half. My mother was Slav. My father was a Magyar."

The Austrian sergeant sighed, already bored with the young man. Gavrilo heard the sergeant's boredom, and it pleased him. He now had the weapon of surprise.

"Address! Date of birth! Prison record?"

To all of these Gavrilo replied in polite and perfect German.

"The arresting officer tells me that you are the nephew of Mayor Donovitch. You should know better than to travel without identity papers."

"I changed schools. My new papers were not ready by the time I was to leave. My father is mailing them to my uncle."

"That's no excuse. It is forbidden to travel without identity papers. Perhaps you think you are above the law because you are the mayor's nephew?"

"No, sir," Gavrilo said quickly.

"You are not a child. You are old enough to know better."

Gavrilo nodded in feigned contrition.

"You Slav students are the worst. You call us swine. You spit on the Austrian flag."

"No, sir."

"Quiet!" the sergeant roared. "You Slav students think of yourselves as liberators. I'll tell you what you really are: bad-mannered children! If Austria has a duty to the world, it is to teach you Slavs some manners."

Gavrilo nodded politely.

"Now," the sergeant continued in a slightly gentler tone. "Have I treated you so badly? Have any of my men struck you? Have I acted like a tyrant?"

The two police clerks who sat at the other desks chuckled at the last question. Gavrilo remained silent and shook his head.

His father's words rang silently in his head: "Learn from what you see, Gavrilo. Watch them bury another Slav. Never forget how easy it is to bury a Slav! Learn that!"

The sergeant went on, "You are too young to understand what Austria is trying to do for Bosnia. You students are blind. You think we are acting out of self-interest. What interest could we have in a land rich only in rocks?"

Gavrilo continued to shake his head. Each gesture of agreement seemed to take greater and greater effort.

"You Slavs would starve without our help. Sometimes I think we should let you have your own way—let you go to the devil. . . ."

Gavrilo stopped listening. It was the patronizing condescension of people like the sergeant that he hated most about the occupation.

Suddenly the sergeant stopped speaking and Gavrilo felt a soldier grasp his arm.

"It will be amusing to see the expression of Donovitch's face when he has to pick up his nephew at the police station," the sergeant announced.

Gavrilo's teeth came together. So that was what was happening. The sergeant had sent someone to get Donovitch. The whole situation changed before his eyes.

He was taken back to the wooden bench and told to sit. The heavy suitcase between his legs, Gavrilo attempted to sort out his chances.

If Donovitch was sympathetic to the Slav cause, if he was quick witted enough, if he didn't get confused and immediately announce that he had no nephew, if he was willing to risk his neck by coming to the police station, and if the police didn't search Gavrilo in the meantime, there was a chance that it would work. Too damned many ifs.

Gavrilo sat on the wooden bench for three-quarters of an hour. His mind seethed with calculations. Twice he came close to shooting the soldier who guarded him.

Suddenly he felt a hand grab his elbow and direct him back into the inner office. He seized the suitcase with his left hand, leaving his right free to grab the handgrip of the Browning beneath his shirt. As he walked, he slipped his hand under his loose shirt and eased the revolver out of his belt.

Before he could pull the gun, a man threw himself on Gavrilo and pinned the young man's arms to his sides.

"Louis, Louis!" the man cried. "I told your father not to allow you to travel without your papers. Now you can see what trouble you have gotten yourself into."

Donovitch held on to Gavrilo while the young man plunged the revolver back into his belt beneath his shirt.

"You were always strong willed, but this time, Louis, you have gone too far!"

Gavrilo nodded meekly.

"You must apologize to the sergeant for the trouble you have caused."

Gavrilo complied with the mayor's demand.

"Come along now. I am sure your aunt will want words with you."

The fat little mayor bowed to the sergeant and caught hold of Gavrilo's arm.

In the street outside the police station the mayor's grip

loosened a bit, and after several hundred meters, Donovitch said softly, "Talk about nothing serious until we reach my house. Your friends are there."

Gavrilo, in the confusion of being arrested, had forgotten about Nedelijko and Trifun. But now it became obvious. When he had not shown up at the cinema, Nedelijko and Trifun had gone to Donovitch's house and had explained the situation to him.

Gavrilo followed Donovitch's instructions and didn't speak until they reached his house. The mayor's house was large, with a living room, a dining room, and four separate bedrooms. It was the largest house Gavrilo had even been in. The trappings made Donovitch's wealth obvious, and Gavrilo found himself puzzled by the man's sympathy with the Slav cause.

Nedlijko and Trifun greeted him warmly and plied him with questions. Gavrilo's eyes, however, were riveted to Donovitch.

"Thank you," Gavrilo murmured.

Donovitch nodded without looking up.

"It is not common that a Magyar helps a Slav."

When Donovitch did look up at the young man, his eyes were filled with anger.

"Your friends told me about your plans," the Magyar roared. "It's lunacy. Madness!" Donovitch broke off in disgust.

"You are a member of the Union?" Gavrilo demanded.

"Yes," Donovitch sneered. "I am a member, and I will remember my oath. I will not betray you. But the blood will not stop with the Crown Prince's. It will not stop with yours, and it will not stop with mine. . . ."

"You have placed yourself and your family in danger," Gavrilo replied.

Gavrilo's comment only made Donovitch angrier. He glared at the young man for several moments until he finally shook his head sadly.

"It is a sad nation that makes heroes out of children."

"We are *komitadji*," Gavrilo snapped.

"Of course you are," the Magyar whispered wearily. "And no doubt you are friends of all the Slav people."

"We will need your help getting out of Tuzla."

"I will make arrangements for getting the three of you on the morning train to Sarajevo," Donovitch replied, and then turned and walked out of the room. The Magyar mayor was aware that if the three young men were successful, his life and the lives of his wife and child would be in great danger.

§   §   §

Gavrilo woke early. He ate a small breakfast with the mayor and discussed the train trip to Sarajevo. Donovitch stressed over and over again that Gavrilo must not be seen at the railroad station.

After breakfast, Donovitch left to get the train tickets, and Gavrilo went upstairs to wake Nedelijko and Trifun. He found it annoying that his companions were still asleep.

The three young men left the house at fifteen-minute intervals. Gavrilo had given Nedelijko a revolver and ammunition. If they were stopped in Tuzla, Gavrilo had decided to shoot first. He had even made up a story claiming that he had come to Tuzla to rob his uncle's bank. There was a slim chance that it might save Donovitch.

But Gavrilo did not run into any police patrols on his way to the railroad station. He arrived ten minutes before the train was due to leave and hid himself in the public toilet until he heard the train whistle and the scream of escaping steam.

He jumped on the train unnoticed just as it was pulling out of the station. He had no difficulty finding a seat in the smoking car. Relief flowed through him. He thrust the suitcase between his legs. Accomplishment, a pure sense of achievement flowed through his mind.

Nervously, he glanced about the carriage. Trifun sat seven rows in front of him. Nedelijko must be in a different carriage.

§   §   §

It was midafternoon when the train puffed its way into Sarajevo. Gavrilo's lips formed a secret smile. He sought Trifun's eyes and found that they too were triumphal. Neither of them offered any sign of recognition.

The station was always crowded, but somehow Gavrilo thought it was more crowded than he had ever seen it before. He wondered for an instant if all the people were present because of what he was about to do.

Vendors huddled on the platform, hand-woven garments and spring flowers were spread beneath his feet. He listened to the cacaphony of chaos. Beneath the soot-stained glass roof that sheltered him from the direct rays of the sun, stood the crowded *wechseln* office, and to his left the great black boiler of the train relaxed into split tongues of hissing steam.

There was not an Austrian soldier in sight.

It was the afternoon of June 27, 1914.

PART TWO

Vidovdan

Audacity, audacity, and more.audacity.
     —Danton's maxim
          for revolutionary movements.

*June 28 is Vidovdan, the Feast of St. Vitus.
To the Slav peoples of the Balkan peninsula
it is a holiday unlike any other. For centuries it
was a national day of mourning because it
commemorates the battle of Kossovo in 1389
when the Turks destroyed the medieval king-
dom of Serbia and enslaved its Christian
subjects. Since 1912 it has been the symbol of
a glorious resurrection—the defeat of the Turks
in the First Balkan War that led.to their virtual
expulsion from Europe.*
     —Edmund Taylor, *The Fall of the Dynasties*

CHAPTER ONE

Preparations

Saturday, June 27, 4:00 P.M.

Preparations for the archduke's visit to Sarajevo were already underway when Dr. Rudolph Cistler left his office on Appel Quay. Uniformed workmen pruned the flowering fruit trees that lined the Miljacka river. Men in dark suits distributed photographed portraits of the Crown Prince to shopkeepers along the motorcade route. They were told to have the archduke's portrait in their shop window by seven the following morning.

Cistler was not in the habit of working on Saturdays. Usually there was not enough work to demand his presence. But this Saturday had been different. He had spent the afternoon drafting a will for a peasant farmer. The farmer was Slav and as such had nothing of any real value to leave to his heirs. But Cistler had taken much time and care with the will. Such was the way he worked.

Cistler rarely worked alone—not because his meager caseload demanded extra attention, but simply because the old lawyer enjoyed his own daughter's company.

Stega was more than a mere daughter to him. She had her mother's strength. She wore her Slav peasant background—at times, even proudly. She was large-boned, with broad shoulders and ample, child-bearing hips. Even in the city, where many Slavs had ceased to wear native dress, Stega continued to do so. Like her father, she knew that she was out of place, but then, she also knew that in the Austrian empire all Slavs were out of place.

The last few years had been difficult for the old lawyer. As a Slav, there had always been questions about his practicing law. Some courts permitted him to argue cases; other did not. As Bosnia went, Sarajevo was probably the most liberal area. He could represent other Slavs. He could not, however, represent Magyars, Austrians, or Muslims.

But Dr. Cistler's real troubles had begun after his wife had died. Maria had been more than just a wife; she had been a companion, friend, teacher, and second mother to the old man. She had calmed his anger, tempered his excesses, encouraged moderation in everything, especially in her husband's consumption of *vinjak*.

Maria had become a victim of smallpox. She had died in her bed in their small house on Vuka Street. The Sarajevo hospital did not admit Slavs.

After Maria's death, Cistler had found himself adrift. He continued working but found little satisfaction in even those cases which had previously excited him. A deep brooding depression set in. All his interests failed him. Even his friend Father Jamis could only hope to raise a thin sardonic smile.

More and more Cistler found himself sharing his leisure time with a *vinjak* bottle. The waiters at a half dozen local cafés greeted him by his first name and smiled with understanding when Stega arrived in the early hours of the morning to take him home.

It was not long before the legal community was buzzing

about old Cistler's decline. Some were sympathetic. Some were amused. Others explained with seriousness that it was to be expected of a Slav. The law school should have rules about admitting Slavs. The general court of Sarajevo was much too liberal.

But Dr. Cistler's disgrace did not take place until two years after Maria had died.

On a pleasant morning in the spring of 1910, the sun was warm and shone brightly upon the street vendors who spread their wares on the pavements of Franz Joseph Street. The shout of these vendors managed to awaken Dr. Cistler.

His head ached, his vision was blurred, and his mouth tasted vaguely like burned toast. The old lawyer gestured to the blurred image of a waiter, who brought him another bottle of *vinjak*.

"It's morning, Dr. Cistler. Shouldn't you be going home?"

"Morning?"

"It's six o'clock."

"Morning?"

Cistler sat in the café until the pain in his head had been reduced to a distant throb. The *vinjak* cleaned his mouth and cleared his vision. Then he realized that he had spent the night slouched over the café table.

"What day is it?"

"Thursday," the waiter replied.

"Christ almighty!" Cistler mumbled, his gray head sinking into the cupped palms of his hands. "I'm supposed to be in court in another hour."

The old lawyer took another large gulp of *vinjak* and stumbled toward the lavatory in the rear courtyard. He used the toilet and splashed cold water on his face. He stared at himself in the cracked mirror.

He looked like hell. His eyes looked like holes made with a red-hot poker. He shook his head. His long gray hair fell in front of his eyes. White-gray stubble covered his chin.

"To hell with them," he murmured to his reflected face.

He walked unsteadily back to the table he had been

sitting at, gulped down a third of the bottle of *vinjak,* and decided to appear in court exactly as he was.

The case was not an important one. Not one he could have hoped to win. A Magyar shopkeeper had accused a Slav boy of trying to steal a blanket. There was no evidence, other than the shopkeeper's word against the boy. But it was enough for a conviction.

Cistler appeared in court promptly at ten o'clock. He waited through several cases, until the judge called his client and himself to the bench. It took the judge only minutes to realize that Dr. Cistler was in no condition to be in court.

"You look ill, Dr. Cistler. I suggest you go home and rest."

That was all the judge had said. But the reek of *vinjak* was too strong for the others in the court to ignore. The rumor was passed. A petition was drawn up. Disbarment proceedings were initiated.

But Dr. Cistler was not disbarred. For one reason or another the proceedings were dropped. Cistler suspected simple laziness on the part of the other lawyers. Father Jamis had argued that he was being given another chance.

During the period of his sickness Cistler did not want another chance. All he really wanted was *vinjak* and oblivion.

The sickness had lasted two painful months. Stega and Father Jamis had been ruthless. There had been many times when he had come to hate them.

§   §   §

A gust of wind blew down Appel Quay, picking up last year's leaves and swirling them in the air. The memory of his sickness was not a pleasant one. Cistler reached the far side of the quay and turned in the direction of Vuka Street.

Just as the old lawyer stepped onto the opposite curb, two men in dark, ill-fitting suits came up on either side of him.

"Austrian security," announced the one on the right, flashing an official-looking identity card. "What's your name?"

"Rudolph Cistler."

"What are you doing on the quay?"

"I was crossing the street, until you stopped me."

"What business do you have being here?"

"I work across the street. I'm a lawyer."

"Search him," the plainclothesman on the right ordered. The man on the left swung Cistler around and made the old man brace himself against the parapet that overlooked the river. They frisked him from his armpits to his ankles.

"You really think an old man like myself would be out planting bombs?" Cistler asked, suddenly finding humor in the situation. "Do I look like a *komitadji*?"

"Keep quiet, old man."

"Do I look suspicious?" Cistler asked, grinning. "A man of my age can not help but be flattered at all this attention. You really thought—"

"You'll spend the night in jail, if you don't keep your mouth shut."

"On what grounds? Don't forget, I'm a lawyer."

The security officer on the right shrugged his shoulders.

"Go home, old man, and stay off the quay. All Slavs found on the quay are being detained for questioning."

"The Crown Prince will be proud of you," Cistler snapped, and walked off toward his home on Vuka Street.

June 27, 5:00 P.M.

Trifun Gabrez left the railroad station in Sarajevo thinking he was a hero. Even though Gavrilo had not allowed him to carry a weapon, he felt proud of himself. He swaggered slightly, allowing his broad shoulders to fall into the rhythm of his stride.

The apelike young man was amused by the other people in the street. For once in his life he knew something they didn't. He knew what was going to happen the following day. He felt powerful.

He rented a small attic room overlooking Barcarsija Square. Although unaware of the nature of what he felt, something bestial in Trifun was excited by the speed of events. He told the Muslim landlord, as Gavrilo had instructed him to, that he was a farm laborer who had come to market and then had become separated from his employer.

The Muslim landlord stared suspiciously at the large young man for a moment but then accepted the money Trifun offered.

Trifun sighed as he entered the tiny room. He had not been asked for his identity card. He had only fourteen hours to wait.

June 27, 5:45 P.M.

Count Harrach stepped from the carriage and ran up the seven steps that led to the entrance of Sarajevo's town hall. A young Austrian officer saluted and pointed toward the streaked marble staircase. Harrach took the stairs two at a time.

There was an emergency. Another telegram had arrived from Pastich.

When he reached the second floor another Austrian officer saluted him and led him down the corridor to the mayor's office. Without pausing to knock, Harrach flung open the door and marched into the office.

There were three men in the office. Harrach knew only one of them, a Lieutenant von Merrizi, an extremely capable security officer sent from Vienna especially to handle the archduke's visit to Sarajevo.

Count Harrach nodded to von Merrizi. Von Merrizi carried out the introductions without wasting words.

"Count Harrach, this is Mayor Sudjic." The fat Magyar stood and bowed from the neck. "And this is Colonel Smyra, chief of Bosnian security."

Smyra, a heavyset, bullet-headed Austrian, rose to his

feet and extended his hand. Harrach shook it and noted the strength in the colonel's grip.

"You have news?" Smyra asked as the four men seated themselves.

"Another telegram from Pastich," Harrach began. "He says that despite Serbian security measures, three students have managed to cross the border into Bosnia. According to Pastich, they are armed and are to be considered extremely dangerous."

"We have names?" von Merrizi demanded.

"Descriptions," Harrach replied, "but no names."

"That's odd," Smyra snapped.

"What's odd?"

"No names. If Pastich knows that these three students have already crossed into Bosnia, he must also know their names. Why hasn't he supplied us with them?"

"They probably wouldn't travel under their real names anyway," von Merrizi suggested.

"But," Smyra replied, "we have security files. If we had their real names we would know who their friends were. We would know where they might be staying if they have managed to get into Sarajevo."

"What are the chances that they've already arrived in Sarajevo?"

"It depends," Smyra answered softly, lighting a cigarette. "As you know, all the roads that come from the Serbian border have been patrolled. All the trains that have come in from the west have been searched."

"Is it possible," von Merrizi asked, "that our three students could have arrived in Sarajevo from either the north or the south?"

"It's possible," Smyra replied quietly, "but it would be out of their way."

"They could have simply taken a train south from Brcko, Slatina, or Tuzla," Harrach announced.

Smyra didn't reply immediately. He didn't enjoy sharing

the responsibilities for the archduke's safety with Harrach and von Merrizi.

When the emperor had paid a state visit to Sarajevo, Colonel Smyra had been solely responsible for the security arrangements. Vienna had sent him three hundred soldiers to line the parade route. But this time, Vienna had insisted that he share the security arrangements with Harrach and von Merrizi, and instead of sending him three hundred men, Vienna had sent only thirty.

Smyra turned his eyes back toward Harrach.

"Yes, it is possible that our students came in from the north. But it would be difficult for them to stay in Sarajevo. When Lieutenant von Merrizi first informed me of Pastich's telegram, I ordered all students with Slavist sympathies arrested. We picked up twenty young men."

"But all those little boarding houses in the souk . . ."

"Possible," Smyra replied, "but unlikely." Colonel Smyra honestly believed that if an attempt on the archduke's life was made, it would not be made in Sarajevo itself. Any assassination attempt, Smyra convinced himself, would have to include an escape plan for the assassins. Escaping from Sarajevo after an attempt on the life of the Crown Prince would be impossible. Everything pointed toward an attempt on the Crown Prince's life either at the hotel or Ilidize or while Ferdinand was en route to Sarajevo.

It was this logic that particularly embittered Smyra. His responsibility for the archduke's safety extended only as far as the perimeters of the city of Sarajevo. Smyra turned to Harrach.

"Do we have a revised schedule for the Crown Prince's visit tomorrow?"

Harrach reached into his pocket and withdrew a page of hastily scribbled notes.

"Ferdinand refuses to change the schedule, even after I told him about Pastich's second telegram. It remains essentially the same. Ferdinand and Sophie will spend the night at the hotel in Ilidze. In the morning, Sophie will attend mass before breakfast. Von Merrizi's men will guard the chapel. At nine Ferdinand and Sophie will have breakfast at the restaurant overlooking the racetrack in Ilidze. While they are having breakfast, the motorcade will form in front of the restaurant. At ten they will enter the cars, and begin the trip into Sarajevo. It should take them about an hour to cover the thirty kilometers between Ilidze and Sarajevo, so they should be arriving at the town hall at about eleven."

The fat Magyar mayor looked up from his desk and interrupted Harrach.

"At which point, I will present the Crown Prince with the keys of the city. Duchess Sophie will be escorted upstairs to meet with a delegation of Muslim women. Archduke Ferdinand will address the assembly. . . ."

Harrach was the only one in the room who had read an advance copy of Ferdinand's speech. He knew as a certainty what the others had heard as merely rumor. Ferdinand was indeed going to announce his support for land reform in Bosnia.

"After the speech at the town hall," Mayor Sudjic continued, "Archduke Ferdinand and Duchess Sophie will be taken to the governor's residence for luncheon. They will spend the afternoon there, resting. The ball is set for seven o'clock, although I shouldn't think the Crown Prince would arrive before eighty-thirty or nine."

"What we must be most concerned about," von Merrizi interjected, "are the few times that Ferdinand will be required to appear in public. My men are covering the hotel in Ilidze. Security on the town hall and the governor's residence should be no problem."

Colonel Smyra nodded expressionlessly. He did not like being instructed in his work.

"What we should concern ourselves with," von Merrizi continued, "is the drive into Sarajevo and the drive from the town hall to the governor's residence."

It was Smyra's turn to interrupt. He could not allow his professionalism to be interfered with, without comment.

"I have deployed twenty of my men along Appel Quay. They have instructions to detain and question any Slav found on the quay. I have another ten men at the train station. They will be searching all incoming trains. This is in addition to the patrols on the roads coming in from the Serbian border."

"Is it worth searching the boarding houses in the souk?" von Merrizi asked Smyra.

"I'd have to pull men from the quay. I'd rather leave them where they are."

"What about the three students?" Mayor Sudjic asked. "If anything happens to the Crown Prince in Sarajevo, I'll be held responsible."

Smyra gritted his teeth and raised his eyebrows in exaggerated futility. He disliked the mayor and made no effort to hide his feelings.

"Count Harrach," Colonel Smyra began, "is there any chance that Ferdinand will change his itinerary?"

"I doubt it," Harrach replied, "but I am going to see him after supper. I'll make another attempt to get him to change plans."

"We should assume that Ferdinand will refuse to alter the arrangements," Smyra added. "In which case, we should probably meet late and coordinate security for the actual motorcade."

Von Merrizi nodded.

"Nine o'clock?"

"Unless something comes up before," Harrach murmured.

The young count rose to his feet. He was already tired, and he was aware that he would not get much sleep that night.

June 27, 6:00 P.M.

Nedelijko Cabrinovitch wandered through the rabbit-warren alleys of the souk. There had been a number of boarding houses at which he could have spent the night, but he was being cautious. That was what Gavrilo had ordered: caution.

He remembered Gavrilo's instructions that morning in Tuzla: "We will travel separately. Even if I bump into you, offer no sign of recognition. Once we get to Sarajevo, go into the souk. Rent a room. None of us will know where the others are staying. If one of us is arrested, even under torture he will not be able to inform upon the others.

"We'll meet in the morning," Gavrilo had ordered. "Nine o'clock sharp. The Putnik Café on Barcarsija Square. There's a window table. The first one there will sit at the window table. If everything is all right he will be holding a fork in the left hand. If something is wrong, he will be holding it in his right hand.

"If the first one at the café is holding the fork in his right hand, it means every man for himself. We'll still try for the archduke, but individually. Understand?"

Nedelijko had understood. The coolness of the revolver beneath his belt had impressed Gavrilo's caution upon him. Success was important to him.

He had seen several Austrian patrols in the souk, but it was not hard to avoid them. The Muslim quarter of the city was riddled with narrow cobblestone streets and alleys. Nedelijko had been brought up on the edge of the souk. It had been his playground as a child. He knew the shortcuts, the cul-de-sacs, the alleys that would lead to the river. He was cautious but not overly worried about being caught.

The young man paused at the end of Voda Street. It would be twilight in another hour. It was time to get off the streets. It would be harder to avoid the Austrian patrols at night. He turned down Voda street and walked to a small boarding house.

The landlady was a plump Magyar whom he had known as a child. She greeted him warmly, asking about his family and his schooling. Nedelijko answered the question, pleasantly and then asked if she had a room he could rent for the night.

The landlady's eyes narrowed.

"Why don't you stay with your family?" she demanded.

"My father is angry."

"You have failed in school?" the landlady asked with annoyance. "Nedelijko, you must learn to concentrate."

"No, no, school is fine. It has to do with a girl."

A broad grin appeared on the plump woman's face. Nedelijko had judged the situation correctly. The woman would help him if she thought it involved an affair of the heart.

"Little Nedelijko has a girlfriend?"

"My father does not approve."

"What is wrong with her?"

Nedelijko thought quickly and decided to gamble. "She is a Magyar."

The grin disappeared from the woman's face. He wondered if he had gone too far.

"That is not good, Nedelijko. Many people have strong feelings . . ."

"But . . ."

"I know what you're going to tell me," the plump woman interrupted. "I'm not that old that I have forgotten the passions of youth. But . . ." She paused. A faint smile formed on her lips as if she were remembering the passions of her own youth.

"Come in, come in," she said with mock impatience. "I will let you have a room for the night, Nedelijko, but we must talk more about this girl. It is not a good thing for a Slav and a Magyar to be seeing each other. Not a good thing at all."

She led Nedelijko up to a small room and left him there to wash up. He sighed silently as she closed the door behind her.

He used the pitcher and bowl to wash his hands and face, and felt reasonably refreshed. Reaching under his shirt, he retrieved the revolver and inspected the room for a hiding place. The dresser drawers were too obvious. He checked for loose floor boards, but finally decided on sticking the revolver beneath the mattress. He smoothed out the bed-clothes and felt satisfied.

He decided to go for a walk. He had an hour before dark. It would calm his nerves. A walk would take his mind off the following day.

While Nedelijko walked through the souk calming his nerves, his plump Magyar landlady came to his room to prepare his bed for the night.

Her mouth formed an oval of surprise when she found the revolver beneath his mattress.

June 27, 6:30 P.M.

At the same moment that Nedelijko's landlady discovered his revolver, Archduke Francis Ferdinand and Duchess Sophie sat in the hotel dining room over a small supper of roast quail.

The Srbija Hotel had been redecorated in their honor, but it had failed to impress Ferdinand.

"Do you remember what you were doing fourteen years ago tonight?" Ferdinand asked with a smile.

"It was the night before our wedding. Henriette was trying to calm me at the same time as she was making last-minute arrangements with the dress makers and the bishop." Sophie chuckled softly. "Fourteen years."

"Good years."

"Little Karl arrived at about this time. I remember because he asked where the rest of his family was, and I had to explain that they weren't coming to the wedding."

Ferdinand nodded. The smile had faded from his face. With Ferdinand's own children unable to succeed him as emperor, little Karl had become next in the imperial line of succession. But, Ferdinand reminded himself, Emperor Franz Joseph could not live forever. And things might change when Ferdinand was emperor.

Ferdinand gestured to the waiter to pour Sophie more wine.

"Your Highness," the waiter began, "Count Harrach is waiting outside. He wonders if it is possible for him to have a few moments of Your Highness's time after dinner."

Ferdinand scowled. He knew what Harrach wanted.

"Tell him I'll see him after dinner."

Ferdinand had not mentioned the threat on his life to Sophie, and he had forbidden Harrach to do so. Even the second telegram from Pastich had not impressed the Crown Prince. There were so many threats.

Suddenly Ferdinand remembered that he had promised to see Governor Potiorek after dinner. He gestured at the white-gloved waiter.

"Tell Potiorek I won't be able to see him this evening." Ferdinand paused thoughtfully. The waiter stood at attention. He had not been dismissed. A cold smile broke on Ferdinand's face. "Tell Potiorek that the rumors that I will announce my support for land reform tomorrow are all true. And that there is nothing he could say that would make me change my mind."

The waiter bowed from the waist.

"Potiorek will be humiliated," Sophie whispered after the waiter had left the table.

"He should learn not to oppose my policies," Ferdinand replied with a grin.

June 27, 7:00 P.M.

An Austrian sergeant snapped to attention before Colonel Smyra.

"Twelve Slavs have been picked up along Appel Quay. They have been questioned. There was an old man who we didn't bother to bring in."

Smyra nodded. "Have you got anything out of them?"

"Not yet, sir. For the most part they appear to be street vendors."

"No one who fits the descriptions of the three Bosnian students?"

"No, sir." The sergeant paused for a moment. "There were two or three of the Slavs we picked up who were reluctant to answer questions. I took the responsibility upon myself, sir, to order the measures necessary for their cooperation."

Smyra nodded. He knew that the "measures necessary" probably meant a beating with rifle butts.

"That was a sensible decision, Sergeant. You did not exceed your authority."

"Shall we release the Slavs we have picked up?"

"Detain them overnight. I'm going to order a curfew for all Slavs. I don't want any of them on the streets after dark. How many men do you have now on Appel Quay?"

"Twenty-two, sir."

"All right. Take six of them and patrol the souk. If our three Bosnian students are in Sarajevo, they're probably hiding out in that maze."

"Yes, sir."

"And Sergeant, if you find anything out of the ordinary, I want it reported to me immediately. Anything! Do you understand?"

"Yes, sir," the sergeant saluted stiffly, turned on his heels, and left the office.

Colonel Smyra lit a cigarette. He was pensive.

June 27, 7:35 P.M.

Nedelijko was horrified to find the sheets on his bed turned down, but he did not feel real fear until he tore the mattress from the bed and found his revolver missing.

He fought panic. Tankosic's words rang in his head: *Panic is the ally of the enemy. The brain is the komitadji's most valuable tool! Use it!*

The landlady must have found it. She would have taken it to the police. How long ago had she found it? How long did he have before the police arrived?

Nedelijko cursed Gavrilo's security arrangements. There was nowhere to hide. But he knew he couldn't stay where he was!

He rushed to the head of the staircase, paused, and listened to the house. Silence. Could be a trap, he thought. They could be waiting for him to come downstairs. He listened again. Still silence. He didn't have a choice. It was lunacy to stay where he was. He went down the stairs as quickly and quietly as possible.

The front hall was empty. The dim gaslights glowed from the street. He listened again. Still there was silence. Without know where he was going, Nedelijko dashed into the street, and rapidly faded into the shadows of the labyrinth of the souk.

June 27, 8:00 P.M.

"But the second telegram tells us that this is more than just an idle threat. We have descriptions of the three students."

"Then arrest them," Ferdinand barked.

"We haven't been able to find them yet."

"That's a problem for Smyra. Why do you bother me with it?"

"Because it's your life that's in danger," Harrach snapped back at the Crown Prince. Harrach was frightened for the archduke, and it was this fear that made him angry at Ferdinand's stubbornness. "As Ernst's godfather, I insist that you change plans."

Ferdinand chuckled at the fury and determination in Harrach's face.

"Since when does being a godfather to my son entitle you to insist upon anything?"

"At least change the motorcade route?"

"Nothing will be changed. The planned route will be followed. The reception will be at noon. Sophie will meet some Muslim women while I am addressing other dignitaries. We will do everything as planned."

"That is your final word?"

"That is my final word."

"May I ride in the car with you?"

"You will ride in the car following mine as was planned."

"Yes, sir," Harrach snapped to attention, and then stormed out of the private lounge. Had Harrach been any other man, Ferdinand would have been furious.

Harrach caught his breath in the hotel lobby. He would have to ride back to Sarajevo. Perhaps Smyra had some news to report. He checked on the security precautions at the hotel, picked a fresh stallion from the stable, and began the twelve-kilometer ride back into Sarajevo. For the third time that day, he wondered if he should have gone to Sophie. She was probably the only one who could make Ferdinand change his mind.

Harrach spurred the horse. He couldn't go to Sophie and he knew it. It would breach his friendship with Ferdinand.

He wondered if von Merrizi and Colonel Smyra had had better luck.

June 27, 8:10 P.M.

Sergeant Borzaga had just ordered two three-man patrols into the souk. He leaned languidly against a gaslight overlooking the dark water of the Miljacka. There was nothing languid about his mind. He recognized the danger.

An angry female cry came from behind him. He turned and saw two of his men dragging a plump woman toward him.

"Fools! Stupid fools!" she screamed.

"What do you have?" Borzaga snapped.

The officer on the right relaxed his grip on the woman's arm.

"She was on the quay, carrying this." The officer handed Borzaga a Browning revolver. The sergeant's eyes registered surprise.

"Where did you get this?"

"That's what I was trying to tell these idiots!" the woman

shouted. "Grabbed me. Like I was a criminal. Wouldn't listen to a word I said. Treated me just like I was a criminal."

"But you are," Borzaga snapped. "You have broken the curfew."

"But—"

"There are no buts. Take her in and lock her up. I'll meet you at the police station."

"Lock me up!" the woman cried, but Borzaga was already walking away.

June 27, 8:30 P.M.

Nedelijko guessed that a curfew had been imposed. The souk was deserted. The cafés were closed. The narrow cobblestone alleys were empty and silent. He stood within the shadows of a doorway.

The brain is the komitadji's *most valuable tool. Use it!*

Nedelijko tried to judge just how much the police knew. They would have his name and his description. It would not take much intelligence to see that the revolver was meant for the Crown Prince. They would probably assume that anyway.

His family would be questioned. Nedelijko winced. Austrians were not known to be gentle when questioning Slavs.

His friends in Sarajevo would be detained.

He would be hunted.

Do the unexpected! Do it suddenly!

But what was the unexpected? He didn't dare leave the souk. But that would be expected. The souk was exactly where the Austrian patrol would look for him. *Calm, now,* he told himself. *Panic is the ally of the enemy.*

What wouldn't the Austrians expect? What would surprise them? What would throw them off guard?

A germ of an idea formed in Nedelijko's mind, but before he had a chance to explore it, he heard the echo of hobnail boots in the narrow alleyways. He drew back into the doorway and held his breath.

A gaslight some thirty meters down the street cast flickering shadows over the cobblestones. The sound of the boots drew louder. His stomach burned with fear, and he couldn't seem to catch his breath.

Three soldiers came into view at the end of the street. They stopped beneath the gaslight. Nedelijko could hear fragments of an argument. The dispute seemed to be over which direction the river was. Nedelijko pressed himself farther back into the shadows of the doorway. If only he knew where Gavrilo or Trifun was staying . . .

The three soldiers continued to argue for several minutes, until one of them turned toward the doorway in which Nedelijko was hiding. Whether the soldier actually saw Nedelijko or whether he just sensed a presence in the doorway Nedelijko did not know.

He did know that the soldier's conversation stopped suddenly, in midsentence. If that wasn't enough of a warning, the soft sound of the boots against the cobblestones was.

Nedelijko bolted. He lept out of the doorway and dashed down the narrow alleyway.

"*Halt!*" roared an Austrian voice. Nedelijko dashed on. Behind him he heard the sound of the soldier's boots as they broke into a run. Then came the sound of a carbine bolt being snapped into place.

"*Halt!*" the Austrian soldier again ordered.

Nedelijko veered into another alley on the left. There were cobblestone steps that led up to the rear of the bey's mosque. He flew up the steps, taking two or three at a time. Behind him he could still hear the steady beat of the soldiers' boots.

Nedelijko had no time to explore the idea he had. The decision was made the moment the soldiers had seen him. Halfway up the stone steps, Nedelijko darted into a footpath that ran directly to the crest of the hill.

The shrill blast of a whistle came from behind him.

"No, he went up here!" an Austrian voice bellowed.

The soldiers were faster on their feet than Nedelijko had anticipated. He reached the top of the hill. Before him stood the deserted courtyard of the bey's mosque. He crossed to the side of the wrought-iron fence and scaled it quickly. It was a shortcut to the river.

Again a whistle blasted, but this time it came from the right. Had another patrol joined the chase? He dashed across the courtyard, leaped across the mosaic fountain, and skirted the minaret.

"Get on the other side! He went in, and he's got to come out!"

Nedelijko paused behind the upthrust branches of a cypress tree. Through the leaves, he watched the soldiers spread out around the wrought-iron fence that surrounded the mosque. Now he had them where he wanted them. They did not know whether he was armed. They would be cautious. Their caution would cost them precious time.

Nedelijko inched his way toward the base of the minaret. He remembered it well from all the games of hide and seek he had played as a child. He prayed silently that some wealthy Muslim had not repaired the fence.

But no repair work had been done. From his left an Austrian bellowed an order. There was the sound of a soldier climbing the fence. Nedelijko slipped between the base of the minaret and the broken fence.

It would take them at least thirty minutes to find the small break in the wrought iron. And in thirty minutes Nedelijko would be out of the souk and off the streets.

He crossed the narrow parapet and found the familiar footpath that led down to the river. He no longer ran. Instead, he kept himself within the shadows of frame houses that lined the path. He crept along cautiously. He would do the unexpected. He would spend the night on Appel Quay!

It would be the most patrolled street in Sarajevo. It would also be the last place the Austrians would search for him.

June 27, 8:50 P.M.

At the same time Nedelijko was squeezing through the break in the wrought-iron fence, Gavrilo Princip sat reading. He was calm and mildly sleepy. All the nervous excitement he had felt earlier in the day had disappeared. He was in Sarajevo. Tomorrow he would complete what he had come to do.

He remembered the worn cyrillic letters over the entrance to the chapel in Grahovo. He remembered his father standing beside him. It had been the same each Sunday. Before they entered church his father would make him read the words out loud: "There is no darkness, nor shadow of death where workers of iniquity may hide."

Nowhere to hide. It was comforting. He did not seek sleep. It was an unnecessary sanctuary.

He glanced down at the Bible that straddled his knees. "By the great force of my disease is my garment changed: it bindeth me about the collar of my coat."

Gavrilo was relaxed. Even the cathedral bell soothed him. It would soon be Vidovdan.

June 27, 9:00 P.M.

"Ferdinand absolutely refuses to alter the itinerary," Harrach announced to Smyra and von Merrizi without any other form of greeting. Smyra sat behind his desk. Von Merrizi slouched wearily in an armchair.

"I have news," Smyra began. "It appears our three students have managed to get into Sarajevo. We picked up a woman on Appel Quay carrying a revolver."

"A woman?" Harrach asked.

"A Magyar woman," Smyra went on. "She runs a boarding house in the souk. She said she had found the gun in a room she had rented to a Bosnian student."

"Could she give us a description of the student?" Harrach demanded.

"There's no question that the student is one of the three that Pastich warned us about."

"Have we arrested him?" Harrach asked.

Colonel Smyra grunted angrily and reached for a cigarette. "We missed him. A patrol spotted him in the souk. They gave chase, but lost him up by the bey's mosque."

Symra leaned over close to Harrach. The colonel's eyes told of his exhaustion. His voice was thin and impatient.

"Now that we are sure the three students are in Sarajevo, Ferdinand must be forced to alter his plans."

"Ferdinand will not discuss it," Harrach replied.

"Would it help if Potiorek talked to Ferdinand?" Von Merrizi asked.

"It would make it worse," Harrach said with a short laugh. "Ferdinand despises the governor."

There was silence in Colonel Smyra's office while the three men digested the new information.

"What are the chances we can pick up the three students before the motorcade tomorrow morning?" Harrach asked finally.

Colonel Smyra considered before he replied.

"We've got a name. Nedelijko Cabrinovitch. The Magyar landlady gave us the address of his family. They live in the Slav quarter of Sarajevo. My men are bringing them in now." Colonel Smyra paused and then shook his head sadly. "I don't think the family will be much help. It would be the last place this Cabrinovitch would go.

"We've had a file of Cabrinovitch for some time. In many respects he's typical. Grew up in Sarajevo. Went to the industrial school for three years. Nothing outstanding there. Disappeared from Sarajevo three years ago, about the same time as the outbreak of the Balkan wars. Presumably he went to Belgrade to join the Serbian army. We don't have anything more on him. But I can make several educated guesses."

Colonel Smyra stubbed out his cigarette and glared out

into space. He was furious with his men for allowing the student to give them the slip.

"But there're two things that disturb me. The first is that we don't know anything about the other two students. The landlady said that Cabrinovitch was alone. Doesn't that strike you as odd?"

"Maybe they separated?" von Merrizi suggested, failing to catch Smyra's meaning.

"Separation would be the safest thing for them to do," Colonel Smyra replied grimly. "And I'll bet you my next month's salary that if we catch Cabrinovitch he won't know where the other two are. We could question him until we're blue in the face. Cabrinovitch can't answer, even if he wanted to. Simple security precaution. The less a man knows, the less he can tell."

"But that doesn't sound like the planning of teenage students." Harrach snapped.

Again Colonel Smyra nodded grimly. "Exactly. Either there's someone else behind the organization, or these young students have been carefully trained. If they have received training in security, then it's a safe bet that they've also been trained in weapons handling."

"The Serbian army?" Harrach asked.

"Possibly. They could also have been recruited as *komitadji.*"

"*Komitadji?*" Harrach repeated. He did not know the word.

"Essentially they're Slav terrorists. They started out as bandits who used Slav nationalism as an excuse to steal. But now, Austrian intelligence tells me that students are being recruited."

"Who's behind these *komitadji?*" Harrach asked.

"We don't know. There's what they call the *gluvonem.* The code of silence. When we've caught *komitadji* alive, we can't get a word out of them."

"Torture?" von Merrizi suggested.

"The Austrian army does not use the word *torture*," Colonel Smyra replied with a short laugh. "Even our techniques of persuasion have not broken them. I would guess that they are taught to endure pain."

"What's our next move?" Harrach demanded. There was a sense of futility in Smyra's voice that annoyed him.

"My men are bringing in Cabrinovitch's family. We'll question them. Maybe we'll pick up a lead there. I've ordered three more patrols into the souk. If Cabrinovitch is on the streets, we'll find him."

"We want him alive. He may know something," von Merrizi added.

"If he's on the streets, my men will find him."

June 27, 10:00 P.M.

Nedelijko was not on the streets; he was beneath one.

At the bottom of the mosque hill, he had slipped onto Adamic Street. He could still hear the soldiers' voices as they searched the grounds of the mosque.

Cautiously he followed Adamic Street toward the river and the quay. There was a spot along the quay that he remembered from his childhood. It was the best place along the river to catch eels. The eels gathered to feed beneath where the sewage flowed into the river.

At low water the large iron sewer pipe was exposed.

At the corner of Adamic Street and the quay, Nedelijko paused and searched for any sight of soldiers. He could make out four or five figures in the flickering gaslight and assumed they were part of a patrol.

But there was no time. Casting one last glance in the direction of the silhouetted figures, and mumbling a prayer, he darted across the quay toward the river.

He did not stop at the edge of the quay but jumped over the embankment down to the huge pipe that extended out into the shallow water. He perched silently on the pipe for a moment, listening for sounds of alarm. The river bubbled and splashed, but there was no sound of running boots.

Carefully he inched his way out to the mouth of the pipe. The smell from the sewage was overpowering. He grasped the iron pipe and swung his legs into it. Something soft scurried between his legs and plopped into the river. By wiggling his hips back and forth, Nedelijko managed to squeeze himself into the pipe. He lay still. The water in the pipe was only a trickle, but it soon soaked through his clothes. He shivered and closed his eyes. The river gurgled behind him.

June 28, 5:35 A.M.

The sun rose at five-thirty-seven in the morning and announced the end of the curfew. Sleepy street vendors began to appear with their carts loaded down with clucking chickens or cabbages as big as human heads. Slowly other sounds began to punctuate the dawn and herald the beginning of another day. The clank of the coppersmith, the mumbled gossip of Muslim women, appearing to be no more than a bundle of clothes, the rumble of an oxen cart bouncing over the cobblestones.

It was Vidovdan.

Father Jamis opened the great double doors of the Orthodox cathedral and hung out the icon of the Madonna. It was the Feast of St. Vitus, and the six-o'clock mass would be crowded.

A crew of workmen appeared on the quay and began the last-minute preparations for the royal visit. Some swept the gutters; other hung Austrian flags from the lamp posts. Sergeant Borzaga watched them in silence. He was in particularly bad temper. Colonel Smyra had handed him his head for losing Cabrinovitch in the mosque grounds. The sergeant sipped a cup of coal-black coffee and imagined what he would do to the Slav bastard if he ever caught him.

The plump Magyar landlady dozed on a wooden bench at the police station. Finally someone had listened to her.

Nedelijko's father and mother sat nervously in front of

Colonel Smyra. They had answered the same question at least a dozen times. They did not know where their son was. The last thing they had heard, he had been in Belgrade. No, they didn't know if he was sympathetic to Slav nationalism. But they didn't think so. He had always been a good boy.

Count Harrach and Lieutenant von Merrizi dozed in the lobby of the Srbija Hotel.

Gavrilo Princip read aloud from the book of Jeremiah: "Those who feasted on dainties, now perish in the streets; those who were brought up in purple now lie on ash heaps."

Stega shook her father's shoulder and whispered that if he didn't hurry he'd be late for church. The old man blinked and groaned, and then remembered that it was Vidovdan.

Trifun Gabrez awoke at six-thirty. For a moment he couldn't remember where he was. And then suddenly it all came to him. His sleepy mind leaped into alertness. Was it real?

The church bells confirmed the reality of Vidovdan.

All Trifun's instincts told him to be careful. He felt hunted already. His head was pulled closer to his broad shoulders. His eyes narrowed dangerously and he looked like a hunted beast.

He was in danger. He was the prey. It would have been difficult to explain to him that he was also the hunter—Trifun had trouble appreciating such distinctions.

At seven the muezzin's chant broke the still morning air. Trifun was not due to meet Nedelijko and Gavrilo until nine. Pacing the room like an animal in a cage did not sooth his nerves.

June 28, 8:00 A.M.

It was warm, warmer than could normally be expected for Sarajevo at that time of year. The morning sun had burned off the mist.

Standing by a row of cypress trees, Archduke Francis

Ferdinand, in full dress uniform, had already begun to perspire. He pushed back the left half of his handlebar moustache and scanned the pillared façade of the restaurant.

In front of the restaurant stood Governor Potiorek, Count Harrach, and an Austrian lieutenant named von Merrizi. As Ferdinand crossed the damp grass on his way to the restaurant, he thought again about the planning that had gone into the trip to Bosnia, the way he had kept it a secret from Sophie, as a surprise, as an anniversary present. A half-hidden smile became visible at the corners of his mouth.

"Your Highness," Governor Potiorek greeted him, bowing from the waist. Ferdinand nodded abruptly to the governor and then turned to the exhausted face of Count Harrach.

"You did not sleep well, Harrach?"

The young count bowed from the waist but did not reply.

"You worry too much. Tonight, my friend, you will sleep like a baby."

Ferdinand turned and passed through the double glass doors that led into the restaurant. Potiorek shot Count Harrach a questioning stare. But Harrach's face remained expressionless. The archduke walked down the four marble stairs and across the red velvet carpet. The smile had disappeared from his face. He listened to the subdued clamor of the officers entering behind him.

"Your Highness slept well?" Potiorek asked as Ferdinand seated himself at the raised table.

"I slept miserably."

"I'm sorry to hear that, Your Highness. Perhaps there is something I could do. . . ."

"Why don't you lose weight? Your stomach is a disgrace to Austria."

An embarrassed silence descended upon the table. Harrach hid his grin. Governor Potiorek fumbled for words.

"Will we have the pleasure of Countess Sophie's presence at breakfast?"

Ferdinand glared at the governor. "My wife is a duchess!"

"Of course, of course. How stupid of me. You must excuse my—"

"Must I?" Ferdinand snarled.

Governor Potiorek sat in silence. His fingers played nervously with a silver coffee spoon, bending it in two and then straightening it. The general was overdue for promotion, and might, upon recommendation, be ordered back to Vienna to become part of the cabinet. But Ferdinand's land-reform announcement would certainly not help his case.

"Will we have Her Highness's presence at breakfast?"

"She's at mass."

"It is a beautiful morning," Potiorek smiled. "We could not have prayed for better weather. There will be a great crowd out to see you today. A messenger has just come from Sarajevo with the news that people are already forming lines along the route you will be taking. It will be a grand day."

"Will it?" Ferdinand scowled. "Count Harrach thinks differently."

Harrach was finally forced to smile, and Ferdinand laughed.

The silver coffee spoon in Potiorek's lap was being bent back and forth so quickly that it looked like a tiny panicked bird.

Ferdinand knew that Potiorek's "countess" slip had not been intentional. The governor did not have the courage to say it deliberately. Ferdinand disliked weak men.

"Does Your Highness really consider it wise to announce your support of land reform today?" Potiorek had finally broached the subject.

"The alternative is civil war."

"Perhaps Your Highness is overestimating the situation in Bosnia. The Slavs are simple, uneducated people. They are not ready to own land. The responsibility would be too great for them."

Ferdinand glared at the governor but remained silent. Potiorek took Ferdinand's silence as an invitation to continue.

"Your Highness need only spend a little time in Bosnia to see that what I am saying is true. The Slavs are little better than savages. Even the church has not been able to civilize them. There are a few vocal Slavs who have managed to educate themselves, but the vast majority are peasants. Land reform would be misunderstood. The Slavs would see it as a sign of Austrian weakness. They would make other demands. Before you know it, they would be demanding an elected official to oversee Slav problems. . . ."

Ferdinand yawned. "You didn't get my message last night?"

"I received your message."

"Then there is no point in discussing the matter further. I have made up my mind. I will announce my support of land reform at the reception today."

Ferdinand was interrupted by the appearance of his wife, standing in the double glass doors, framed on either side by handmaidens. Duchess Sophie stood graciously above the four marble steps. There was about her a quiet, unobtrusive dignity—a dignity that hushed the restaurant and brought the breakfasters to their feet.

Ferdinand crossed the dining room, took his wife's hand, and whispered something to her. She smiled. Together they walked, hand in hand, across the velveteen carpet back to their raised table.

The officers at the other tables bowed from the waist as they passed. Women swept gracefully into curtseys. Sophie was again reminded of Ferdinand's anniversary present. A week of being a queen, a week of being treated as the empress she could never become.

June 28, 8:30 A.M.

Before starting to wriggle out of the pipe, Nedelijko listened to the bell of the Orthodox cathedral toll the half hour. From the sounds that filtered down from the quay, he could tell that crowds of Muslims and Magyars had already begun to form. Even with the cover of the crowds there would be danger.

He guessed that the Austrian patrols would have his description. He could not afford to draw attention to himself.

He used his arms to pull himself clear of the pipe and then swung himself quickly up to the embankment. He squatted on the cobblestones. His legs were stiffer than he had imagined. The quay was crowded. The Austrian soldiers had their hands full keeping the crowds out of the street. Nedelijko winced at the pain in his legs and rose to his feet. The Putnik Café on Barcarsija Square. He slipped into the crowd and headed toward the meeting place.

Gavrilo Princip stood by the horse trough in the center of Barcarsija Square. The bell in the Orthodox cathedral struck the quarter hour. His narrow eyes watched the entrance of the Putnik Café. The window table was still empty.

By the side of the horse trough was an old Slav woman selling dried corn as bird food. Gavrilo bought a handful.

"Nobody buys corn this morning," the toothless old woman complained. "They're all over on the quay waiting to see the Austrian prince. My little pigeons will go hungry."

Gavrilo scattered some corn for the pigeons. His eyes panned around the square. Nothing seemed to be unusual. He threw some more kernels to the hungry birds.

Nedelijko appeared first. Gavrilo saw him the moment he turned onto the square. His appearance puzzled Gavrilo. His hair was matted and his clothes clung to his body as if wet.

Nedelijko paused on the far pavement and then turned back into an alleyway. Why didn't he go into the café? Gavrilo wondered. Was something wrong? But if something was wrong Nedelijko would have used the prearranged signal. Why wasn't Nedelijko following directions?

Gavrilo scattered the remains of the dried corn. The birds pecked at it furiously. He was worried. It wasn't like Nedelijko to ignore directions. Something was wrong. He wished Trifun would appear so that they could get off the streets.

He crossed the square and entered the café, seating himself at the window table. He stared at the knife and fork that lay neatly on the table. Slowly he moved his left hand toward the fork. He paused and stared out over the square to the alley Nedelijko had ducked into. There was no sign of his friend.

"You want to order?" a waiter said from behind him.

"Coffee," Gavrilo replied without turning. His left hand seized the fork and he held it within full view of the window. The bell in the Orthodox cathedral struck nine. Why was Trifun late?

Trifun watched Gavrilo raise the fork in his left hand and smiled. Everything was all right. He crossed the square and entered the café.

"Where's Nedelijko?" he asked.

"He's in the alley on the far side of the square," Gavrilo replied. Trifun turned his head toward the alley. "Don't stare!" Gavrilo whispered.

"Why doesn't he come into the café?"

"I don't know. Something must be wrong. We'll give him ten minutes and then go on without him."

"Without him?"

"That's what I said."

"But shouldn't we—?"

Gavrilo silenced Trifun with his eyes. The waiter came to their table and deposited Gavrilo's coffee.

"You want coffee too?"

Trifun nodded and cast a glance at the clock above the bar. Nedelijko had four minutes left. What had gone wrong?

"I don't like it," Gavrilo finally murmured. "Nedelijko may have been followed."

"Then the police would try to arrest us."

"Not if Nedelijko knew he was being followed. He wouldn't bring them to the café." Gavrilo threw some coins on the table. "We'll leave separately. Walk to this addresss. Make sure you're not followed." Gavrilo thrust a scrap of paper across the table at Trifun.

Trifun read the address slowly and painfully. "I'll meet you there. And forget about Nedelijko. He's in some kind of trouble. There's just you and me."

Gavrilo rose from the table and walked back out to the square. He was concerned and frightened. They were so close to realizing their plan, it seemed incredible that something should go wrong.

Trifun waited another five minutes, and then he, too, left the café. He did not follow Gavrilo. He, too, was frightened. They hadn't done anything yet. How could there be trouble? The big boy walked to the far side of the square and then turned into a narrow street. He had recognized the address Gavrilo had given him. It was only two blocks away, but he couldn't go directly there. First he had to discover if he was being followed.

Three blocks further up the side, Trifun paused to stare into a merchant's window. He looked behind him. No one appeared to be following him. He turned left at the next corner and waited out of sight to see if anyone would turn after him. Again, no one appeared.

The bell in the Orthodox cathedral struck the half hour. Trifun caught his breath.

The address Gavrilo had given him was occupied by a small frame boarding house. Trifun entered through the side door and climbed to the second floor. He knocked softly on the warped door.

Gavrilo opened it.

"You weren't followed?" Gavrilo demanded.

"I don't think so," Trifun replied, closing the door behind him.

"You didn't see Nedelijko?"

Trifun shook his head.

"We'll have to go ahead without him."

"No you won't," said a voice from behind them. Gavrilo spun toward the doorway. Nedelijko stood in the doorway grinning. "Sorry I couldn't join you at the café, but I didn't think they'd let me in."

Nedelijko's clothes were still wet, and he smelled strongly of the sewer.

"You stink," Trifun announced.

"Where the hell have you been?" Gavrilo demanded.

Nedelijko explained briefly the events of the previous night. Gavrilo listened intently. When Nedelijko was finished Gavrilo questioned him:

"How did you find your way here?"

"I followed Trifun."

Gavrilo turned to glare at the large boy.

"The police know your name?"

"Probably."

"What do you mean, probably? I haven't come this far to fail because of your stupidity!" Gavrilo whispered furiously.

"How was I supposed to know that woman would look under the mattress?"

Gavrilo turned his head away. He had to think. Had Nedelijko alerted the police to the fact that the three of them were in Sarajevo? And, if so, would security around the Archduke be tighter? Should they alter their plans? Should Nedelijko remain behind?

"Listen carefully," Gavrilo began quickly. "We're going to continue as planned. If they spot you, you've got to take the cyanide. Do you understand?"

Nedelijko nodded.

"Trifun, you know where to stand? Right by the side of the Cumurija Bridge. When the archduke's car is ten meters in front of you, twist the cap on the grenade and hit it against something hard. They're twelve-second grenades. That means after you knock the cap off you'll have twelve seconds before it explodes. Do you understand?"

Trifun nodded. He had heard all this before, but he didn't interrupt Gavrilo.

"The archduke's car will be moving slowly. After you knock the cap off your grenade, you must count to eight. Don't throw it before you get to eight. And for God's sake don't hold it any longer than that!"

Trifun nodded.

"Try to toss it in Ferdinand's lap. As soon as you've thrown it, run like hell! If we're successful we'll meet in Belgrade."

Gavrilo handed Trifun a grenade from the suitcase. He then handed Nedelijko the second revolver and a grenade.

"Don't lose them."

"Don't worry, I won't."

Gavrilo then pocketed a grenade. It was heavy and made his jacket lumpy. He felt the revolver beneath his belt.

He nodded to the other two. "Good luck."

"God go with you!"

At ten minutes after ten, the three young Bosnians left Gavrilo's room and separately made their way to Appel Quay. The archduke was not due until eleven, but to be on the safe side, they would be early.

CHAPTER TWO

A State Visit

The motorcade awaited the royal couple outside the restaurant. Seven officers snapped to attention as Ferdinand and Sophie approached the five open-topped cars. Governor Potiorek walked at Ferdinand's side. Harrach and von Merrizi were four steps behind.

Count Harrach watched Ferdinand and Sophie enter the third car. Von Merrizi shrugged despondently. From now on the security was up to Colonel Smyra. Harrach sighed as he entered the car behind Ferdinand's. The crown Prince was in God's hands.

The motorcade began slowly. Ferdinand leaned back in his seat, enjoying the warm morning sun. He had always enjoyed riding in motorcars. He had one at Belvedere, and although the emperor had refused to allow him to use it in royal processions, Ferdinand had had ample opportunity to play with his new toy. He had managed to terrorize half of Vienna one afternoon, roaring through the streets at thirty miles an hour, honking his magnificent brass horn and shouting at people to get out of his way.

Sophie opened her yellow parasol and shaded herself from the sun. Her thoughts lingered on a morning fourteen years before.

The ride into Sarajevo was slow and bumpy, but otherwise uneventful. The road was a dirt track, worn and rutted by countless cart wheels. Sophie and Ferdinand bounced gently against the leather seats. If it had been a different day, the bumpy ride might have annoyed Ferdinand. But it was their anniversary, and Ferdinand felt something akin to happiness.

The car bounced on. A cool breeze rustled in the olive groves on either side of the road. Ferdinand smiled. Perhaps in a year or two Slavs would own similar groves.

Sophie's hand rested on his knee, transmitting to him the knowledge that she shared his contentment.

On the outsikrts of Sarajevo the road changed from dirt to cobblestone. Small clusters of curious peasants stood along the side of the road. Some waved at the royal couple. Others just stared.

In the car behind, Harrach watched the clusters of peasants nervously. His hand rested on the hilt of the ceremonial sword that was part of his dress uniform. He recognized the absurdity of trying to stop revolvers and bombs with a cavalry saber, but he did not unclench his white knuckles.

§   §   §

Trifun stood across from Cumurija Bridge. He placed himself in the center of the crowd. He could not see Nedelijko or Gavrilo, but he knew where they were. Nedelijko was next to Lateiner Bridge, a block farther up the quay. Gavrilo stood across from the Kaiser Bridge. It was a gauntlet of assassins.

Trifun knew he would be the first to see the cars. The first to act. He was nervous and had trouble standing still. To his right was a Magyar boy waving a small Austrian flag.

To his left was a Muslim in a red fez. It seemed to him that he was the only Slav in the crowd.

As eleven o'clock approached the crowds grew larger and people began pushing for better views. Trifun withstood the pushing and kept his position near the curb. His eyes were glued to the quay and his ears listened intently for the sound of motorcars.

A man tapped Trifun on the shoulder. Trifun's stomach was suddenly on fire with adrenaline. He clenched his fists and turned.

"Do you mind letting my children stand in front of you?" he asked. Trifun glanced at the little boy and girl. His brain lumbered over the consequences of this act of charity.

"I was here first," Trifun snapped. "Take your children somewhere else." If Trifun had not been so large the man might have argued with him.

It was then that Trifun heard the sound of a motorcar. He forced himself to be calm and peered over the heads of the crowd. He could just make out the car as it turned onto Appel Quay. His heart pounded as he waited. He would have to push through the crowd when the car was opposite him.

He looked both ways and calculated the distance to the closest policeman—about twenty meters. The policeman would have trouble getting through the crowd. Trifun estimated that he had an even chance of escaping.

The motorcar moved slowly up the quay. Trifun suddenly became aware of another car following it. Gavrilo hadn't told him that there would be more than one car. He was confused. He didn't even know what Francis Ferdinand looked like.

The car came closer. Trifun trembled. In desperation he turned to the woman next to him and asked: "This is the Crown Prince's car?"

"No. He's in the third car. It was announced earlier."

Trifun watched the first car pass. It was full of Austrian

army officers. He turned his large head toward the second car. It, too, passed.

The woman next to him nudged his arm. "This is his car," she said.

Trifun saw it. The car was still a half block away. He search for something hard to bang the cap of the grenade against. There was only the cobblestone street. The archduke's car came closer. Trifun's muscles tightened. The woman grabbed his arm. As if this had been the cue he had been waiting for, Trifun plunged forward into the crowd, knocking people out of his way, struggling towards the curb.

He broke out onto the quay and turned toward the archduke's car. He suddenly stopped and stared. His mouth fell open and his hand grasped the grenade beneath his shirt.

The car came closer. Trifun didn't move. He seemed frozen. A uniformed policeman shouted at him to get back up on the curb. Trifun didn't respond. What he had seen when he had first leapt from the crowd prevented him from throwing the grenade. He felt tears of rage creep into the corners of his eyes.

He thrust the grenade deep beneath his jacket and watched the archduke ride by. Why hadn't Gavrilo told him about the woman? Trifun had been prepared to kill a man, not a woman.

"Get back in the crowd!" the uniformed policeman shouted.

Trifun turned slowly. There was defeat written on his face. Why hadn't Gavrilo told him about the woman in Ferdinand's car?

A puzzled look came over the policeman's face. He stared after Trifun. Suddenly there was recognition. "*Halt. Stop him!*"

The shrill blast of a whistle came to Trifun's ears as he plunged back into the crowd.

§   §   §

Nedelijko watched the first car turn onto the quay. He suddenly remembered that neither he nor Gavrilo had told Trifun that there would be more than one car. He calculated the chances of running down to warn Trifun, but there was not enough time.

He had situated himself on the corner next to Lateiner Bridge, one block down from where Gavrilo stood. He placed himself next to a lamp post in order to have something to smash the cap of his grenade against.

The first car came alongside Trifun. Nadelijko held his breath. The crowd surged forward, but there was no explosion. He craned his neck and stared out over the heads of the crowd. There were five cars in all and even Nedelijko was not sure which one the archduke was in.

The second car passed Trifun without an explosion.

The first car was now level with Nedelijko. He had his hand on the grenade beneath his shirt. He waited. There was no one in the car he recognized. Suddenly he wished there were enough grenades to blow up all the cars. Something that resembled greed came over him. He wanted more than just the Crown Prince—he wanted all of them. No one was truly innocent.

The third car had passed Trifun and the fourth was directly opposite him. Still there was no explosion. Nedelijko cursed. Why had Gavrilo put Trifun first? Nedelijko knew almost nothing about imperial protocol, but he assumed that the guest of honor would not ride in the last car.

Trifun had failed. Trifun had let them down. Nedelijko turned his intent, catlike eyes toward the road. It was all up to him.

The second car passed Nedelijko. The crowd that surrounded him cheered and waved little Austrian flags.

The third car seemed to be going faster than the others. Nedelijko's first glimpse of it was over the heads of the crowd. He couldn't make out the faces of the occupants, but his heart leaped at the sight of Ferdinand's plumed helmet. When the car was about twelve meters down the quay from where he stood, Nedelijko jerked the grenade from inside his shirt and struck it against the lamp post. The cap popped off.

Nedelijko howled in pain. The grenade hit the post the way it was supposed to, but between the grenade and the post was one of Nedelijko's fingers. The grenade fell from his injured hand, and rolled into the legs of the crowd.

"It's a *bomb!*" Someone screamed. "Oh, God! *He's got a bomb!*"

Nedelijko panicked and scrambled after the grenade, forcing his way into the forest of legs.

"*Policija! Zaboga! Policija!*" a woman screamed.

Nedelijko seized the grenade, leaped to his feet, and threw it instantly. In his panic, he forgot about the count of eight. The Archduke's car was ten meters past him, but Nedelijko did not wait to see if the bomb had found its target.

He turned and plunged back through the crowd.

§   §   §

Something heavy struck the back of Ferdinand's car. Sophie turned at the sound. The driver must also have heard the dull thud, because he immediately stomped on the accelerator. Ferdinand and Sophie were thrown back in their seats.

There was a long moment of silence.

Nothing happened. Ferdinand caught a glimpse of the surprised expression that flashed across his wife's face. Her smile was gone. Puzzlement had replaced contentment.

Ferdinand watched the black grenade bounce off the bumper of his car and roll beneath the car that followed.

The roar of the explosion was deafening.

§   §   §

"They've blown up the archduke?" Stega cried from a window overlooking the quay. Cistler stood at his daughter's side by the window. His eyes were wide in surprise and horror.

The street below was total confusion. The quay was

covered in a blanket of thick, acrid smoke. Governor Potiorek was trying to climb into the back seat of the archduke's
car.

"It's not the right car," Cistler whispered breathlessly
to his daughter. "There's the Crown Prince."

At that moment Ferdinand was climbing out of the car,
arguing the whole time with Potiorek. Sophie remained
seated. She looked frightened.

The car behind Ferdinand's had been actually thrown in
the air, had twisted almost ninety degrees, and then had
fallen to earth like a bird shot in flight.

"Who did it?" Stega demanded.

Cistler shrugged. He didn't know.

The driver of the damaged car was on the cobblestones.
The crowd surged about his body. The sight of blood seemed
to excite them. Uniformed and plainclothes police tried to
force the crowds back onto the curb. Harrach and von Merrizi remained in the back seat.

Stega flung open the window. The chatter of the excited
crowd filled the small office.

Ferdinand suddenly broke away from Governor Potiorek
and sprinted to the side of the wounded driver.

"Is he mad?" Cistler whispered. "Why is he just standing
out there in the street? Does he want to be killed?"

A man tried to break through the police line.

"I'm a *doctor!*" the man shouted. "*I'm a doctor.* For God's
sake, *let me through!*"

The doctor burst through the police lines and ran to the
side of the driver. The doctor glanced up at Ferdinand and
shook his head. He then made for the car and felt for von
Merrizi's pulse. Ferdinand watched the doctor count silently
to himself. Then the doctor moved to the far side of the car
and felt for Harrach's pulse.

"Well?" Ferdinand demanded. The doctor looked up and
for the first time actually recognized who was standing next
to him. He bowed deeply from the waist.

"Are they dead?" Ferdinand barked.

"This one is, Your Highness." The doctor moved Harrach's head slightly and exposed a great gash in his throat. "The other one," the doctor continued, pointing at von Merrizi, "will live. He's unconscious and in shock. It is doubtful that the driver will live."

Anguish and pain flooded Ferdinand's expression.

Governor Potoriek was suddenly at Ferdinand's side leading him back to his own car. From the far side of Lateiner Bridge came the frantic ringing of ambulance bells. The police forced the crowd back to make room for the ambulance.

§ § §

"Why?" Stega murmured. "Why do they do it? Why are they so crazy?"

"A damned good question," Cistler replied wearily.

§ § §

At the sound of the explosion, ˙Gavrilo Princip pulled a small tricolor Serbian flag from his pocket and waved it. He reached into his groin and pulled out the vial of cyanide, toasted the unification of all Slav peoples, and drank the poison in one gulp.

He was ready to die. They had been successful. He ran towards the blanket of brown smoke, staying within the crowd that surged forward in excitment. Suddenly he caught sight of Nedelijko on the edge of the embankment. His friend was running. Gavrilo grasped the handgrip of the revolver beneath his shirt. It would be an act of mercy to kill his friend.

But the distance was too great, and Gavrilo was forced to watch the crowd knock Nedelijko to the ground. Even from a distance Gavrilo was able to share Nedelijko's pain as a policeman's boot repeatedly slammed into his groin.

They handcuffed Nedelijko and searched him.

Suddenly Gavrilo's attention was torn from Nedelijko's plight. Through a break in the crowd he saw Archduke Francis Ferdinand get back in his car and drive off toward the town hall. He didn't believe his eyes.

Just as the cyanide began to burn in the pit of his stomach, Gavrilo realized that Nedelijko had blown up the wrong car.

§ § §

When Trifun heard the explosion, he was three blocks away. He had given the policeman the slip in the crowd. Tears of rage poured down his cheeks. He had failed. He had let his friends down. He had failed to obey a direct order. But he wasn't a coward! He could have killed Ferdinand with his bare hands. But why hadn't they told him about the woman?

He walked quickly down Franz Joseph Street. He had no doubt that the explosion meant that the Crown Prince was dead. Probably the woman too. He winced. It also meant that Gavrilo and Nedelijko were either dead or dying. How could it all happen so quickly?

When Trifun arrived at the train station, he found it full of soldiers. They were searching all passengers. Trifun turned in the entranceway. The train station was where they would expect to find him. He must think. He must use his brain.

At that same moment a soldier slammed his rifle butt into the small of Trifun's back and sent the large boy sprawling on the pavement. Instantly, two other soldiers had their rifle barrels leveled at the back of his head. A fourth soldier tore open his shirt and grabbed the grenade.

"You're a bit young to have playthings like this," the fourth soldier muttered as he snapped handcuffs on Trifun's large wrists.

§ § §

There was silence in the car. The mood of the morning had been shattered. Sophie trembled and clutched at Ferdinand's arm. She had not asked about the occupants of the other car.

Ferdinand sat in a furious silence. The bomb had been meant for him. His jaw was set with bitterness and fury. His anger sought a focus. Where the hell was Potiorek's security?

Finally and reluctantly Ferdinand shifted the full weight of his anger against himself. It became mingled with guilt. He should have listened to Harrach. He should have listened at Konopischt. He should have listened last night at the hotel in Ilidze. He should not have come. He could risk his own life, but not the lives of others. It was a bitter irony that Harrach, who had been so concerned about the safety of the Crown Prince, should himself be killed. What had Harrach called the trip? Suicidal. Perhaps the young count had been more accurate than even he had imagined.

Ferdinand closed his eyes. He knew that his own stubbornness, perhaps even his vanity, had killed Harrach just as much as the bomb had.

The driver slammed on the brakes and jolted the car to a stop before the imposing façade of the town hall. The crowd had been pushed back by a line of uniformed soldiers. A man dressed in livery opened the car door for Sophie. Ferdinand could not bring himself to look at the crowd.

The royal couple walked quickly up the stairs and into the central rotunda of the town hall, where the mayor met them and in a brief ceremony presented them with keys to the city.

The mayor, a short, bald man with thick glasses and a bristling moustache, whose reaction to the explosion was to pretend it had not occurred, led Ferdinand into the meeting hall. Sophie was escorted upstairs, to where she would meet a delegation of Muslim women. Although Sophie felt

uneasy about being separated from Ferdinand, she said
nothing.

The meeting hall was already full of various minor dignitaries. Ferdinand knew from past experience that he
would now be subject to verbose speeches in his honor and
in the honor of Austria. Ferdinand wasn't in the mood.

Before he sat at the head table, Ferdinand turned to
Governor Potiorek.

"After the reception upstairs, I want my wife taken
directly back to the hotel in Ilidze. The driver is to use
side roads. If anything happens to her, I will hold you
personally responsible. Understand?"

The speeches were everything that Ferdinand had expected. They praised him, they praised the emperor, they
praised Austria, and they bored him. But his boredom led
him to think again about Harrach, and his anger returned.

"With open hearts," the mayor intoned, "and outstretched
arms, the people of Sarajevo—"

"Throw bombs at me!" Ferdinand shouted suddenly. The
mayor stumbled and stuttered, and there was a full minute
of awful silence.

But Ferdinand's mind was elsewhere. He thought of all
the violence that had beset his family. Rudolph's suicide at
Mayerling. His uncle Maximilian executed in Mexico,
gunned down by a firing squad. He remembered the telegram that had arrived. Telegrams had always announced
death. There had been that other telegram, the one that had
come from Switzerland. Aunt Elizabeth had been visiting
the Baroness de Rothschild. Elizabeth, empress of Austria,
queen of Hungary, wife of Franz Joseph, had been stabbed
by an anarchist. She had bled to death in the gutter.

Perhaps assassination was a Hapsburg curse. But then
it wasn't species specific. It was the professional hazard of
royalty as being gored was the professional hazard of the
bullfighter.

His mind went to Spain. It was the summer of 1906. He

had left Sophie at Belvedere and had traveled to Spain to attend the wedding of King Alfonso and Victoria Eugenia of Battenberg.

The newspapers had called the marriage "beautiful beyond words." The royal procession had left the cathedral in the afternoon. The warm Spanish sun beat gently down on the crowded streets of Madrid. The golden bridal carriage was pulled by eight pairs of white horses. The crowds that lined the route cheered, waved, and roared out their best wishes. They tossed flowers into the streets until the pavement itself became a bed of roses, marigolds, and carnations.

About halfway along the route, a bouquet of flowers was tossed from a window overlooking the street. The bouquet landed on a balcony and exploded. It tore a woman's head off, ripped the balcony from the side of the building, and sent it crashing into the street below. The balcony landed on a horse, killing it instantly.

Alfonso and Victoria had not been hurt, but the bride's white grown was splattered with blood and brain. Ferdinand remembered his horror. It had been his first experience of attempted assassination. . . .

Potiorek slipped a small square of paper into Ferdinand's hand. The archduke opened it beneath the table and read it quickly. It was a note from Sophie. Under no circumstances did she want to be separated from him. She refused to leave the town hall before him.

Ferdinand crumpled the note and stuck it in his pocket. The speeches continued. He had half expected such a note. If he was going to put himself in danger, then Sophie would insist upon accompanying him.

Suddenly there was silence in the hall. It was time for Ferdinand to make his speech, his announcement of support for land reform. He had a prepared speech in his pocket, but he did not reach for it.

How could he give land to the man who had killed his friend?

Potiorek fiddled with a button on his coat. The mayor used his handkerchief to clean his thick glasses. The hall was tense.

Ferdinand refused to address them.

§　§　§

For the fifth time Gavrilo tried to vomit. He stuck his finger down his throat but with no result. He retched and convulsed but could not vomit. A man tried to comfort him, thinking perhaps the scene of violence had made the young man ill.

The sight of Ferdinand alive had crushed Gavrilo. One minute hope, the next total failure. The cyanide burned in his stomach as if to remind him of the completeness of his failure.

He walked away from the quay, wondering how long it would take the poison to work. The police would torture Nedelijko until he talked. Gavrilo wondered whether he would be dead before the police found him. He looked for a quiet place to die.

§　§　§

Colonel Smyra nodded at Sergeant Borzaga's salute.

"Arrested two," the sergeant announced.

"Cabrinovitch?"

"Cabrinovitch and a chap named Gabrez, Trifun Gabrez. We recognized him at the train station. He had a grenade on him."

"It was Cabrinovitch who threw the bomb on the quay?"

"No question about it, sir."

"And the third one?"

"Haven't found him yet, sir."

"You know his name?"

"Cabrinovitch hasn't talked yet, but he will. My men are questioning him now."

"You are to use whatever measures necessary. I want that

third young man arrested. Every minute he's on the loose, the Crown Prince is in danger."

"I understand, sir."

"Would it be easier to crack Gabrez?"

"We'll try both of them, sir." Sergeant Borzaga saluted and turned toward the door.

"Sergeant," Colonel Smyra called after him. Borzaga turned. "Don't scar their faces. They'll have to appear in court. We don't want a bad press."

§   §   §

Ferdinand's refusal to address the dignitaries of Sarajevo was accepted in an embarrassed silence. Ferdinand simply rose to his feet and stalked out of the room.

Potiorek was quickly at his side.

"Your Highness," Potiorek whispered breathlessly. "I want to apologize for what happened this morning. As governor, I must take full responsibility. The emperor will have my resignation tomorrow."

Ferdinand looked at the exhausted, worried face of the Bosnian governor and suddenly felt pity for the man. It had not been Potiorek's fault.

"I don't think that will be necessary," Ferdinand replied quietly. "Have you caught the assassin?"

"Two of them. Colonel Smyra's men are questioning them now. We shall soon have the full story."

"My wife will not leave without me. The ball this evening will be canceled. Arrangements will be made to transport Harrach's body back to Vienna. Sophie and I will go to the coast tomorrow and meet the imperial yacht."

"I will make the arrangements, Your Highness." Potiorek almost snapped to attention. "May I suggest that we do not continue with the afternoon as planned? I believe it would be advisable to change our plans."

Ferdinand listened to the words and secretly cringed. They were almost the same words that Harrach had spoken the night before. If only he had listened then . . . If only he had not been so stubborn . . .

"Sophie and I will drive directly to the hospital. I want to see Lieutenant von Merrizi. Then we will go back to the hotel in Ilidze."

"I will make all the arrangements, Your Highness."

Sophie was still upstairs with the Muslim women and Ferdinand had a ten-minute wait for her. He abruptly made it known that he did not want to be entertained, and the bald mayor showed him to a private office.

Ferdinand fell into a reverie of jumbled memories—the attempt on the lives of Alfonso and Victoria, the deluge of flowers; the carnations, the marigolds, the roses. He thought of his own roses, the great spreading faces of his roses at Belvedere. And the onions and garlic the gardener had planted at Konopischt. It was an indignity, but the irony was lost on Ferdinand. Here the onion and the rose bloomed together. Sophie, many years before, had announced her affection for wildflowers.

But even the tenacious offspring of that match were considered bastards, their birthright stolen.

And the poachers. Was there no way to stop the poaching without becoming a poacher?

Long ago, after Rudolph had killed himself, but before Ferdinand's marriage to Sophie, Ferdinand had had the answer. The answer to every problem lay in the death of the emperor. Then the power would have been in his hands. He would have seized the helm, righted the ship, barked an order into the storm, and shot the man who dared disobey.

But the emperor had not died. His golden jubilee had come in 1898—a half century on the throne. Franz Joseph of Austria and Victoria of England were the grandparents of all Europe. Victoria had died and Europe had mourned. But still the Austrian Emperor had lived on. The Diamond Jubilee had come in 1908. It too had passed.

Few people could remember an Austria without Franz Joseph; still fewer could imagine one without him.

Ferdinand knew, better than most, that no one is the heir of a living man. Franz Joseph was the empire, tired and frail, his skin scaled and tanned with age and suffering, his soul the soul of Austria, weakened by each passing hour. His portrait was as immovable as the flag, something that would never change—so Austrian, so stable. . . .

Stability in the stormy sea of Europe. That was the watchword of the day—stability. Don't rock the boat unless you can swim and don't give a damn about anyone else.

But the war that had been declared fifteen years earlier was not quite over. Ferdinand had one last recourse. One day Franz Joseph would die. One day he would be emperor. Vienna would squirm. Montenuovo would be banished. Ferdinand would renounce his morganatic oath. He would be a liar, but his wife would be queen and his children would be Hapsburgs.

Sophie entered the room without knocking. She looked exhausted, ten years older than she had looked earlier that morning. He motioned for her to sit next to him.

"How was it?"

"I was not at my best," Sophie replied, "but the Muslim women were understanding. I'm tired now." She paused and stared directly into her husband's eyes. "Please don't make me leave without you. I'm frightened. I want to stay with you today. It's important."

He nodded and forced a smile.

"I have made the arrangements. We'll leave together. I want to see how von Merrizi is doing at the hospital. We will go there directly and then back to the hotel. I ordered Potiorek to cancel the ball this evening."

She nodded, but her face clouded over. The blood drained from her cheeks. She had just realized what Ferdinand had said, or rather what he had failed to say.

"We will not be seeing Count Harrach at the hospital?"

Ferdinand shook his head. "Harrach was on the side of

the car closest to the explosion. Part of the bomb struck him in the neck. He was dead before the ambulance arrived."

Tears crept into Sophie's eyes, and her lips quivered. "Why do they want to hurt us?" she cried, the pain of Harrach's death heavy in her voice. He took her hand and held it gently.

She had not really asked a question, and she didn't really want an answer. She had received what she desired most—his hand holding hers. Harrach had been close to them. He was Ernst's godfather. His death would upset their son.

A knock came at the door. Potiorek entered and announced that the car that would take them to the hospital was waiting for them. Ferdinand rose. Sophie hid her face and dabbed at the corners of her eyes with a handkerchief.

They left the town hall together, hand in hand.

§   §   §

Sergeant Borzaga hurried down the upper corridor of the police station, knocked once on Colonel Smyra's office, and entered.

"Sir," Borzaga announced with a salute, "Gabrez has started to talk. We've got the name of the third young man. Gavrilo Princip."

"We have a file on him?" Smyra demanded.

"I checked that, sir, before I came up. We've got quite a bit of information on Princip. He's nineteen. Brought up in Grahovo, a mountain village to the east of Travnik. Went to cathedral school in Sarajevo for two years. An honor student. Three years ago he disappeared. Presumably, he crossed into Serbia."

"Any relatives?"

"Father died in prison, doing a sentence for assaulting an Austrian official."

Smyra raised his eyebrows. "Perhaps violence runs in the Princip family."

"Mother died of smallpox."

"Friends in Sarajevo?"

"None."

"Have you alerted your men?"

"Yes, sir. We've covered the train station, and we've set up checkpoints on all roads leaving the city."

"Good. I want Gavrilo Princip arrested."

"Yes, sir."

Colonel Smyra turned back to the papers on his desk.

"One other thing, sir."

"Yes, sergeant?"

"Both Gabrez and Cabrinovitch had vials of cyanide taped in their groin."

Smyra's eyebrows rose again in surprise. *"Komitadji?"*

"It would appear so, sir. The grenade we took from Gabrez is Serbian."

"In that case, sergeant, I think it is unnecessary to take Princip alive. Tell your men that I don't care how they bring him in."

"Yes, sir." Sergeant Borzaga saluted and hurried back out of the office.

§   §   §

An hour had passed since the brown smoke of Nedelijko's bomb had clouded the quay. Gavrilo Princip had fully expected to die, and had been surprised to find that the poison was so slow in producing death. Finally, he had no choice but to assume that the poison had been tampered with.

Standing in front of Moritz Schiller's elegant food shop on the quay, Gavrilo tried to think things out. Nothing made sense.

Some of the crowd had drifted into Franz Joseph Street on his right. Gavrilo watched them disinterestedly. He knew he couldn't leave Sarajevo. The train station and the roads would be guarded. He could not be sure what to do next. Why hadn't the poison worked?

Suddenly bits and pieces of the puzzle fell together in

his mind. The diluted poison. The order to close the Serbian border to three young Bosnians. The informer. It all began to make sense to the young man.

Before Gavrilo had any more time to think about the conspiracy within the conspiracy, he heard shouts of *Zivio!* and saw two cars roaring back down the quay.

§ § §

All pretense of a state visit was gone. The crowds slipped by silently. Ferdinand had hold of Sophie's hand. In the morning they had shared their joy. In the afternoon they would share their grief.

Suddenly the driver braked and began to turn the car into Franz Joseph Street. Potiorek shouted something. The driver looked confused.

"Not this way!" Potiorek bellowed at the driver. "Continue on the quay. To the hospital."

The driver nodded and brought the car to a stop, engaged the clutch, shifted into reverse, and stalled the engine.

Ferdinand silently cursed Potiorek. All the arrangements had been made, he thought sarcastically, except someone had forgotten to tell the driver where he was going. It was little wonder that Austria was dying.

§ § §

Gavrilo was calm again. His stomach no longer burned. Order had been reestablished. The sight of the roaring cars on the quay had reminded him of his purpose. The diluted poison had been a reprieve of sorts. Perhaps it was not quite as easy to bury a Slav as his father had thought.

The crowds re-formed along the quay. Police hustled them back to the curb. The cars were going much too fast for him to act. Gavrilo wished, more than anything else in the world, for that first car to slow down.

Slow down, he repeated to himself. For God's sake slow down! His right hand found the grip of the revolver. Slow down, he silently ordered the car. Slow down. And suddenly the car did slow down. Gavrilo's eyes widened, and his heart leaped into his throat. It couldn't be true!

And yet the car was slowing down. It was turning into Franz Joseph Street. Gavrilo spread his legs and balanced himself in a low crouch.

The car passed him. Gavrilo reached for the revolver. The trigger guard caught in his belt, and he struggled with it. By the time he had wrestled the gun free, the archduke's plumed helmet was twenty meters past him.

Stop! Stop you Austrian bastard! Stop! Gavrilo silently screamed after the car. *If there is any justice left in the world, stop that car!*

To his amazement, the car did stop and stall. He could see the green feathers Ferdinand wore in the ceremonial helmet. It was his chance. There *was* justice left in the world. He jumped forward and crouched a shadow's distance from the Crown Prince.

He held the revolver in two hands and gently squeezed the trigger. Just before the gun exploded, Ferdinand turned toward Gavrilo. The two men stared at each other. The Crown Prince did not look surprised. It was almost as if Ferdinand had recognized his assassin.

A sharp crack. Ferdinand's neck exploded. His eyes remained open. The ceremonial helmet slipped forward, and bits of green feathers hovered like insects in the air.

A second explosion. Sophie jerked. A bullet crashed into her abdomen and severed her spinal cord. She slumped forward and crumpled upon the floor of the motorcar.

Potiorek acted quickly. He leaped from the front seat of the car and drew his ceremonial sword. Potiorek ran at the young Slav who was wrestling with the crowd, trying to get the barrel of the revolver into his own mouth. The revolver fell to the cobblestones.

Potiorek struck at Gavrilo twice. Neither thrust hurt the young man. Police arrived in force and threw Gavrilo to the ground. Potiorek was surprised at the expression on the murderer's face. The young man appeared so calm—almost serene.

The governor returned to the car and ordered the driver to take them to the governor's residence. Two military doctors and the bishop of Sarajevo met them at the residence. Not until they arrived at the residence did Potiorek realize that Duchess Sophie had also been shot.

Countess Lanjus, Sophie's lady in waiting, assisted Dr. Wolfgang in examining Sophie. The doctor sent two of the governor's aides in search of ether. Wolfgang had no trouble finding the small red hole in Sophie's belly, and it was but minutes before he closed his eyes and shook his head. Countess Lanjus burst into tears.

The bouquet Sophie had received from the Muslim women at the town hall was placed on her body.

As soon as Dr. Wolfgang had declared Duchess Sophie dead, he rushed into the adjoining room to assist Dr. Payer, who was already examining Ferdinand.

The Crown Prince lay on an ottoman. He was in a deep coma, and his breathing was shallow and irregular. Blood flowed freely from the back of his neck.

Potiorek knelt next to Ferdinand and asked him if he had any message for his children. Ferdinand was beyond replying. The bishop of Sarajevo stood in the doorway, his hands folded in prayer.

At twelve-fifty-one on June 28, Dr. Payer looked at Dr. Wolfgang, and the two men nodded silently. Payer reached out and closed Ferdinand's eyes, while Wolfgang beckoned the bishop.

"Nothing more can be done. His Majesty's sufferings are over."

Bishop Stadler gave Ferdinand and Sophie absolution *in extremis* and administered the last rites.

The imperial couple died fourteen years to the minute after they had left the small mountain chapel as man and wife.

PART THREE

A Political Trial

Our ghosts will walk through Vienna and roam through the palace, frightening the lords.

—GAVRILO PRINCIP
THERESIENSTADT PRISON

Among the Serbs every peasant soldier knows what he is fighting for. When he was a baby his mother greeted him: "Hail, little avenger of Kossovo!"

—JOHN REED

CHAPTER ONE

Dr. Rudolph Cistler

There was nothing routine about Monday morning for Dr. Rudolph Cistler. For the fourth time he brushed his silver-gray hair from in front of his eyes. It was almost lunchtime, but he felt little hunger. He could hear the buzz of conversation in the outer office. Stega had her hands full making appointments.

At nine-thirty a messenger had summoned him to the general criminal court of Sarajevo. At ten o'clock Investigating Judge Pfeffer had assigned him the defense of the three Bosnian students charged with murdering the Austrian Crown Prince.

His gray eyes reflected his excitement. They darted eagerly within their slightly hammocked sockets. Age and suffering had not dulled his mind, had not slurred his speech, had not reduced his conversation to a repetition of self-serving reminiscences. Time had refined the old lawyer, eroded the sharp edges of his temper, fused hope and despair into irony, and blended caution and spontaneity into a wildly optimistic cynicism that is not uncommon in oppressed peoples.

The small oak door opened, and Stega entered.

"Good morning, Buttocks," Cistler chortled, his gray eyes twinkling.

"Papa!" she replied sternly. "You mustn't call me that."

"But with that bottom, with those magnificent hips—how can you expect me to call you anything but Buttocks?"

Cistler winked at his daughter, lit the briar pipe, and watched the blue tobacco smoke rise.

"Papa," Stega began, but hesitated. She knew what she wanted to say but couldn't find the words.

"What is it?"

"This case is not good."

"Few criminal cases are good," he chuckled.

"No, I mean this one." She took a deep breath. She would say it, even if it offended her father. "Papa, don't you see why this case was assigned to you?"

"I am a Slav. The defendants are Slavs."

"It is a dangerous case. They picked you because of your reputation. . . ."

Cistler's eyes narrowed. "I'll tell you why they picked me," he snapped angrily. "Because I was the only one. You're right, it's a dangerous case. None of these bright young lawyers have the courage to take it. I have the courage. I am an old man with a bad reputation, but I have courage."

Stega was forced to smile at her father's vehemence.

"You must not overwork. The first case in years, and you will overwork. I'll bring you up some lunch."

"I don't want lunch," the old man barked. "I want coffee and an obedient daughter, not a mother. One mother is too much for most men, but two mothers . . . dear God in heaven, preserve us!"

Stega frowned gently at her father. His excitement

pleased her. The case had revitalized him. He was suddenly
the man she remembered from her childhood. It was as if
the sickness had not happened. But the case also worried
her. The Austrians had their reasons for assigning the case
to her father. And those reasons frightened her.

"I'll bring you up some coffee."

"Who's waiting outside?"

"The Cabrinovitches, Trifun Gabrez's uncle, and an
Englishman named Watson."

"An Englishman?"

"He told me he just came in from Vienna. I think he's a
newspaper reporter."

Cistler nodded thoughtfully. "Send in the Englishman.
We might as well get that out of the way first. And Stega,"
Cistler smiled, "please remain in the office during the inter-
view with the Englishman."

Ernie Watson was in his thirties, slightly overweight and
slightly overbearing. He shook Cistler's hand just a little
too eagerly and smiled just a little too broadly.

"I can't tell you how grateful I am, Dr. Cistler, for a few
minutes of your time. I'm a correspondent from the *London
Times*. Came down on the train from Vienna to cover the
assassination case. I suppose you haven't had time yet to
interview the students."

"Mr. Watson," Cistler said slowly, "I would like you
to meet my daughter, Jeanne-Marie. She will be assisting
me on the case."

Stega's eyebrows rose in surprise. Why had her father
introduced her as Jeanne-Marie?

Watson jumped to his feet a little too eagerly.

"A pleasure, Jeanne-Marie, a pleasure."

"Now, Mr. Watson, as you can understand I am rather
pressed for time. If you have any questions . . ." Cistler
broke off and turned his attention to Stega. "If you have
things to do, Jeanne-Marie, I'm sure Mr. Watson will excuse
you."

Stega rose and crossed to the door. Her expression was one of puzzlement. Why had her father called her Jeanne-Marie?

"My paper is interested in the politics of the trial," Watson began as soon as Stega had closed the door. "The police seem to have no doubt that they've arrested the guilty parties."

Cistler nodded.

"But I suppose the real question lies in how deep the guilt goes."

"What are you trying to say, Mr. Watson?"

"Well, it's no secret that Austria is looking for an excuse to invade Serbia. Anyone who reads the newspaper knows that. Do you think Austria will try to prove that Serbia was behind the assassination?"

"That's a question for the investigating judge."

"But do you think Serbia was behind the murders?"

"From the little I know now," Cistler said cautiously, "I do not believe the Serbian government had anything to do with the murders."

"But you agree that Austria would like an excuse to annex Serbia the same way it annexed Bosnia?"

"That is a question for the Austrian foreign minister," Cistler replied. He felt the interview was going well. With caution and care, he would use Watson in his investigation.

"But you don't think these young students were acting alone?"

"I don't want to be quoted," Cistler said, knowing full well that he would be. "I don't think the students acted alone."

"Who do you think was behind them? Who do you think supplied the weapons and the grenades, if it wasn't the Serbian government?"

"How much do you know about Balkan politics?"

"Not very much, I'm afraid."

"You have heard the word *komitadji?*"

"It means something like terrorist, doesn't it?"

"That's close enough. Have you ever heard of an organization called the Union or Death?"

Watson shook his head.

"The Union or Death is a secret network of terrorists, as you call them. It is devoted to unifying all the Balkan Slavs. Other than that, not much is known about it. But I would bet that our young students know a great deal more about the Union."

"You think that the defendants are *komitadji?*"

"I don't want to be quoted."

"I understand. But you have evidence?"

"There is always evidence for someone with eyes to find it," Cistler murmured cryptically. He was almost finished with Watson, and he welcomed Stega's interruption as she brought a cup of coffee to his desk.

"You must excuse me, Mr. Watson. I have suddenly become a busy man."

As soon as Watson had been shown out of the office, Stega turned to her father. "Why did you introduce me as Jeanne-Marie?" She demanded.

The old man laughed and settled back in his chair.

"Stega, you must learn cunning. It is the only weapon the Slavs have. I wanted that young man to publish the interview. The reactions to it will be very interesting. But it may become necessary for me to deny that it ever took place. When I call that young man a liar, I can point out as *prima facie* evidence that he didn't even get your name right. Old Cistler may be ancient and a little senile, but he certainly knows the name of his own daughter." Cistler grinned.

"Papa, this case scares me."

Cistler ignored his daughter's remark and relit his pipe. "We must proceed with caution, Stega. With extreme caution."

"Is there any chance we can win the case?" she asked.

"Of course we can win!"

"You always were an optimist."

"All Slavs are optimists. We have to be! We have no choice. Our life is so bad," the old man laughed. "Our life is so bad we cannot afford the extravagance of pessimism. To be a cynic is a luxury to be enjoyed by Muslims and Magyars. Slavs are romantics—we never grow up. The key to success is excess. We dance, we fight, and we make love like madmen!"

Stega hid her smile as she left the office. Cistler turned his attention back to the papers that lay scattered across his writing table. It would be a difficult case. He was not as sure of himself as he had pretended in front of Stega. He chewed on the amber stem of his pipe. It was national guilt that concerned him. The Englishman was right. Austria was looking for an excuse to invade Serbia, to annex Serbia the same way it had annexed Bosnia. But Austria still had to prove, even as a formality, that the Serbian government was behind the assassination.

Cistler read on. The official confessions lay on the writing table. Lies and more lies. He knew how the Austrians extracted confessions.

"Papa," Stega called from the door to the outer office, "there's a man to see you, but he doesn't have an appointment."

Cistler would have replied that he was busy, but he wasn't given the chance. The man burst through the door, brushing Stega aside, and stalked to the edge of Cistler's desk.

Cistler did not stand.

"You need to talk to me," the man began without any other form of greeting.

"It's all right, Stega," Cistler said and watched her close the door behind her.

The man who stood before Dr. Cistler was in his mid-thirties, tall and slender, with short-cropped hair and a pair of almond eyes that seemed to watch everything while concentrating on Cistler alone. The man had a purple scar on his cheek.

"I need to talk to you?" Cistler asked.

The man turned to assure himself that the door was closed. "I understand you will be defending the three students accused of murdering the Austrian archduke."

Cistler nodded.

"I have advice for you."

"Advice?"

"There's no need for a trial. The three defendants should plead guilty at the arraignment next week."

"And why should they do that?" Cistler asked pleasantly.

"There were scores of witnesses. A trial would waste everyone's time."

"Time is about the only thing old men have a lot of. But tell me, who does this advice come from?"

A thin, almost effeminate smile broke on the man's lips, and his scarred cheek twitched nervously. "From a friend of the Slav people."

Cistler did not recognize the greeting. "I will consider what you have said," he replied.

"You will take my advice, if you know what is good for you."

"That sounds like a threat."

"I am not here to play with words. That is *your* job." There was an edge of impatience in the man's voice. "There must be no trial. No investigation."

"You're trying to put me out of work," Cistler said with a short laugh. "Old men need work."

"The trial might prove embarrassing to important people. Sometimes it is dangerous, embarrassing important people."

Cistler leaned back in his chair and ponderously lit his pipe. He had expected to be visited, but he had not expected it to come so soon. These important people must be very worried.

"You must understand the seriousness of the situation. There are consequences to this trial that you are not aware of. You read the newspapers. You must realize that the three students are not on trial alone. Serbia is on trial. Serbia as a nation!"

Cistler's face remained expressionless.

"The trial might provide Austria with an excuse to invade Serbia."

"Are you trying to tell me," Cistler asked, "that the Serbian government was behind the murders?"

"Not at all. But the trial might give that impression."

Cistler smiled coldly. He had learned a great deal from this scarred young man. He wondered how much more the young man would divulge.

"Whom do you represent? Who are these important people who seem so easily embarrassed?"

"You do not need to know. What may interest you is how powerful they are." The scarred man's voice had grown thin and menacing. "The defendants will plead guilty next week. You may wish to argue that they are insane. It's not that far from the truth. But under no circumstances are they to testify."

"That sounds more like an order than advice."

"I tried to be polite with you."

"And who exactly is issuing the orders?" Cistler snapped. "The Union or Death?"

The name caught the scarred man off-guard. His scarred cheek twitched furiously.

"It would be sensible for you to cooperate. If it is a question of money . . ."

"It is a question of justice!" Cistler roared. "You and all the other *komitadji* have forgotten justice. In your bombings, your arson, your murders, you have forgotten justice! There will be a trial! My clients will have justice!"

"A nice speech, but you'd better save it for the judges. I know your background Dr. Rudolph Cistler. I know what you're really interested in. You don't give a damn about justice. You're interested in making old Dr. Cistler look good. You've got quite a reputation to overcome. Why do you think you were assigned this case? Because you are a

Slav?" The scarred man shrugged. "There are other Slav lawyers. The court picked you, Dr. Cistler, because you were the lawyer least likely to present a coherent defense. Do you really think the Austrians want a competent lawyer handling the defense?"

"*Get out!*" Cistler roared.

The scarred man rose. "I was just leaving, but if I don't read in next week's newspapers that the defendants have pleaded guilty, I will be back to have another chat."

The scarred man turned and walked casually out of the office. He felt pleased with himself. Despite the old lawyer's anger, the scarred man knew that Cistler was frightened.

CHAPTER TWO

Kmet Prison

The harsh electric light glared into the cell from the rough-cut stone corridor, casting elongated shadows upon Gavrilo Princip.

The young prisoner sat motionless, as if in a trance. He wore the gray prison uniform and was barefoot. The shirt was several sizes too large and hung limply from his narrow shoulders.

Beside Gavrilo, on the blanketless bench that served as his bed, was a tin bowl half-filled with turnip gruel. Opposite the young man was a rust-encrusted bucket. Otherwise, the small cell was empty. Gavrilo was in the maximum-security wing of Kmet Prison.

The investigating judge, an old Austrian named Pfeffer, had visited him earlier in the day. Gavrilo had not broken the *gluvonem*. But he was concerned about the others. The judge had told him about Trifun's arrest. Gavrilo wondered if Trifun had been tortured.

A soft tapping came from the wall behind him. Instantly, Gavrilo's eyes took on a new alertness. He counted silently to himself. He knew the code. It was the simple alphabetic code that Tankosic had taught them.

	1	2	3	4	5
1	A	B	C	D	E
2	F	G	H	I	J
3	K	L	M	N	O
4	P	R	S	T	U
5	V	W	X	Y	Z

Sharp knocks meant the vertical column of letters, and deliberate knocks indicated the horizontal.

The message sender identified himself: Nedelijko. Gavrilo tapped back his greeting. Again Gavrilo counted silently. "Donovitch and family hung without trial." Gavrilo closed his eyes in pain. Reprisals! Nedelijko's coded message continued. "Visited this AM by Judge Pfeffer. Claimed reprisal executions widespread. Six Slavs hung in Trebinje. Also claimed we have been assigned a lawyer to defend us. Don't know what to believe."

Gavrilo replied: "Believe little. Say less. Has Trifun been contacted?"

Nedelijko: "Trifun must be in other part of prison. No contact made."

Gavrilo: "Torture?"

Nedelijko: "Head held under water in bathtub. Didn't reveal anything."

Gavrilo: "Silence must be our companion. God's mercy will come soon."

There was silence again, this time interrupted by the sound of the guard's boots in the corridor.

"Give me the bucket," the guard ordered. Gavrilo picked up the bucket and handed it to the guard.

"You have a visitor."

"A visitor?"

"Someone has come to see the Slav pig!" the guard sneered, and turned away from the cell.

When the guard returned, he was followed by an old man with gray hair. The guard opened the section of bars that served as a door and held it for the old man.

"I'll be down the hall," the guard murmured. "Call me when you're finished, Dr. Cistler."

"You're a doctor?"

"A doctor of the law," Cistler replied with a smile.

"You're a Slav?"

Cistler nodded.

"Which Austrian ass did you have to kiss to become a lawyer?"

Cistler chuckled. "As a matter of fact, I had to kiss a great many. I'm glad to see that jail has not broken your spirit."

"My spirit does not matter."

"My name is Rudolph Cistler. I've been appointed to defend you."

Gavrilo stared past the old lawyer into the gray cement of the opposite wall.

"You will be coming to trial soon. Together, we must plan a defense. I'm here to help you."

"I need no help other than God's."

"You don't care what happens to you?"

"It's unimportant."

"Did you murder the archduke?"

"Ask the police who arrested me."

"You are prepared to die for what you did?"

"I am prepared to die," Gavrilo replied matter of factly.

Cistler watched the prisoner's empty Slav-black eyes gaze belligerently into nothingness. The young man looked not only prepared to die, but as if he were already dead.

Cistler laughed. "Spoken like a true *komitadji!* A true hero! You have served your purpose, and now you are expendable."

"Old men and cattle worry about death."

"Death does not concern you. A hero is never concerned about death," Cistler said, still chuckling. His opinion of the young man was confirmed. Princip was playing a role, wearing the mask he believed he was expected to wear—that of a fanatic nationalist hero.

"Perhaps this fact will change your mind. According to your statements to Judge Pfeffer, you are twenty years old. Even Austrians do not execute children. You have to be at least twenty-one to die a hero's death. How does a *komitadji* react to the prospect of life imprisonment?"

"Why should I care what happens to me?" Gavrilo countered. "Does a book that has been read worry about which shelf it is stored upon?"

"Are you proud of what you did?" Cistler demanded. He watched the prisoner closely.

"I am a Slav."

"So am I. But are you proud of killing the archduke?"

"He was the enemy."

Cistler had anticipated the young man's reply. "Are you also proud of killing his wife?"

"An accident," Gavrilo snapped, his dazed expression fading like a flame in the sunlight.

"Is that what I should call it in court? Perhaps I should call it a regrettable accident. Your aim was not good . . . your training was not sufficient."

"I don't care what you say."

"You may not care about yourself, but perhaps you still care about the Slav people?" The question angered the prisoner. Cistler was pleased by the reaction. "It is not just Gavrilo Princip who is on trial. You must start understanding that. You have placed all the Slav people on trial. Whether you like it or not you have come to represent the Slav people."

The prisoner would not meet Cistler's eyes.

"Are you proud of killing the Crown Prince's wife?"

"Do you think I have no feelings?" the prisoner demanded. "Do you think I am an inhuman animal? I have a conscience, and it is more powerful than a thousand witnesses. Her death was useless. As useless as Monja's."

"Monja?"

"My sister."

Cistler was suddenly confused. Perhaps the young man was not acting, not wearing a mask. Perhaps he really was a fanatic, the totally dedicated man. Cistler was frightened of totally dedicated men. Saints and heroes led short lives.

Cistler said finally, "I will defend you to the best of my abilities, but you must help. You must answer some questions."

Gavrilo's eyes became empty once again.

"Where did you get the weapons?"

"Anyone can get weapons, if they know where to look."

"Who are you protecting? What are you hiding?"

"Why is it that blind men always accuse others of hiding things?"

"Where did you get the weapons?"

"From in here," Gavrilo slapped his palm against his heart.

"Why are you protecting the Union or Death?"

Gavrilo had not been prepared for any reference to the Union, and it caused momentary surprise to register on his face.

Cistler smiled. He had the reaction he wanted. The old lawyer was not displeased with the first step of his investigation.

Later, after the old lawyer had left the cell, Gavrilo tapped out a message to Nedelijko: "Visited by Slav lawyer. Yes, there really is such a thing. Claims to be defending us in court. I think he's telling the truth. But much too early to trust him. Be cautious and silent. Perhaps later we can use him. Slav lawyer tells me we are to be arraigned next week."

Nedelijko replied: "The wheels of Austrian justice move swiftly when Slavs are in the dock."

CHAPTER THREE

The Arraignment

It was early in the morning of Tuesday, July 7, when Stega knocked on the door of her father's office. She was worried about her father. He had worked late into the night. Again she knocked on the door.

The man who stood behind her was Austrian and impatient.

"Is he asleep?" the man demanded.

Stega knocked on the door again. This time a little harder. From within the office came a soft groan. Stega waited no longer. Fearing some accident, she pushed open the door and marched into the office. She was followed by the Austrian.

Stega caught her breath and blushed. She was greeted by the sight of her father, stripped to his underclothes, touching his bare and bony toes. Cistlers' back was turned toward the door so that the Austrian had a strange view of the old man's withered legs arching out from his bony pelvis like a giant wishbone.

Cistler caught sight of his visitor as he touched his toes, seeing the Austrian upside-down between his knees. The old lawyer grinned at the astonishment on the Austrian's face.

"You might have knocked."

"I did," Stega mumbled sulkily, before she turned and walked quickly out of the office.

"Please sit down," Cistler invited. The Austrian remained standing. "You'll excuse me, I hope. I do not make a habit of holding interviews in my underwear. As you may have realized, you interrupted my morning exercises. It's the only way to keep the body in shape. I'm seventy, or will be in two months."

Cistler turned to his chair and began to dress himself.

"I take off my clothes when I exercise so I don't smell them up with perspiration. Sometimes I think old men perspire more than young men. Do you perspire a lot?" Cistler turned to stare at the Austrian.

"Do you know who I am?" the Austrian demanded.

Cistler smiled and shook his head.

"I am an assistant to the prosecutor general. I have been sent down from Vienna especially for this case."

"Would you hand me my shirt?," Cistler asked, flashing a grin at the younger man.

"I came here to remind you of the arraignment this morning."

"Did you think I had forgotten?"

"The prosecutor general was concerned."

"Please put his mind at rest and advise him that he has better things to worry about. Would you hand me my tie?"

"Will the defendants plead guilty?"

Cistler's grin remained frozen on his face. Why did this man want to know?

"Why don't you wait and see?" Cistler replied. "The defense might have a surpirse or two."

"That's exactly what this case does not need. We have

had enough surprises." The Austrian walked to the window overlooking the quay and stared out over the skyline of the city. "Perhaps you are not aware of the stir this case could create in Vienna. It would be wise for us to cooperate."

"Cooperate?"

"A guilty plea by your clients might calm Bosnia. Might even put an end to the reprisals. And your clients are young; perhaps the court would be lenient."

"Vienna does not want to see a trial?" Cistler asked.

"The three young men are clearly guilty. We have thirty witnesses. But more importantly, the grenade the police took from Gabrez was manufactured in Serbia."

"You think the Serbian government was behind the murders?"

"It is plausible."

"And you don't want the trial to prove it implausible?"

"The trial is unnecessary."

"I'm hearing that more and more. No one seems to want to see a trial. But I'll tell you something. The more people tell me that the trial is unnecessary, the more suspicious I become that the trial is essential."

"You will not be reasonable?"

"I am always reasonable. But not always cooperative. The two words are so easily confused."

The Austrian stalked toward the door. It was obvious that he did not enjoy Cistler's lesson in semantics.

"Don't be late for the arraignment, Dr. Cistler. Your reputation depends upon it."

Cistler's smile disappeared the moment the Austrian left his office. So the Austrians didn't want to see a trial either. Perhaps they were concerned about what might be said. It might interfere with their plans. Plans to invade Serbia? Cistler couldn't be sure.

Perhaps the Austrians had guessed that the Union or Death was behind the assassinations. If they had, they would not want that information to come out in the trial. The

Austrians would want the responsibility for the murders to rest upon the shoulders of the Serbian government, not upon a terrorist organization.

Cistler began to see the difficulties the trial presented and its importance.

At quarter to ten the old lawyer left his office and strolled casually toward the courthouse. His mind was occupied with the pressure that had been put upon him. So far everyone had been gentle. How long would it be before advice became threats and words became actions? Cistler shrugged. He had never expected it to be an easy case.

The small courtroom was already jammed with people when Cistler entered. The back rows were full of newspaper reporters, relatives of the accused, and curious spectators. Cistler made his way to the front row on the left. It was reserved for the defendants and was still empty. The old man could feel the eyes of the court upon him. He could almost hear the whispered gossip. He could not forget the other lawyers' contempt.

The courtroom fell into silence as the defendants were led in.

Each of the young men was chained to an Austrian guard. Nedelijko was in the lead. His stride was bold, almost a swagger. Following him was Trifun, who lumbered awkwardly and self-consciously across the courtroom. Behind Trifun was Gavrilo. A reporter attempted to ask him something but was silenced by the guard. Gavrilo walked slowly and casually. His expression was distant and unconcerned.

The court rose to its feet as the three judges entered and climbed the three steps to their bench. The presiding judge, seated in the center, was unknown to Cistler. An Austrian, probably sent down from Vienna especially for this case. Just to the right of the judge's bench were an Austrian flag and a portrait of the emperor.

The prosecutor general began to intone the charges against the three young men.

Cistler turned and whispered to the defendants, "You will

be asked to plead innocent or guilty. My advice to you is to remain silent. I will ask the judges for a postponement. It will give us time to prepare a defense." Cistler turned his attention back to the prosecutor general and wondered how long it would take the scarred man to visit him again.

When the prosecutor general had finished reading the charges, the center judge asked Nedelijko Cabrinovitch if he wished to plead guilty. Nedelijko remained silent, glaring defiantly at the judge.

"Your Honor," Cistler said, "is it possible for the defendants to plead at the trial? We have not had sufficient time to prepare a defense."

The center judge appeared surprised. He turned to the black-robed judge on his left and whispered. The prosecutor general asked for permission to approach the bench. More whispered conversation.

Cistler suddenly understood. The center judge had expected the defendants to plead guilty. A deal had been struck between the court and the prosecutor general's office. The Austrian judge didn't want to see the case come to trial any more than the union did.

Finally the prosecutor general returned to table, and the presiding judge addressed Cistler.

"Due to the seriousness of the charges, the court cannot allow a postponement. The defendants must answer the charges today. You may have a few minutes with your clients, Dr. Cistler."

A few minutes! Cistler thought angrily. What was the hurry? Why this sense of urgency?

Before Cistler could turn to consult with the defendants, the prosecutor general rose and crossed to where Cistler stood.

"Dr. Cistler," the Magyar greeted him. Cistler nodded and shook the man's hand. "I apologize for sending my assistant this morning. We should have taken a few minutes before the arraignment to consult personally."

The prosecutor general touched the older lawyer's elbow

and led him away from the rows of newspaper correspondents.

"You are no doubt aware of the political implications of this case?"

"I am."

"I assure you, Dr. Cistler, that Vienna is not looking for vengeance. In fact, my instructions from Vienna have been to calm the situation. The reprisal executions of Slavs in Trebinje have been reported widely and have generated a number of questions."

"Questions?"

"Both the British and Russian newspapers have openly asked whether a Slav can receive a fair trial in Bosnia."

"Can a Slav receive justice in Bosnia?"

The prosecutor general did not reply to Cistler's question. He pretended not to hear it.

"We have over thirty eyewitnesses who are ready to testify that they saw Princip fire the shots that killed the Crown Prince and his wife. The case is not complicated. It might be a serious error to complicate it, to turn it into a forum for radical speeches on Slav nationalism."

"I have no intention of doing that," Cistler replied coldly. The prosecutor general had still not made his point. Cistler was becoming impatient.

"I spoke with the presiding judge this morning. As I said before, Vienna is not looking for vengeance. If the defendants plead guilty as charged, the court is willing to be lenient with Trifun Gabrez and Nedelijko Cabrinovitch. They are young and easily misguided. The presiding judge has agreed to five-year sentences. Of course, the court cannot be lenient with Princip. In Princip's case, I'll have to ask the court for the maximum penalty allowed by law."

"You have it all worked out!" Cistler snarled.

"A case like this must proceed swiftly."

The prosecutor general's logic was simple. Suddenly Vienna's plans became apparent to the old lawyer. They weren't going to try to prove anything. They weren't going to waste time showing that the Serbian government was behind the murders. It was unnecessary. Once they had a guilty plea from the defendants, they could assume whatever conspiracy theory suited their plans. And Cistler had no doubt that Vienna's plans included the invasion of Serbia.

Cistler turned his back on the prosecutor general and crossed back to his clients.

"The prosecutor general has worked out a deal with the presiding judge," Cistler whispered to the three young men. "If you plead guilty, Trifun and Nedelijko will be sentenced to five years. Gavrilo, you will receive the maximum, twenty-five years' hard labor."

The three young men did not reply. Their expressionless eyes stared back at the old lawyer.

"However, I should tell you that the Austrians do not want to see a trial. If I'm right, the Austrian politicians would much prefer to make up their own minds as to who was responsible for the murders, without interference from anything you three might say in the course of a trial."

"I don't understand," Nedelijko whispered.

"If the Austrians are looking for an excuse to invade and annex Serbia, they will want the rest of the world, especially Russia, to assume the Serbian government was behind the assassinations. Perhaps Vienna doesn't feel that it can prove in court the complicity of Serbia, so Vienna would rather act on assumption, rumor, and suspicion."

"We will have to plead today?" Trifun asked.

Cistler nodded.

"I will not recognize the jurisdiction of the court," Gavrilo announced in a whisper. "I am a Slav, and the Austrians have no right to try me."

Trifun and Nedelijko nodded their agreement.

The presiding judge gaveled the courtroom back into order and called upon Nedelijko Cabrinovitch to plead.

Nedelijko remained silent. Gavrilo rose to his feet. The reporters in the back rows scribbled furiously.

"May I ask a question?" Gavrilo shouted.

"You should consult your lawyer before you speak," the presiding judge advised.

"I speak for myself. I want to know if this court is really interested in justice."

The presiding judge exchanged a worried look with the prosecutor general.

"If you plead innocent," the judge replied, "you will have a chance to defend yourself. You will be confronted with all witnesses who speak against you."

"In that case," Gavrilo sneered, "you will not mind removing that portrait from the courtroom."

All eyes in the court focused on the large portrait of Emperor Franz Joseph, the uncle of the man Gavrilo had killed.

§   §   §

After the court had adjourned, Cistler returned to his office. Gavrilo Princip's demand that the portrait of the emperor be removed was, of course, denied. The judges had had no choice but to accept the defendant's refusal to recognize the court as a plea of innocent. There would be a trial. It was scheduled to begin in three weeks.

That surprised Cistler. Three weeks to prepare a defense!

He entered his twilit office and lit a small oil lamp. Then he saw the outline of a man behind his desk.

"I have been waiting for you."

"I don't suppose we could postpone this meeting," Cistler asked, the forced cheerfulness in his voice belying his exhaustion.

In the flickering lamp light the scar on the man's face seemed even more hideous.

"How did the defendants plead?" the man demanded.

Cistler walked to the window overlooking the quay. He stared out over the river, over the twilit city, and felt a twinge of fear in his stomach.

"They refused to recognize the jurisdiction of the court.

But you could have learned that from tomorrow's papers."

"There will be a trial?"

"In three weeks there will be a trial. But you could have learned that too, from tomorrow's newspapers."

"You're a fool," the scarred man snapped. "You're a damn fool."

Cistler turned from the window and faced the scarred men. He wondered how far the man would go. If the man was working for the union, he would probably go to extremes. The thought made Cistler shudder.

"Who are you?" Cistler demanded.

"My name is unimportant. I am a friend of the defendants. I wish the best for your clients."

"And what do you consider the best?"

"What they desire most—death."

"Death?"

"You look surprised." The scarred man's voice had dropped to a hoarse whisper. "They have served their purpose. What is the use of continuing to exist without a purpose? Especially when they are so dangerous alive. Had you obeyed orders, had they pleaded guilty, perhaps their deaths would not be necessary. But now, we have no choice. The defendants must die. You see what your foolishness has led to. I tried to warn you, but you wouldn't listen—"

"And I do not intend to listen to this nonsense!" Cistler barked. "I refused to advise my clients to waive their right to a trial. That is that. If you're planning on killing them, you'll have your work cut out for you. They're in maximum security. They're guarded round the clock."

The scarred man chuckled. "I know where the defendants are, Dr. Cistler. We are not all as foolish as you are. It is not hard to dispatch young men who want to die. It is as easy as this." The scarred man snapped his fingers. "Do you understand?"

Cistler sighed audibly and impatiently. He crossed the small office and threw himself into a chair opposite from where the scarred man sat.

"No, I don't understand. I don't understand a damned thing."

"In the top drawer of your desk you will find three vials of cyanide. You will take them to the defendants and explain that they are presents from the friends of the Slav people. The defendants will know what to do with them."

Cistler stared incredulously. The man really expected Cistler to carry the poison to the prisoners. He really expected Cistler to be an accessory to suicide. Or would it be considered murder?

The scarred man rose to his feet and from within the folds of his coat withdrew a small nickel-plated revolver. The gun caught the lamplight and sparkled.

The man walked around the side of the desk, keeping the gun leveled at Cistler's head. The old lawyer's hands trembled. He reached forward and grasped the edge of the desk.

"I will be back if the newspapers do not announce the death of the three prisoners," the scarred man whispered. His breath was warm and sticky. "I will leave you with a taste of the future—should you continue to be foolish."

The scarred man cleared his throat before he smashed the handgrip of the revolver down on Cistler's hand. Cistler heard himself scream as the little finger on his left hand splintered.

CHAPTER FOUR

Sour Milk

It was almost midnight before Cistler left the doctor's office. His finger had been braced with a splint and then bandaged. The doctor had shook his head. The bone was too soft. Cistler was an old man. He would never recover the use of the finger.

Cistler had grinned and mumbled something about being too old to play the piano, but the news had shaken him. Despite his age, Cistler had not grown accustomed to the idea that one day he would die.

As he walked down Franz Joseph Street toward his apartment, he tried to think calmly about the alternatives. No one wanted to see a trial. But the alternatives to a trial could be war. Was he being melodramatic? He was sure the prosecutor general would say so. Was he taking too much of a burden of responsibility upon his own shoulders? It was his job to defend his clients, not to prevent wars. He was forced to smile. It did sound absurdly egotistical when he thought about it that way.

The pain in his finger reminded him of the scarred man's visit. What would he do about that? It was absurd. None of it made sense. But there was no question about the pain. He was not calm. The beat of his heart filled his ears and his mind. What if he didn't take the poison to the prisoners? What would the scarred man's next move be?

Only once had he thought about going to the police. He had discarded the idea almost instantly. The police were always too busy to take Slavs seriously.

Cistler strained to be rational. He had to think analytically as they trained him to do in law school. But he failed again. His mouth was parched, and all he could think of was vinjak.

He entered his rooming house and climbed the two flights of stairs, pausing after the first flight to catch his breath. He used his key and opened the apartment door. He was greeted by a frantically happy dog, who wagged her tail and jumped playfully at him.

"Papa?" Stega called from the far room.

"Down, Breskva," Cistler whispered to the dog. "Down, girl." Cistler ran his uninjured hand over the dog's head.

Stega appeared in the doorway to the bedroom.

"It's after midnight!" she announced. "You will overwork yourself!" She paused and took note of her father's injured hand. "What happened to your hand?"

"It's nothing. The clumsiness of an old man."

"Did you break a finger?"

Cistler nodded. He had decided not to tell Stega about his visit from the scarred man. It would serve no purpose other than to frighten her. "I slipped and fell."

Stega examined the injured hand and, discerning that there was nothing further she could do to help, instructed her father to get a good night's sleep, and then proceeded to follow her own advice.

But the old lawyer did not sleep well. His nerves were on edge. He was not sure what to do next. His mind was seized by a sense of urgency that was as inexplicable as it was immediate. He had to make a decision. He threw off his shoes and fell into an armchair. Breskva curled up at his feet.

It was clear that the Union, if that was who the scarred man represented, was not bluffing. They expected him to carry the poison to the prisoners. The dull ache in his finger reinforced that reality. Cistler had heard about how the Union exceuted people who did not obey them. There was nothing quick about it. They made examples of people who did not cooperate with them.

A body had been found only three weeks before, some Magyar official. The top of its head had been sawed off, and the brain cavity was empty. The newspapers had speculated that the killers had begun to saw the man's head before he was dead.

Cistler shuddered and forced the image from his mind. The cravings returned. He wanted a drink. He needed a drink. But that wasn't going to solve anything, he told himself. Another voice shouted that there was nothing to solve. A little *vinjak* would soothe his nerves. A single drink would help him think.

He resisted the temptation and thought of the poison in his desk drawer.

But what was he thinking of? For a moment he had actually considered taking the poison to the young men.

There had to be another alternative. Cistler had never killed anyone.

Suddenly his own words echoed in his mind: *If you're planning on killing them, you'll have your work cut out for you. They're in maximum security. They're guarded round the clock.*

Maximum security! That was the key. The Union couldn't get at the defendants. Cistler was the only Slav allowed to visit them. He was the only contact the Union could have with the prisoners. The old lawyer was not expendable. He was important.

The Union wouldn't kill him. He was sure of that. But

that didn't mean they wouldn't hurt him. Suddenly he thought of Stega and shuddered again. Even if they couldn't kill him, they could get to him through his daughter.

More now than before, he wanted a drink. He shouldn't put his daughter in danger. But there didn't seem to be a way to prevent it, other than taking the poison to the defendants. He wasn't a killer. He had a conscience. Was it possible that the prison guards would discover who brought the poison in? But if all three died, there would be no evidence against him.

Evidence against him! He was already thinking like a criminal. Was that what fear did? What effect would the death of the three boys have on him? He wouldn't sleep for a week. But he would still be alive. Stega would still be alive. There would be no trial. The Austrians would be pleased. The Union would be satisfied. And everyone would happily go off to war! It was madness. Stark raving madness!

Perhaps it would be kinder to the defendants themselves. A quick death from cyanide or a long-drawn-out death in an Austrian prison. It could be an act of mercy.

There was only one agent of mercy in Cistler's world, and that was *vinjak*. His mouth could almost taste it. Finally, his exhaustion overcame his confusion and fear, and the old lawyer drifted into a troubled sleep.

Breskva did not stir.

§　§　§

The following two weeks were busy ones for the old lawyer He scheduled interviews with relatives of the accused young men and attempted to make some sense out of the contradictory evidence The scarred man made no further attempt to contact him. The full-time business of defending the young men preoccupied him, and gradually the old lawyer came to believe that the union had decided to ignore his existence However, Cistler had forgotten that the easiest lies to accept are those one tells to oneself.

§   §   §

Stega broke the silence of the breakfast table.

"Trifun Gabrez's parents are due in your office at ten."

Cistler nodded. He did not expect much from the Gabrezes. They were typical Slav peasants, ill-educated and intimidated by Austrian authority. But if he was going to ask the court for leniency, he would need some background information.

The old lawyer put his spoon in the empty bowl and prepared to leave for his office. Stega would meet him there later in the morning.

The morning was hot and humid, and before he had gone far he started to perspire. He reminded himself to stop by the court on his way to his office. He wanted a copy of Cabrinovitch's statement to the police. The trial was set for a week from Friday. There was too damned much to do! The dull ache in his finger had diminished a little. Perhaps, he thought, he should attempt to see Princip in the afternoon. Of the three defendants, Princip was unquestionably the leader. The other two would obey Princip. Perhaps Princip could be reasoned with. Perhaps together they could plan a coherent defense.

Cistler turned from Vuka Street onto Franz Joseph Street. Despite the heat of the early morning, the old lawyer was enjoying his walk. Not until he crossed Milkov Street did he first begin to suspect that something was wrong.

He paused and looked into a shop window. Suddenly he snapped his head to the right. Another man, one he had never seen before, was also looking into a shop window a hundred meters behind him.

He walked another block, trying to ridicule his own suspicions. His imagination was out of control. He turned the corner and walked another hundred meters before stopping to stare into a shop window. Casually he glanced over his shoulder.

It was not his imagination. The man was still there, still behind him.

By the time Cistler got to the courthouse, he had no doubt that he was being followed. He had taken a long, round-about route, crisscrossing many side streets, but the man had stayed almost exactly a hundred meters behind him.

By the time the old lawyer climbed the steps of the courthouse, his nerves were in a state of near collapse. His hands trembled and his breathing had become irregular.

Cistler had no question in his mind that the man who was following him was a member of the Union. No one else would want to follow him. The Union wanted to make sure he would obey orders. The Union wanted to make sure he didn't go to the police.

Police protection? Cistler had been both a lawyer and a Slav too long to believe in the myth of police protection. If the police wanted you as an important witness, then it was a different story. But for an old Slav lawyer? The police would not waste their time.

Cistler stood in the lobby of the courthouse, wondering what he should do next. Finally he left by the rear exit and cut across several side streets to his office. Outside his office, he turned and cast his gaze over the street behind him. To his relief, he did not see the man who had been following him. He climbed the steps and entered his office.

It was not long before his relief left him and his common sense returned. His office was the most obvious place for him to go. The man who had followed him was certain to check there. Cistler shook his head and shrugged wearily.

Even sitting behind his desk with the testimonies spread before him he could not force himself to concentrate on the case. They were out to get him. They would hunt him down like an animal. He thought about resigning. He could tell the judge that his health was bad. It would be a coward's way out, but it was better than no way out.

Let some young lawyer risk his neck. He was too old. He should have retired after his sickness. It was foolish for him to become so involved with such an important case.

Cistler might have returned to the courthouse immediately and announced that he was withdrawing from the case, had Stega not knocked on his office door and announced the arrival of Trifun Gabrez's parents.

The parents were obviously nervous about being in a lawyer's office. If Cistler had not been so preoccupied, he would probably have tried to put them at ease.

The interview lasted less than thirty minutes. Cistler's mind was elsewhere, and he allowed Mrs. Gabrez to mumble on about how her son was a good boy, how she couldn't imagine his getting into trouble like this, and how he must have been influenced by other young men. Cistler nodded impatiently and fired several questions at them about Trifun's whereabouts for the past few years. The old lawyer was not surprised to hear that Trifun had been in Belgrade since 1912. It fit into everything he knew about the Union.

Finally Cistler thanked them for their time, avoided several questions about what was going to happen to their son, and showed them to the door. When he opened the door his heart leaped into his throat.

Sitting calmly in the outer office was the man who had followed him to the courthouse. Cistler gagged on his words, nodded abruptly to the puzzled parents, and disappeared back into his office.

Stega opened the door to his office and looked at him. The sudden fear Cistler had felt had distorted his face, and at the sight of him, Stega's eyebrows shot up in concern. She came into the office and closed the door behind her.

"Are you all right?" she asked, coming over to the side of his desk. "What's the matter?"

Cistler forced a smile. "A little tired, perhaps."

"Papa, you must get some rest. You know what the doctor—"

"I know," Cistler murmured. "I remember what the doctor said."

"There's a man outside who would like to see you. Shall I tell him to come back later?"

Cistler almost smiled at his daughter's innocence. One did not tell a *komitadji* to come back later.

"No. I'll see him now."

Stega returned to the office door, held it open, and nodded for the man to enter. The man crossed the small office and stood by a chair. There were several moments of silence.

"May I sit down?" the man asked.

"I'm too old to stop you."

"Thank you," the man replied, but his expression registered surprise at the harshness of Cistler's reply. The man slipped into the chair.

"I have come to see you about the case you're handling. The defense of the three young men accused of—"

"This doesn't help me concentrate!" Cistler barked, holding up his broken finger.

Again the man's expression registered surprise. But he chose to ignore the old man's comment.

"I just wondered if the defendants were talking freely to you?"

The casualness of the young man annoyed Cistler. It was as if the man didn't really care whether he got an answer.

"They wouldn't talk at all if you get your way," Cistler blurted out.

"I beg your pardon?" the man asked, clearly confused.

"You know what I'm talking about!"

"I have no idea what on earth you're talking about."

"Why were you following me this morning?"

"Was I that bad?" the man asked, and chuckled. "I'm sorry I frightened you. I just didn't know what time you would arrive at your office, and it was important for me to speak with you."

The man's casualness began to confuse Cistler. There was nothing threatening or menacing about the man's manner. In fact, the man seemed to go out of his way to be pleasant.

"Who the hell are you?" Cistler demanded.

"My name's Moyen. Jovo Moyen. I'm a special assistant to Prime Minister Pastich."

"You're a *komitadji?*"

"I'm a civil servant," the man replied with a laugh. "But it's obvious from your reaction to my presence that the Union has been in touch with you. Did they break your finger?"

Cistler did not reply. He was surprised by the man's mentioning the Union.

"What did they want?" Moyen asked. "Why did they threaten you?"

Still Cistler remained silent.

"Well, Dr. Cistler, let me give you some answers. The Union probably doesn't want to see a trial or an investigation. You've probably guessed the reason why—because the Union was behind the murders. The assassination was planned in Belgrade. The three defendants had the idea, and they requested weapons from a man named Milan Ciganovitch, a captain in the Union. Ciganovitch took their idea to the leader of the Union, Colonel Apis. Apis thought it over and approved it. Ciganovitch supplied the three young men with weapons and assisted them in crossing the Serbian border into Bosnia."

"Why are you telling me this?" Cistler demanded.

"So that you can prove to the court that it was the Union that was behind the murders, not the Serbian government."

"How long am I supposed to live after I prove the Union guilty? A day?"

"If you'll help make the truth known at the trial, the Serbian government will help you get out of the Balkans."

Cistler sighed and reached for his pipe.

"You know," Moyen started again, "the Austrians may use the assassinations—"

"I know. I know," Cistler interrupted impatiently. "As an excuse to invade Serbia. I am sick and tired of hearing it."

"You would be performing a service to all Slavs."

Cistler remained silent. Once again he wanted a drink.

"I can give you proof that the Union organized the assassinations," Moyen coaxed Cistler gently. "For a number of years we've had an informer. I can give you names, locations, dates. . . ."

Cistler listened as Moyen explained how the three students had been recruited and trained. The old lawyer found himself growing interested. It sounded plausible. It seemed that Moyen was telling the truth.

At the mention of Tankosic's name, Cistler involuntarily reached for a fountain pen. "Spell it," the old man commanded.

Moyen spelled it and went on to outline the type of training the new *komitadji* received. He described Tankosic, Apis, and finally Ciganovitch.

"Ciganovitch has a scar?" Cistler repeated.

Moyen nodded.

"He was the man who broke my finger."

"It's possible," Moyen replied. "Apis sent him to Sarajevo as soon as he learned that the three students had been captured alive."

"Why don't you just pass all this information to the Austrians?" Cistler asked. "Why come to me?"

Moyen smiled. He had expected the question, and he knew his answer would not satisfy the old lawyer.

"The Austrians are probably already aware that the Union supplied the weapons for the assassination. They don't want to admit it, because then they would lose their excuse to invade. If the Serbian government passed the information about the Union to the Austrians, we would be playing into their hands."

"Playing into whose hands?"

"The Austrians. Vienna would respond by demanding

that we extradite Apis so that they could try him for murder. That would mean that we would have to arrest him."

"I don't see any problem with that. From what you're told me, Apis should have been arrested years ago."

"And he would have been arrested years ago," Moyen replied, "if he wasn't so damned powerful. Most of the army is loyal to him. If we arrested him there would probably be a military takeover, which we would be powerless to stop."

"So what exactly do you want me to do?" Cistler asked. Moyen's casualness had put the old lawyer at ease, and he reached for his pipe.

"Just tell the truth at the trial. Except don't mention Dragutin Dimitrievitch."

"Dimitrievitch? Who's he?"

"That's Apis's real name," Moyen replied. "Tell the court about the Union. Explain about the organizing of the murder in Belgrade. Mention Ciganovitch and Tankosic by name. Naturally, the Austrians will demand their extradition. We may have to arrest them. But Apis may sacrifice them rather than provoking something which might well resemble civil war."

Cistler leaned back in his chair thoughtfully puffing on his pipe.

"And what happens to me after I tell the truth?"

"The Serbian government will assure you safe passage out of the Balkans."

"Terrific!" Cistler muttered sarcastically. "You don't even dare arrest the man responsible for the Crown Prince's murder, and yet you're assuring me safe passage out of the Balkans?" Cistler pointed the amber stem of his pipe at Moyen. "What do you suggest I do the next time I'm visited by Ciganovitch?"

"Don't worry about Ciganovitch. We'll take care of him. He's outlived his usefulness. It is time to repair the *gluvonem*."

"The what?"

"It's nothing," Moyen replied softly. "If someone from the Union visits you, then you must appear cooperative, appear to be obeying their orders. You know the old saying: 'When the milk goes sour, make yogurt.' Pretend to obey the Union, and then speak the truth at the trial. The Serbian government does not break its promises. We'll get you out of the Balkans."

Cistler curled his lips into a sneer. "Sour milk stinks, and so, for that matter, does your advice."

"Think about it, Dr. Cistler," Moyen whispered with an almost sad smile. "Just think about it. It may be your only alternative."

It was almost lunchtime when Moyen left the small legal office. Cistler was convinced that Moyen had spoken the truth about the Union.

Perhaps Moyen had been right. Perhaps there was only one way for him to stay alive. Pretend to be obeying the Union. Appear cooperative.

The afternoon went slowly for Cistler.

Stega and Cistler left the office together at six. They stopped at a small café on Milkov Street and ate a light supper of cold ham and crusty Bosnian bread. Cistler told her nothing about what Moyen had said. It would frighten her unnecessarily.

After coffee, the old man and his daughter headed home. Several times on the way to his apartment, Cistler paused to stare into shop windows, casting surreptitious glances over his shoulder. But the street behind him was empty.

Stega took her father's arm as they climbed the two flights of stairs to their small apartment. Standing before the apartment door, Cistler pulled the key from his pocket, but he paused and stared at the lock. Part of the outside casing had been filed away. It was scratched. He suddenly pushed Stega away from the door. She opened her mouth as if to protest, but the expression of urgency on her father's face silenced her.

Cistler inserted the key quickly, turned it, and flung the door open.

"*Jesus Christ!*" he cried. His living room was in chaos. Furniture broken and smashed. Cabinets and chests ransacked. In the center of the room lay his dog, Breskva, in a pool of blood. Her throat had been cut.

CHAPTER FIVE

Entropy

It had taken Cistler fifteen minutes to calm Stega and another two hours to straighten out the apartment. Cistler had dragged the dog's carcass down the stairs and deposited it in the narrow alleyway that ran beside the building.

Fear had returned to him. Cold and unwelcome. His dog stabbed to death. His apartment torn apart. It was a warning. Another warning. The Union was telling him that they had not forgotten about him. There was nowhere he could hide from them.

He climbed the stairs back up to their apartment. Curious neighbors closed their doors as they heard him panting and puffing up the stairs. Through the open door he saw Stega crouched in the livingroom sweeping up the remains of a shattered mirror. She turned to stare at him. "Now are you going to tell me what's going on?"

Cistler did not reply at once. He had made a decision, and now he wondered only how to implement it. Exhaustion and shock were written all over his daughter's face.

He sighed and slipped his pipe between his lips. "There are people who would prefer not to see a trial."

"I know. Is that the only reason you refused to call the police?"

"What would the police do? They would not find the man or men who did this." Cistler paused and lit his pipe. "You will catch the morning train to Mostar. You will stay with your aunt until the trial is over."

"I will not!" Stega replied.

"I am not going to argue with you!" Cistler barked. "At this point I'm safe. Nothing is going to happen to me. But certain men might try to get to me through you. You must leave Sarajevo until the trial is over. There will be no more discussion. I have made up my mind."

"Then you'll have to unmake it, because I'm not going anywhere. Listen to me, Papa."

Cistler turned away from his daughter and walked toward the kitchen.

She went on, "Someone broke your finger. It wasn't an accident, was it? You've lied to me about the case. You've been trying to protect me so that I wouldn't be frightened. Well, I am frightened. And I'm not leaving you alone."

Cistler turned back to face his daughter's anger. "You are very much like your mother," he whispered softly.

"You need someone to help you," Stega snapped. "You know what will happen if I go away."

"No one will hurt me."

"That's not what I mean, and you know it. If I go to Mostar, you'll start drinking again."

"I was the one who went through the sickness," Cistler bellowed. "All you did was watch it. You're going to be on that train in the morning even if I have to physically place you on it."

Stega turned on her heel and stalked into her bedroom, slamming the door behind her.

Neither father nor daughter slept well, and both were up early the following morning. Stega was silent, almost sullen, until they were both seated at the breakfast table.

"Papa," she began softly, "you are my father, and I will obey you, but I think it is the wrong time for me to go away. You need me here. If you would only tell me the whole truth about the case, I could help you."

Cistler looked up from his bowl of barley and milk. There was love in his daughter's expression, and it hurt him to look at her. There was no question about him needing her just as he had needed her mother. But there was also danger.

"You are my daughter, and a father should never have to send his daughter away. But I have no choice."

"You won't start—"

"I promise you I won't drink."

"If you need me, you will send for me?" Stega asked. Her father nodded, still finding it difficult to look directly into her eyes.

"It won't be for long," Cistler added, changing his tone of voice. He smiled and winked at Stega. "The Austrians seem to be in a hurry to get the trial over with. I don't think your holiday in Mostar will last very long."

"It won't be a holiday. I shall spend every day worried about what's going on here."

"That will be foolish. I am safe, and you have my promise. After this trial is over, we'll have a real holiday together." He grinned at Stega. "I'll find you a man. That's what you really need, a man."

Stega forced a thin smile onto her lips. She kissed her father on each cheek and withdrew to her room to pack.

At eight-thirty they walked together to the train station. Cistler gave her money for the train ticket and instructed her not to write to him. He would contact her when the trial was over.

He walked from the train station to his office. It was still early, and he was somewhat surprised to find a court officer waiting for him. The man was a Magyar and made no effort to conceal his contempt for the older Slav lawyer.

"You're to be in court at ten."

"I don't understand," Cistler replied. "The trial's not until next week."

"I don't care whether you understand or not. Just be in court at ten. The prosecutor general said he was going to cut your Slav tongue out."

"That's one way to prevent someone from speaking the truth."

"Just be in court at ten. Try not to forget."

The Magyar turned and strolled out of Cistler's office.

At five minutes to ten Cistler was in court. The courtroom was almost empty. The prosecutor general and his assistant sat at their table on the right side of the court, and a half dozen reporters were scattered through the back rows. The prosecutor general made no attempt to greet Cistler; in fact, the Austrian avoided looking toward the old lawyer.

At ten o'clock the single presiding judge entered the courtroom and climbed to the bench. The prosecutor general remained standing after the rest of the court had sat.

"Your Honor has received the translation?" The prosecutor general inquired. The presiding judge nodded and turned his glaring eyes to where Cistler sat.

"Dr. Cistler," the Judge began, "have you seen yesterday's copy of the *London Times?*"

Suddenly everything made sense to Cistler. He had forgotten about his interview with the reporter named Watson. Fear returned in earnest. He wasn't frightened of what the court might do. He was frightened of the Union's reaction. How could he have been so stupid as to talk to that reporter?

"You were interviewed by a man named Watson?"

Cistler thought hurriedly about the consequences of lying. The prosecutor general would probably haul Watson into court. The judge might even charge him with perjury. How could he have been so stupid? Even using a false name for Stega had been ridiculous. Cistler decided to risk telling the truth.

"I answered some of the reporter's questions."

"This story has created quite a stir in Vienna," the presiding judge continued angrily. "A number of important men have been embarrassed. Do you have any evidence that this Union or Death was involved in a conspiracy to murder the late Crown Prince?"

Cistler did not reply immediately. If he told the truth and repeated what Moyen had told him, he was sure that he would not live out the day. However, if he didn't tell the truth, it would be almost impossible to do so later. From behind him he heard the whisperings of the reporters.

"At the moment, Your Honor, I have no evidence that there was a conspiracy."

"Then, Dr. Cistler, you agree that your statements as quoted in the *London Times* are misleading and false?"

"Your Honor, I'm afraid my statements were drastically misinterpreted."

"Drastically misinterpreted," the presiding judge repeated. "You will then authorize a complete retraction and refrain from speaking to any journalists about the case for the duration of the trial. Do you understand, Dr. Cistler?"

"Yes, Your Honor."

"The reporter, Watson, has already been expelled from Bosnia. As I am sure you will appreciate, Dr. Cistler, this case needs no more sensationalism than that which already surrounds it."

"I understand, Your Honor."

Cistler left the courtroom worried and puzzled.

What to do next? The thought of going to his office frightened him. It was the logical place for him to go. If Ciganovitch was looking for him, his office would be one of the first places. He sighed and rubbed his temple. He just needed some time to think. He was already missing Stega.

It was then that Cistler made a decision, or rather refused to make a decision. His mind blotted out the memory of his sickness. The cravings made his hands twitch. The dull ache in his finger demanded medication. One drink would steady his nerves. Allow him to think clearly. One drink would ease the sharp tension in his stomach. One drink would not really be breaking his promise.

He made his way to a small, dimly lit café three blocks from the courthouse and ordered *vinjak*. The café was almost empty, but the waiter did not consider it unusual for an old Slav man to be drinking at that hour of the morning. There was very little else for Slav men to do.

The *vinjak* did calm the old man's nerves. It settled his stomach and stilled the dull throbbing of his injured finger. He ordered another, and then a third. Drinking was automatic, a mechanical process that required no thought. His mind was not present in the café; it drifted away from the immediacy of the *vinjak*. It remembered the past, it anticipated the future, it traveled the entire span of his life in a moment. But it was forbidden to dwell on the fact that he had started drinking again.

The *vinjak* acted as a catalyst in converting fear to anger. At first his anger was directed toward himself. He cursed himself for being fool enough to talk to that Englishman. But he recognized that he had spoken the truth even before he knew for a fact it was the truth. It was always the same way. Slavs were taught to turn their fury in upon themselves. They were taught how to blame themselves for their miserable lot in life. The victim became the victimizer.

It was all a matter of education.

He recalled his own education. The red brick law school in Zagreb and its bitter motto: *Truth is the wellspring of all justice.*

The well had gone dry. Bone dry. No one cared a damn for truth or justice. Everyone wanted a bloodbath. There was a thin fiber in the human brain that had suddenly snapped and unleashed man's lunatic desire to destroy.

Suddenly Cistler found himself laughing at the absurdity of the situation. Laughing at himself. At the *vinjak* bottle that now stood half-empty on the table. Laughing at the pompous Austrians, at the melodramatic Union or Death, at the prosecutor general and the presiding judge. None of it mattered really. They all existed in separate worlds, constructed out of self-told lies. The civilization that Austria brought to Bosnia was just as much a fantasy as all the rhetoric about Pan-Slav unity. All of it was madness.

Cistler's hand shook as he poured himself another inch of *vinjak*. He was the link between the separate worlds. He giggled and fumbled in his pocket for his pipe. Everything seemed bent upon achieving the maximum state of disorder. Entropy was lord of the universe. Cistler raised his glass and toasted entropy, gulped the drink, and passed out on the table.

It was evening before he was conscious again, and he was somewhat surprised to find himself lying on his own bed. His hangover was terrific. A sharp pain shot through his head, and his mouth felt as if something had died in it.

He could not remember how he had got home or how he had managed to climb the two flights of stairs to his apartment. He was disgusted with himself.

Slowly he rose from the bed and wandered toward the kitchen. In the living room sat Milan Ciganovitch.

"It's a good job we keep an eye on you," Ciganovitch greeted him. "You might have spent all night slouched over a table in that café."

Cistler groaned and continued on his way to the kitchen. His brain was clearing rapidly. The Union had been watching him. Ciganovitch had taken him home.

"You should be more moderate in your vices, Dr. Cistler," Ciganovitch called from the living room. "After all, what would people say if they saw the venerable old Cistler passed out over a *vinjak* bottle? It might damage your reputation." Ciganovitch laughed loudly.

"Go to hell!" Cistler shouted from the kitchen.

"That would be convenient for you, I suppose. But my travel plans do not include hell. However, they do include Mostar."

All the blood had drained from Cistler's face when he

appeared in the doorway to the living room. His heart beat rapidly, and he perspired freely.

"Mostar is pretty this time of year. Don't you think so? I have an aunt who lives there. I might stay with her for a while. Perhaps you know someone in Mostar. Someone you'd like me to visit."

Cistler was cold all over. He realized that he had been an even greater fool than he had thought. Of course the Union would be watching him. They had followed him to the train station. They had watched him put Stega on the train to Mostar. His very act of sending her away had announced his weakest, most vulnerable spot.

"If you hurt Stega—" the old man began but Ciganovitch cut him short.

"That was her name. Stega. A good Slav name. I would be sorry to see anything happen to her. But you are not following orders." Ciganovitch's tone changed. It became thin and threatening. "If by tomorrow night the three defendants aren't dead, your daughter will be. Understand?"

Cistler stood in the doorway speechless. Rage and fear boiled within him. Ciganovitch rose to his feet and almost as an afterthought smiled at the old man.

"Take it easy with the *vinjak*. Your daughter's life may depend on it."

The scarred man walked out the front door.

Cistler felt all the fear of the past three weeks settle and congeal in his stomach. He was trapped. They would kill Stega the same way they had killed his dog, Breskva. Murder meant nothing to them. And after they had killed Stega they would kill him. They would probably kill him anyway. He knew too much. But Stega must live. He was too old to escape. But she was young. She deserved a chance. He wanted another drink. He couldn't escape that either. Perhaps there never had been such a thing as escape.

Choice had been taken from him. He could not allow them to hurt Stega. He would take the bottles of poison to the prisoners.

The next morning found the old lawyer still vaguely hung over. He had not slept well. Dozing between nightmares that were as vivid and nonsensical as reality. He blinked the remains of sleepiness from his eyes and shuddered. There was no choice.

He was aware that the Union could not allow him to live after he had delivered the poison. He would know too much. But Stega would be safe. Reluctantly the old lawyer faced the fact that this might well be his last day alive.

Strangely, this thought calmed him. After all, he mused, the news couldn't get much worse. *My last day,* he repeated silently to himself. He even found himself smiling the way a man does when he realizes that the time for action has arrived.

My last day should begin with a smile, he told himself. And three fingers of *vinjak* for breakfast. *Vinjak* drinkers didn't go to hell. Who had said that? It must have been Father Jamis. There probably wasn't a hell anyway. And it there was, the chances were that it would make a great deal more sense than the world he presently inhabited.

On his way to his office, he stopped at a small café and ordered three healthy fingers of vinjak. The alcohol erased the last remnants of his hangover and soothed the dull pain in his injured hand. Although he was tempted to have another, he remembered Ciganovitch's warning and resisted.

When he arrived at his office, he made straight for the drawer in the writing table and withdrew the blue vials of cyanide. Without a second thought, he pocketed the small bottles and left the office.

He was kept waiting only ten minutes at the prison, before a uniformed guard led him up the curved stone staircase and through the rough-cut stone passageways that led to the maximum-security wing.

The guard opened the section of bars that served as a door and ushered Cistler into Gavrilo Princip's cell.

"I'll be right down the hall," the guard announced as he locked Cistler in the cell. "Call when you're finished."

Gavrilo stared at the lawyer in silence until the sound of the guard's boots indicated that he was out of earshot. Again Cistler became aware of the intensity of the young man's eyes.

"What happened to your finger?" Gavrilo demanded.

"I broke it."

"How?"

"Caught it in the door."

Gavrilo chuckled and rose from the blanketless bench. He crossed to the small barred window that overlooked the courtyard, before he turned and smiled bitterly at the old lawyer.

"You want me to tell the truth, and yet you come here and lie to me. You didn't catch your finger in a door. It was broken for you."

Cistler stared silently at the young man. He had not been in the cell more than a minute, and already the prisoner had turned the tables, had managed to put him on the defensive. Cistler's calm was fading.

He laughed nervously. "You're right. I didn't catch it in a door."

"I've seen that before," Gavrilo murmured, pointing at the old lawyer's injured finger. "It's used as a warning. You have been warned. But why? Why have you been warned?"

Cistler's composure was shattered. The young man was sharper and quicker than he had imagined, but he saw no reason to avoid the truth. Not now that he had made his decision. In fact, Cistler thought, it was probably the opportunity he had been waiting for.

Cistler proceeded to tell Gavrilo about his visits from the Union or Death, about how his finger had been broken, his dog killed, and his daughter's life threatened.

Gavrilo nodded thoughtfully, perhaps even sympathetically.

"I believe you really wanted to help us," Gavrilo finally murmured.

Cistler went on to tell about Ciganovitch's ordering him

to bring cyanide to the three prisoners. Gavrilo's eyes became even more intense at the mention of the name.

"Ciganovitch ordered you to bring us poison?"

"Yes. He said you would know what to do with it."

A sardonic smile formed at the corners of the young prisoner's lips.

"Did you bring the poison?"

This was the moment Cistler had been waiting for. All he had to do was reach in his pocket and pull out one of the blue vials. He wouldn't even have to say anything. Then he could call the guard and get out of the damp little cell. Cistler reached into his pocket. The coolness of the three little bottles was foreign, and it shocked him. His hands trembled. There was no escape. But he could not allow them to hurt Stega.

"Did you bring the cyanide with you?" Gavrilo asked again, the sardonic smile still in place.

Cistler's mind suddenly opened to a flood of confusion. There could be no escape, but he could not bring himself to be party to a murder. Fear returned to him. His composure splintered like thin glass. He wasn't a killer. He was a man interested in truth and justice. He was not an executioner. He envisioned Stega as a mutilated corpse. Beads of perspiration broke out on his forehead. He grasped the vial in his right hand and squeezed it until his knuckles turned milk-white and ached.

"Ciganovitch was not bluffing," Gavrilo muttered softly and somewhat sadly. "He will kill your daughter as quickly as the Austrians and Magyars killed my father."

Suddenly the old lawyer was flooded with anger. The fatalistic helplessness that had produced his calmness disappeared in an instant. He was not helpless. He was not a killer. Even if the entire world had gone stark raving mad, he would remain sane. To hell with the Union! To hell with the Austrians!

"Of course I didn't bring the poison!" Cistler barked. "I'm a lawyer. I'm here to defend you, not to execute you."

A thin sad smile spread across Gavrilo's lips. He had watched the old lawyer's hand fumble in his pocket. He knew the old man was lying.

"Why didn't you bring it?" Gavrilo asked.

"I will not be party to murder!"

"Murder?" Gavrilo chuckled. "Murder is nothing more than dying at the wrong time. The art of life is learning when to die. You should have brought the poison. I don't think it would have helped you or your daughter, but it might have helped us."

"I am going to try to help you," Cistler countered. "I was visited by a man named Moyen. Have you ever heard of him?"

Gavrilo shook his head.

"He claims to be a special assistant to Prime Minister Pastich of Serbia. He knew all about your activities in Belgrade. He told me all about Colonel Apis, Tankosic, and Ciganovitch."

"Did he tell you how he knew?" Gavrilo demanded.

"He said something about having an informer."

"Did he name the informer?"

"No. He just said something about cracking the *gluvonem*."

Gavrilo chuckled and shook his head.

"I know who the informer is," Gavrilo announced. "And perhaps that information *can* help you. Before we crossed the border into Bosnia, we were aware that Pastich knew about our plan to assassinate the Crown Prince. Pastich closed the border to us and ordered our arrest. There were only six men who knew about our plan: Apis, Tankosic, Ciganovitch, Nedelijko, Trifun, and myself. At first I suspected that either Nedelijko or Trifun was the informer."

"Pastich ordered the border closed to you three?" Cistler interrupted excitedly. Gavrilo nodded. Cistler continued eagerly, "That's why the Austrians are so frightened of a trial. If it becomes known that Pastich ordered your arrest, then Vienna will have no excuse to invade Serbia."

Gavrilo was amused at the old man's interruption. He had grown to like the old lawyer. There was a simplistic honesty about the old man that Gavrilo respected.

"Have you read the police reports?" Gavrilo asked. Cistler nodded. "Then you know that the police found cyanide on Nedelijko and Trifun?" Again Cistler nodded. "But they didn't find any cyanide on me. Did you ever think to wonder why one of us would not have the means of suicide?"

"Why didn't you have poison?"

"I did, but I drank it."

"You drank the cyanide?"

"Immediately after I heard Nedelijko's bomb explode. I thought we had succeeded. There was no point to continue living after we had accomplished our purpose."

"You drank the cyanide?"

"Whatever was in the vial I drank was not cyanide. It burned my stomach, but as you can see, it did not kill me. It was then, when I realized that the poison wasn't working, that I knew who the informer was. Someone had deliberately tampered with the poison. Someone wanted to keep us alive. Someone wanted us to testify in court. It was the same person who had informed Pastich of our plans. It would suit Pastich to have us arrested; then we could testify against the union, not against the Serbian government."

"Who tampered with the poison?" Cistler demanded.

"There was only one man who could have—Ciganovitch."

"Ciganovitch?" Cistler repeated, genuinely surprised. "But that doesn't make any sense. If Ciganovitch is working for the Serbian government, why the hell did he break my finger? Why did he kill my dog?"

"Ciganovitch is loyal to no one," Gavrilo snapped. "When it suits him he works for the Union, when it doesn't, he works for the Serbian government He's loyal only to himself. That makes him dangerous. You can never tell what he's going to do next."

"Does Apis know he's an informer?"

"I doubt it. Ciganovitch wouldn't be alive if Apis knew."

Suddenly Cistler had an idea. "How do I find Apis?" the old lawyer demanded.

"Why do you want him?"

"To tell him about Ciganovitch, of course." Cistler took a deep breath. The idea might work. Apis would then take care of Ciganovitch, and Cistler would appear to be co-operating with the Union. Stega would be safe, and he might enjoy the luxury of dying from old age.

But Gavrilo shook his head sadly. "You won't be able to find Apis. Not after the assassination. He's probably not even in Belgrade. Anyway, even if you found him, I don't think he'd believe you. You're not a member of the Union." Gavrilo paused for a moment and thought. "But I'll tell you what you could do. You could go looking for Ciganovitch. Tell him you brought the poison to the prison but that we refused to take it. Tell Ciganoivtch that Gavrilo Princip called him a traitor to the Slav people. It might panic him, but it might also save your daughter."

Cistler stared at the young man and sighed. Events were becoming too complex. He was confused and frightened once again. Ciganovitch was a double agent. No one knew who he was working for. Perhaps even Ciganovitch had trouble keeping his roles straight. But that didn't stop him from killing. Cistler wiped the perspiration from his forehead and flicked the gray hair from in front of his eyes.

"The most sensible thing for you to do," Gavrilo suggested quietly, "would be to bring us the poison. It would solve a great many problems."

"You want to die?"

"I have fulfilled my purpose. I would prefer death to life imprisonment."

"I am a lawyer. Not a *komitadji*. I am after the whole truth!"

"Truth?" Gavrilo chuckled. "What can you do with truth? Can you eat it? Can you plant truth in the spring and harvest it in the autumn? Will truth satisfy the tax collector? Truth is a weak poison. It does not kill—it merely cripples."

"Nonsense!" Cistler barked. "A man who forgets justice also forgets his humanity!"

"There can be no justice," Gavrilo barked, "until all of Bosnia is fertilized with Austrian blood."

"Do you really believe that rubbish?"

"I believe you made a serious mistake in not bringing us the poison. But you still have a chance to change your mind." Gavrilo nodded at the bulge in the old lawyer's pocket. "It would save both of us a great deal of inconvenience."

The sight of a young man so eager for death disgusted Cistler. The young prisoner's eyes seemed to sparkle with hope. Cistler shuddered. There was something mad about a world that made a young boy want to die so much that he could hardly contain his anticipation.

"I will not change my mind."

"Then I'm afraid we shall both pay the penalty of your reluctance. But *I* am prepared to die."

"I suppose," Cistler mumbled, "we all must be." The old lawyer paused as he heard the guard's boots in the stone passageway. The sound of the boots came closer and then disappeared off in another direction.

Cistler finally asked, "If Ciganovitch tampered with the poison once, what makes you think he hasn't done so again?"

"Why would he go to the trouble of breaking your finger and killing your dog, if the poison was not genuine?"

Cistler felt tired and drained of energy. Defeat settled upon him and his eyes clouded with the anticipation of pain, failure, and grief. More out of desperation than out of any real curiosity, Cistler asked, "What did you do after you arrived in Sarajevo?"

"I killed the archduke," Gavrilo replied, puzzled at the question.

"Where did you spend the night?"

"At a boarding house in the souk."

"Did you leave the boarding house the night before the state visit?"

Gavrilo shook his head.

"Not even to eat?"

"I wasn't hungry."

"What did you do in the room alone?"

"Read and thought."

"What did you read?"

"The Bible."

"The Bible?" Cistler repeated, watching the young man very carefully. It seemed almost inconceivable that this young man could have sat reading the Bible the evening before he was to commit murder.

"You believe in God?"

"Of course," Gavrilo replied. "Only fools and rich people doubt the existence of God."

"What's your God like?" Cistler asked.

"What's anybody's God like?"

"No," Cistler murmured softly. "Your God must be different. You have killed a man and a woman, and yet it appears that you feel no guilt."

"Guilt is for sentimentalists." Gavrilo's voice had an edge of impatience. "God cares for a man who cares for his people. I care for my people. I killed the archduke because he was an enemy of my people. I feel no guilt." Gavrilo's voice had risen in volume and intensity.

"Morality is for the well fed," the young prisoner continued. "Distinguishing right from wrong is the business of file clerks. History will call me a patriot."

Gavrilo fell into a nervous brooding silence.

The old lawyer rubbed his temple. Who was speaking? A madman? A patriot? A frightened young man pretending to be a hero? Was it heroic to wait, armed with guns and bombs, for an unarmed man and woman and then shoot them dead?

"Why did you fire the second shot that killed the archduke's wife?"

Gavrilo didn't answer at once. His narrow, bony fingers rubbed his cheek slowly. His eyelids seemed suddenly heavy. But it was as if his exhaustion had come, not from his external act, but from somewhere within himself—as if the act of murder had been incidental to some much greater purpose.

"The second shot was for Potiorek in the front seat. I was nervous. My aim was bad," the prisoner mumbled softly through his fingers, which stretched across his face like a confessional screen.

"Do you think you're a hero?"

"A hero?" Gavrilo repeated wearily. "There was nothing heroic about what I did. It was something that had to be done. It was my duty." Gavrilo paused and then looked sharply at the old lawyer. "You haven't told the police that the weapons came from Ciganovitch?" Cistler shook his head. "It would be better for you not to mention it. It will not serve any purpose."

"Not serve any purpose?" Cistler repeated. "At this point the Austrians want the rest of the world to think that you were operating on the instructions of the Serbian government."

"The source of the weapons is not important. It will not stop the politicians. If they have decided that there'll be a war, then there will be a war. We can't stop it. The truth is not as powerful as you like to believe."

Cistler frowned, and Gavrilo continued, "If it came out during the trial that the Union had supplied the weapons, Pastich would be forced to arrest Apis, or at least try. The army is loyal to Apis. You would have civil war. Do you think Austria could resist the temptation of invading Serbia while it was divided against itself?"

"You have everything worked out, haven't you?" Cistler grumbled bitterly.

Gavrilo closed his eyes. If he had ever been tempted to pity another human being it was now. Gavrilo doubted very much if he would ever see the old lawyer alive again.

CHAPTER SIX

An Ultimatum

It was after two in the afternoon on July 23 when Cistler finally left Kmet Prison. Surprise filled his brain. He had discovered that there were certain things he couldn't do. He had discovered that his actions were limited. He could no more have given the poison to the prisoner than he could have deliberately hurt his own daughter. Even at seventy Cistler had been surprised by this sudden discovery.

He had also been somewhat surprised at the young prisoner's reaction. He could understand Princip's desire to die, although it still disturbed him. What he had trouble understanding was why Princip hadn't taken the poison from him. Princip had known that he had the cyanide in his pocket, and yet the prisoner had made no attempt to take it from him.

Secretly Cistler had hoped Princip would grab it away from him. The responsibility would no longer have been his. Perhaps that was one of the reasons he had fumbled with the vials in his pocket so long. But Princip had made no move to release the old lawyer from his moral dilemma. Perhaps the young man understood Cistler's inability and in some strange way respected it. Perhaps the young man was perverse enough to refrain from interfering with Cistler's opportunity to remain human.

Outside the prison, Cistler walked in the direction of Milkov Street. He was hungry and thirsty and planned on having lunch at a café there. But two things would interfere with his plans, and it would be quite some time before old Dr. Cistler regained his appetite.

At the corner of Franz Joseph Street there was a young Slav boy selling copies of the early-afternoon paper. At first Cistler paid no attention. But the boy was shouting something that caused Cistler to cross the street and buy a copy of the paper.

"Austrian ultimatum sent to Serbia! Crown Prince's murder linked to Pastich government! Read all about it!"

Cistler snatched a copy of the thin newspaper out of the boy's hands and then, almost as an afterthought, dropped a few pfennigs in the boy's hand. The headlines glared up from the page: AUSTRIAN ULTIMATUM SENT TO SERBIA. MILITARY IN STATE OF GENERAL MOBILIZATION. PASTICH GIVEN TWENTY-FOUR HOURS TO REPLY.

Cistler stopped in the middle of the cobblestones to continue reading. The paper announced that a link had been discovered between the assassins and the Serbian government, but it didn't mention what the link was. Austria demanded that the Pastich government take immediate action against pan-Slav terrorists, suppress all publications inciting hatred of Austria-Hungary, arrest all individuals engaged in anti-Austrian propaganda, arrest all Serbian frontier officials guilty of aiding in the illicit traffic of arms and explosives into Bosnia, and arrest without delay all individuals having sympathy with pan-Slav nationalism.

Cistler's mouth fell open. If the last demand was complied with, three quarters of Serbia would be in jail. The old lawyer shook his head. The ultimatum had been written in such a way as to make Serbian compliance impossible. It was a jumble of nonsense. They started out saying that the Serbian government was responsible and ended up ordering the Serbian government to arrest those responsible. The ultimatum made as much sense as everything that had happened to Cistler since he had accepted the defense of the three young men

A wagon driver roared something at Cistler, and the old lawyer leaped out of the way. How would the ultimatum effect the upcoming trial? As if the editor of the paper had anticipated Cistler's question, the old lawyer's eyes came to rest on a small article in the lower-right-hand corner of the front page. ASSASSINATION TRIAL DATE MOVED UP. Cistler's mouth fell open for a second time as he read that owing to the immediacy of the ultimatum, the trial would begin on Friday, July 24. Cistler didn't need a calendar to know that Friday the 24th was tomorrow.

The trial was going to begin tomorrow! Cistler shook his head with disbelief. He knew what the hurry was. But what was he supposed to do? Come up with a responsible defense in one night! The presiding judge was mad.

And how would the Union respond to the ultimatum? How would Ciganovitch respond? Who was Ciganovitch working for today? Would Stega be safe in Mostar? Too many questions and not enough answers.

As if in frustration, Cistler withdrew the three blue vials of cyanide from his pocket and threw them into the gutter. With exaggerated anger he brought his heel down on the three of them, smashing the glass and sending the colorless liquid splattering over the cobblestones.

Slowly Cistler bent over the gutter and sniffed at the colorless liquid. It smelled strongly of almonds. Ciganovitch was working for the Union. The poison was most certainly genuine.

Cistler's brain functioned as fast as the fear that raced through him. There was nothing he could do for Stega at the moment. Even if he sent a telegram to warn her, she would be watched, and the warning might provoke whoever was watching her. There was no question that he had to prepare a defense for the following day, but first he had to make sure he would be alive the following day.

He had to find Ciganovitch and tell him that Gavrilo Princip had called him a traitor to the Slav people. He wasn't sure what that would accomplish, but it might save Stega, and it might cause Ciganovitch to change sides once again.

He crumpled the newspaper under his arm and set off in the direction of his office. How did one go about finding a *komitadji* in a city the size of Sarajevo? Where would Ciganovitch be hiding? Cistler had no doubt that if he waited long enough Ciganovitch would find him, but that might be too late to save Stega.

At the corner of Appel Quay Cistler stopped in a small grocery store and bought a bottle of *vinjak*. For medicinal purposes only, he told himself. Just in case his nerves needed calming.

As Cistler turned out of the grocery shop, he snapped his head to the right just in time to see a young Slav man duck behind a wheelbarrow filled with vegetables. Cistler spun on his heels. It was the opportunity he had been waiting for. The wheelbarrow vendor was only ten meters behind him. He prayed the young man wouldn't run off before he could question him.

Cistler rounded the end of the large wheelbarrow and saw the young man still squatting, clumsily attempting to pick up two dropped potatoes.

"Who are you working for?" the old lawyer demanded.

The young Slav man turned away from the old lawyer, as if he wanted to avoid Cistler's stare.

"Do you want to buy potatoes?" the young man asked.

"I want to know who you're working for and why you're following me."

"I'm not following you," the young man snapped, still

holding his head down so that Cistler could not see the front of his face.

"Liar!"

"I sell vegetables here every Thursday. I have a permit from the Austrians."

"Where's Ciganovitch?" Cistler roared, reaching out and grabbing the young man by the collar. Still the young man kept his face turned away from Cistler. "You lying bastard! You'll tell me where I can find Ciganovitch or I'll make such a goddamned scene that the Austrian police couldn't ignore it even if they wanted to!"

"You're crazy!" the young man shouted.

"Not as crazy as all you goddamned *komitadji!*" Cistler shook the young man by his shirt, but still the young man refused to meet Cistler's eyes. Several passersby paused to watch the scene.

"Let go of me!"

"Where's Ciganovitch?"

"I don't know anyone named Ciganovitch!"

"Let go of him!" shouted another Slav man in the gathering crowd.

Cistler turned and seized the handles of the wheelbarrow. He tipped it over, spilling its entire contents over the cobblestones.

"*Hey! Don't do that!*"

"Now call the police," Cistler snapped. "Call the police and show them your permit!"

The young Slav vegetable vendor turned and swung his fist in Cistler's direction. The punch did not connect; it glided clumsily over the old lawyer's left shoulder, but for the first time Cistler had a glimpse of the young man's face. Cistler took a step backward. The young man had no eyes. His upper and lower eyelids hung loosely over the empty sockets.

"You crazy son of a bitch!" the blind man shouted.

Cistler took another step backward, now fully aware of the hostile crowd he had gathered.

The blind young man took another swing at the old lawyer. His fist made a harmless crescent in the air. "Come back here! I'm going to kill you, you crazy bastard!"

Cistler retreated quickly through the crowd, ignoring the glares of the witnesses, and walked quickly toward the corner. The fact that he had made a mistake was easier to bear than the reason for the mistake. Was he going crazy? How could he mistake a blind vegetable vendor for a *komitadji*?

Cistler turned the corner, the bottle of *vinjak* still tucked underneath his arm, and listened to the sounds of confusion fade behind him. Even though he walked quickly, Cistler could not shake the image of the blind man lashing out with his fists, spiraling a punch gracelessly and harmlessly through empty space. It was a mad, ugly image. A summation of impotent and humiliated rage.

A swirl of gray pigeons passed over the old lawyer's head. He closed his eyes for a moment and tried to imagine the comfort and sanctuary of harmlessness. Suddenly he found himself chuckling. He wanted a drink. He turned into the entranceway to his office and climbed the flight of stairs to his office door.

There, tucked beneath his office door, was an envelope that bore the official seal of the general criminal court of Sarajevo. Even before he opened it, Cistler knew that this was the official notice that the trial date had been moved up to tomorrow. Again, he became aware that he would have to prepare a defense before the following day. A sense of urgency passed through him.

He unlocked the door and entered the outer office. Stega's desk was cleared of papers and her seat was empty. He suddenly felt terribly alone. He needed her strength.

Cistler placed the bottle of *vinjak* on her desk and opened it. He did not bother with a glass. He took a large swig directly from the bottle. The warm brown liquid burned his throat, but it would, if given time, return some sense of normalcy to his world.

Cistler swung open the door to his inner office and froze in the doorframe.

The shades were pulled at the window, and very little of the late-afternoon sunlight penetrated the small office. But even through the dim twilight of the office, Cistler could make out the figure of a man sitting in the chair behind his writing desk. The old lawyer remained framed in the doorway, waiting for the figure to move.

As the old lawyer's eyes grew more accustomed to the dim light he was able to make out the outline of Ciganovitch.

"I've been looking for you," Cistler announced, not moving from the doorway. "I won't ask you how you got into my office. It was probably the same way you got into my apartment when you killed my dog. Anyway, I'm glad you're here. I have a message for you."

Cistler waited for Ciganovitch to reply, but the seated figure made no response.

"I've spent the morning at the prison. I did as you asked. I took the cyanide. But I'm afraid the defendants aren't as eager to die as you believed. It seems that they don't trust you. Gavrilo Princip said that he had already sampled your poison. He won't take any more. In fact, he called you a traitor to the Slav people. . . ."

Cistler broke off and stared at the figure sitting behind his writing desk. The man made no movement. Suddenly Cistler was aware that samething was wrong. He crossed quickly to the window overlooking the quay and threw open the shade. The orange sunlight poured into the room.

The old lawyer now understood why the figure had not responded. The blood drained from the old lawyer's cheeks. It was Ciganovitch, but a Ciganovitch who no longer cared about cyanide or prisoners. He was tied to the old lawyer's chair. His head was thrown back, and his swollen tongue protruded from his parted lips. His bulging eyes stared life-lessly at the ceiling.

Cistler remained motionless for several minutes. The shaft of golden-orange sunlight formed a pool around the dead man, illuminating and exaggerating his distorted features. His cheeks were blown up like balloons and his throat was so swollen that his neck disappeared entirely. Flecks of coagulated blood hung from his flared nostrils. His purple scar had turned a dark shade of blue against his bloated cheek.

Ciganovitch's swollen tongue protruded black and bloody from between his puffy lips.

Cistler crossed the room to the side of the writing desk. He gasped and gagged, then stumbled back from the desk. When he reached the outer office, he vomited.

Ciganovitch was naked from the waist down. Where his sexual organs should have been was nothing but a reddish-black crater of raw flesh surrounded by tufts of public hair. Suddenly Cistler had realized that what protruded from Ciganovitch's mouth was not his tongue. Ciganovitch had been choked to death on his own penis.

Cistler braced himself against Stega's desk. His life had turned into a series of brutal images. He seized the *vinjak* bottle and gulped at it. He couldn't keep up with the flow of madness. Again he gulped at the *vinjak*. There was no question that Ciganovitch had deserved death, but that kind of death . . . Who was responsible? Moyen? The Union? It really didn't matter. But why in his office. Was it just a matter of convenience? Or was there some other reason? The police could hardly believe that an old man like himself was responsible for a murder like that?

The police!

He should fetch the police. There would be an investiga-tion. He would be questioned. Had he known the murdered man? What was his relationship with Ciganovitch? How much should he tell them?

He could almost hear the investigator's voice: "So, you

met Ciganovitch less than a week ago. He broke your finger, killed your dog, and threatened your daughter's life. And now we find this man Ciganovitch dead in your office. You had a motive to kill him, didn't you? As a lawyer, I'm sure you will appreciate how tightly this case fits together. For some reason you have not yet explained to us, Ciganovitch threatened your daughter's life. You wished to protect your daughter. Perhaps you had too much to drink. You do have a reputation for overindulging in *vinjak*. In a drunken rage you attack a blind vegetable vendor. Do you remember that, Dr. Cistler? Do you remember what you were shouting at the blind man? We have four witnesses who will testify in court that you were demanding to know where Ciganovitch was.

"And so, after tipping over the blind man's vegetables you returned to your office and found Ciganovitch waiting for you. Full of *vinjak* and rage, you attacked the younger man. By some stroke of fortune you managed to knock Ciganovitch unconscious, tied him to the chair, and then castrated him. Perhaps Ciganovitch was having a liaison with your daughter?"

Cistler seized the *vinjak* bottle and gulped at it. He couldn't go to the police, and yet he had to. It would only be a matter of time before they found the body in his office. Would the police really think him capable of such a murder?

How would Ciganovitch's murder affect the trial? Would Stega be safe? Who had killed Ciganovitch?

The questions rattled through his old brain like a train, but as before there were too many questions and not enough answers. Suddenly Cistler's mind cleared. There was no question about going to the police. A murder had been committed. He had to go to the authorities. Just because his reputation as a lawyer was not what it should be, didn't mean that he would be accused of murder.

Again he felt that he had let his imagination run away from reality. He placed the *vinjak* bottle in the bottom drawer of Stega's desk and left the office, locking the outer door after him.

He tried to rehearse what he would say to the police, but each statement sounded more absurd, more lunatic than the last: There's a man in my office who choked on his penis. He tried again: There's a *komitadji* in my office. He works for both the Union or Death and the Serbian government. He's been murdered. Cistler shook his head. Better leave out the part about Ciganovitch being a *komitadji;* it would generate too many questions.

As it was, Cistler simply announced to the duty officer at the police station that he had found a corpse in his office. The duty officer did not look surprised, and Cistler wondered whether it was usual for people to walk in off the street and make such announcements.

The duty officer ushered Cistler down a narrow hallway and into a rear office. A sergeant sat behind an oversized desk. Cistler explained to the sergeant that he had returned to his office and found a corpse there. The sergeant nodded to the duty officer and rose to his feet.

"We'd better take a walk over to your office," the Austrian sergeant murmured.

The sergeant gathered two other policemen, and the four of them made their way down Franz Joseph street toward Appel Quay. As they walked the sergeant fired questions at Cistler. Most of the questions were for information: name, address, occupation, etc. But the sergeant did ask Cistler if the old lawyer knew the dead man. Cistler hestitated before answering. He chose to lie.

"I've never seen the man before."

When they arrived at the office building, Cistler led the way up the single flight to his office door. He unlocked the door and pointed to the inner office.

"In there. Behind the desk."

The sergeant and the two policemen entered the inner office. Cistler remained in the outer office, leaning wearily

against Stega's desk. He was exhausted, and the prospect
of hours and hours of police questioning frightened him.

"Cistler," the sergeant's voice came from the inner office,
"come on in here!"

Cistler sighed silently to himself and entered the inner
office. To his amazement the chair behind his writing desk
was empty.

"You said there was a corpse in here!" the sergeant
snapped. "Perhaps you'll show us where it is."

Cistler's eyes darted around the room. There was no sign
of Ciganovitch. The old lawyer crossed the room to the
edge of the desk. There were no signs that Ciganovitch had
ever been there.

"But there was a body here!" Cistler insisted. "There
was! Someone's been here and moved it. While I was out
at the police station, someone broke in and moved the body.
There was a body here."

The sergeant knelt behind the desk and inspected the
floor.

"There's no body here now. There's no bloodstains. There's
no sign of a struggle." The sergeant rose and walked over
to Cistler. He stood very close to the old lawyer and sniffed
at Cistler's breath.

"Had a couple of drinks?"

"The body's been moved. I saw it. There behind the desk.
I saw it there! I really did!"

The sergeant was growing impatient. "I asked you if you'd
been drinking."

"I'm not drunk. . . ."

"But you have been seeing things." The sergeant curled
his thick lip into a sneer. "You damned Slavs can't hold
your liquor. It's against the law to falsely report a crime.
I've half a mind to stick your old Slav ass in jail. You call
yourself a lawyer."

One of the policemen fumbled through the papers that
covered the top of Cistler's desk.

"Those are important papers," Cistler announced.

"I've never met a Slav who could read and write," the policeman replied

"They don't have the brain for it," the sergeant snapped. "Old Cistler here has strained his brain. He's seeing dead bodies under his desk." The sergeant seized a handful of the papers that Cistler had called important and flung them across the room.

The sergeant pointed at Cistler's injured hand. "Listen, you old Slav bastard, if you waste my time again, I'll break every one of your goddamn fingers." He turned on his heel and stalked out of the office, followed by the two policemen.

Cistler stood silently and watched them slam the outer door. Once the sound of their boots on the stairs had disappeared, Cistler turned toward the empty chair behind his desk. He had seen what he had seen. Or could it have been his imagination? Was he going mad? First he attacked a blind vegetable seller for no reason; then he imagined Ciganovitch's body in his office.

No, he was sure he had seen it. He bent over and inspected the floor around his chair. There was nothing. No evidence that a body had ever been tied in the chair. Perhaps he was going mad. Perhaps he couldn't distinguish reality from fantasy. Perhaps he would go home and find Stega and Breskva waiting for him. Maybe the whole thing was a product of his imagination.

But then he saw the faint rope marks on the back of his chair, and he knew that he was not mad, that Ciganovitch's body had been in his office, and that it had been moved.

He shuddered. Again there were too damn many questions and too few answers.

CHAPTER SEVEN

A Defense

Dr. Cistler finished the bottle of *vinjak* he had placed in Stega's desk, and bought another two bottles on his way home. He was not drunk. In fact, the *vinjak* seemed to have very little effect upon him.

At the corner of Vuka Street, he bought a late edition of the afternoon paper and scanned the front page for any recent news of the Austrian ultimatum to Serbia. The headlines revealed that Prime Minister Pastich would not reply to the Austrians until the following day. The article speculated freely and, Cistler thought, not very responsibly on how Pastich might respond. The writer felt that war was inevitable, well-deserved, and on the whole desirable. "After all," the writer editoralized, "who will teach these Slavs a much-needed lesson if Austria turns her back upon her duty?"

Cistler groaned and turned his attention to a series of smaller articles that dealt with troop deployment along the

Austro-Serbian border. "Military experts, familiar with the Balkan situation, speculate that an Austrian invasion of Serbia would take less than a week."

On page two Cistler found a small filler about a young boy winning an athletic contest. The old lawyer found the article reassuring. There were still athletic contests. Young boys still won them. Somewhere, normal people did normal things.

With this conviction tenuously implanted in his mind, Cistler entered his apartment and threw the newspaper down on the kitchen table. The paper was thrown with too much violence, perhaps reflecting Cistler's disgust with its contents. It slid across the varnished surface of the table and flopped onto the floor. Cistler left it where it lay and poured himself an inch of *vinjak*.

Cistler knew he could not hope for a sympathetic court, but he still held out hope for an open-minded one. The single fact that allowed the old lawyer hope was that none of his clients was old enough to be executed. The presiding judge might not be so inclined to show off Bosnian justice if the trial could not end in an execution.

Cistler threw a pad of paper and pencils onto the kitchen table and then sat down. He had to work out some kind of coherent defense. The defendants would be required to plead. Princip would probably continue to refuse to recognize the jurisdiction of the court. Cabrinovitch and Gabrez would probably do the same. The image of the heroic patriot martyred by foreign invaders was too enticing for them to ignore.

Cistler's head slipped into his cupped palms. Questions filled his mind. What about the Union? Should he mention the Union in court? Prime Minister Pastich had actually ordered the arrest of the three defendants before they had crossed into Bosnia. What if that became known? How would that affect the Austrian ultimatum? Would Pastich be forced to arrest Apis? Would that arrest result in civil war in Serbia?

The old lawyer yawned and turned back to the empty pad of paper that lay before him. He was worried now, and the wooden splint on his injured finger tapped compulsively against the surface of the table. Time was passing too quickly. He needed a defense. He turned his head toward the gray twilight of the window and decided he needed more light.

As he returned to the kitchen table with the flickering kerosene lantern in his hand he paused and stared at the floor. There lay the newspaper he had thrown across the table. A small article caught his attention. He put the lantern on the table and retrieved the newspaper.

OFFICIAL OF SERBIAN GOVERNMENT DROWNED

SARAJEVO—Police reported today that at nine fifteen this morning they found the body of a Serbian government official floating in the Miljacka river. From papers found on the body, police sources were able to identify the body as Jovo Moyen, 41 years old. According to other papers found on the body, Moyen was a special assistant in the office of Prime Minister Pastich. Why Moyen was in Sarajevo was not immediately known.

Police sources speculated that Moyen lost his footing while walking along the Miljacka embankment. Due to the current political situation between Austria and Serbia, the police declined comment on whether Moyen's body would be transported back to Serbia for burial. A spokesman for Colonel Smyra, Chief of Bosnian Security, did say that the police did not suspect foul play.

The police didn't suspect foul play! Cistler threw the newspaper back down on the floor. First Breskva had been killed, then Ciganovitch, and now Moyen. Everyone who knew anything about the case was murdered. The old man shuddered and poured himself another inch of *vinjak*.

Moyen was dead, and so was his promise to get Cistler safe passage out of the Balkans. Cistler's mind became keen with desperation. It was only a matter of time before someone came to kill him. He knew too much.

His mind went back over the defense. Princip would certainly refuse to recognize the court. Cistler pulled his pipe from his pocket and held it like a revolver, aiming it at the empty pad of paper before him. The phrase turned over and over in his mind. "I will not recognize the jurisdiction of this court!"

The old lawyer suddenly wondered if there was any reason why his clients *should* recognize the Austrian court.

He rose from the table and made his way into the living room. Placing the kerosene lantern beside him, he began to search through a large bookcase. After several minutes, he withdrew a fat volume and returned with it to the kitchen table. He used the index quickly and found what he was looking for.

Cistler was not fool enough to fail to see that his idea was far-fetched, but since it was his only idea, he explored it with a ferocity that banished all else from his mind. The idea had come from what Princip had said: "I refuse to recognize the court." Cistler had suddenly wondered why the young man should recognize what was essentially a foreign court.

Cistler had grabbed a volume of diplomatic history and had quickly read everything that had to do with the Congress of Berlin. His thirst for information had led the old lawyer to Article 25.

The Congress of Berlin in 1877, Cistler remembered, had been called to solve a number of diplomatic and military problems that had developed out of a series of international crises. In 1875, a rebellion in Turkish-controlled Bosnia had deeply concerned Austria. The slipping grip of the Turks had greatly perturbed Austria, since if the Turks were forced out of Europe, it would leave Serbia with an open path across Bosnia to the sea. The possibility that Serbia might have access to the sea was intolerable to the Austrians.

And so the Austrians signed a secret agreement with the Russians, the protectors of the Serbs. If the Turks were thrown out of Bosnia, Austria would take over its administration and so block Serbia from the sea.

This in itself was quite simple, but the issue was further complicated when the Turks recovered their strength and put down the Bosnian revolt. However, Russia, as always desirous of a warm-water port, took the opportunity in 1877 of attacking Turkey in hopes of capturing the Dardanelles. The war was going well for the Russians, and this infuriated the British.

The British, who considered the Mediterranean their own private domain, sent their fleet into the Dardanelles and demanded that the belligerents convene a conference. The British fleet was exactly the kind of pressure that the czar understood, and the result was the Congress of Berlin.

Article 25 of the Congress of Berlin dealt with the fate of Bosnia. It was agreed that Austria would take over the administration of Bosnia from Turkey. The exact wording was that "Austria would occupy and administer." Occupy and administer! But not, Cistler thought triumphantly, *annex!*

Bosnia was, according to the Congress of Berlin, a trust territory, not part of the empire itself. In 1908, Austria had annexed Bosnia, forced it to become part of the Austro-Hungarian empire. This was contrary to Article 25 and, as such, illegal. Gavrilo Princip had every right to call the Austrians foreign invaders. He had every right to refuse to recognize the court.

Even in his enthusiasm, Cistler doubted that this argument would stand up in court very long. He sat back and relit his pipe. He had just begun to make the necessary notes on Article 25, when he heard the tumblers click in the lock on his front door.

A knot of fear formed just below the old man's Adam's

apple. He started to rise from the kitchen table, but before he was standing, two *komitadji* burst through the door, each with a machine pistol leveled at him.

"If you make a sound, you will be shot," the first *komitadji* whispered. He was a short, muscular man in his thirties, stoop shouldered and completely bald. In the flickering orange lantern light his hairless dome looked like the pointed end of a varnished Easter egg.

The second *komitadji* was older and thinner, but no less menacing. He wore a full beard that hid most of his facial expression and, Cistler thought, probably covered a weak chin.

The two *komitadji* stood on either side of the door like sentries, keeping their machine pistols aimed at the old man.

My executioners, Cistler thought. His hands trembled, and his stomach felt as empty as the coffin he assumed he was soon to occupy. The bald *komitadji* cast a glance in the direction of the open door. Cistler followed the man's eyes.

Standing in the doorway, in the outermost circle of the flickering lantern light, was a third man, larger than the first two, bullet headed, with a thin, cruel mockery of a smile spread across his lips. The man's eyes were concealed beneath the visor of a worker's cap.

"My apologies for having to call so late," the bullet-headed man announced, stepping briskly into the apartment. Although his clothes were civilian, his mannerisms and clipped speech were military.

The bald *komitadji* on his right closed the door behind him, never once taking the machine pistol off Cistler.

"We thought you might work at your office," the bullet-headed *komitadji* said as he walked toward where Cistler stood. "But instead, you chose to work at home."

The bullet-headed *komitadji* was clearly in charge. He gestured for Cistler to sit at the table and then did so himself.

"We would have arrived earlier, but we have been extremely busy."

Cistler remembered the small blue-black crater between Ciganovitch's legs and thought he understood what the word *busy* really meant. The old lawyer steadied himself and tried to match the composure of the man who sat opposite him. But Cistler's apparent calm did not unnerve the man as it had done with Ciganovitch.

The bullet-headed man removed his worker's cap and threw it on the table next to the *vinjak* bottle. He nodded at the almost full bottle.

"You've started drinking again, Dr. Cistler. Not very good for your reputation, but certainly understandable under the circumstances." The seated *komitadji* curled his thin lips into a sneer, and in the orange lantern light Cistler saw a row of sparkling gold-capped teeth.

"I presume you will not mind," Cistler snapped with more ferocity than he actually felt, "if I help myself to my own *vinjak*?"

The bald *komitadji* and the bearded one, both still by the door, laughed.

"We have a great deal to discuss," the seated *komitadji* announced.

"Just discuss?" Cistler replied, pouring himself four fingers of *vinjak*

"That depends entirely upon you."

"Who the hell are you?" Cistler demanded. "Who are you working for?"

"I thought a man of your intelligence would have already guessed."

"The Union or Death."

"Of course."

Cistler nodded. He had expected that, but not the casualness of the man who sat opposite him. Cistler fumbled with his pipe.

"You have me at a disadvantage," Cistler replied, failing to see the absurdity of his understatement. "You know my name, but I still do not know yours."

"My name is Dragutin Dimitrievitch," the bullet-headed *komitadji* murmured softly.

The name rang a bell in Cistler's head. Someone had mentioned that name before. He couldn't remember who. Ciganovitch hadn't mentoned anyone's name. Had Princip said anything about Dragutin Dimitrievitch? Cistler's eyes drifted across the table and came to rest on the fallen newspaper. Moyen was the one who had mentioned the name. Cistler remembered now.

"Although I was baptized Dragutin Dimitrievitch, I expect I am better known as Apis."

The knot of fear in Cistler's throat tightened, and he had difficulty breathing. Colonel Apis, chief of Serbian military intelligence, leader of the Union, assassin of King Alexander and Queen Draga, the organizer of the murder of Archduke Ferdinand, and a man so powerful that his own government was too frightened to arrest him.

"My name means something to you?" Apis asked.

Cistler nodded, trying to hide his fear.

"I have been frank with you, Dr. Cistler. Now, I hope you will be frank with me. What do you know about the assassination of Francis Ferdinand?"

To stop his hand from shaking, Cistler grasped hold of the glass of *vinjak* and took a large gulp. He wondered how he should reply. Whatever reason Apis had for paying him a personal visit, it had to be extremely important. Cistler did not think that Apis was a man who tolerated circumlocutions, to say nothing of lies.

Apis said: "I want to talk to you as a civilized man. I am not a breaker of fingers. If you tell me the truth frankly and candidly, you have nothing to fear."

"I know the Union was behind the murders," Cistler blurted out. Apis nodded mildly and gestured for Cistler to continue. Cistler couldn't find any reason not to tell Apis what he knew. He began with what he had guessed about the Union and then went on to describe Ciganovitch's visits. Occasionally Apis would nod and gesture for him to go on.

Cistler told Apis about his visit from Moyen. Again Apis nodded as if he had known all this before.

"Moyen was the one who told me that the defendants were *komitadji*. He said he had an informer in the union. It wasn't until I was talking with Gavrilo Princip, that I knew who the informer was."

"Princip knew who the informer was?" Apis snapped.

"He guessed that it was Ciganovitch. He called Ciganovitch a traitor to all the Slav people."

"Princip was able to put two and two together and come up with four. A rare ability in these troubled times."

"You killed Ciganovitch?" Cistler asked.

Apis smiled almost philosophically before he replied. "You know quite a bit, Dr. Cistler, but there are several things you haven't guessed. I will tell, and then you will be in a better position to understand." Apis paused and lit a cigarette.

"First of all, Dr. Cistler, you must understand that I am a Slav before anything else. I love my people and will be glad to give my life for them. Second, what I am going to tell you was done for the good of the Slav people. This, I think you will understand in a short while.

"You were right about the defendants' being *komitadji*. I interviewed Gavrilo Princip myself. The three of them were recruited in Belgrade and trained in southern Serbia. But initially it was their idea to assassinate the Austrian Crown Prince. They were Bosnians, and the Crown Prince's visit was a great insult to them. They approached Ciganovitch and asked him for weapons. Ciganovitch in turn came to me and asked me what I thought of the idea.

"I knew, of course, that Ferdinand was coming to Sarajevo. But I also knew the real reason behind Ferdinand's trip. He was going to announce his support for land reform in Bosnia."

Cistler's eyebrows rose in surprise.

"Does that surprise you Dr. Cistler? Yes, Francis Ferdinand was coming to announce his support for Slav ownership of land. Naturally, the Crown Prince would have become an overnight hero to the Bosnian Slavs. I couldn't allow that to happen. It would have set our plans back by years.

"Major Tankosic and I discussed the planned assassination. You recognize the name Tankosic? Yes, I thought Moyen would know about him, too. Regardless, Tankosic didn't like the idea. He was worried that it might provide Vienna with an excuse to invade Serbia. As I am sure you can imagine, Tankosic and I studied a great many possibilities before we acted.

"I took what Tankosic said seriously, and I sent him to see the Russian military attaché in Belgrade, a man named Artonov. His name means nothing to you, Dr. Cistler? No, your friend Moyen did not know about him. Artonov promised Tankosic to make discreet inquiries in St. Petersburg as to how Russia would respond to an Austrian invasion of Serbia. A week went by before we had a reply from St. Petersburg. The telegram stated in no uncertain terms that an Austrian invasion of Serbia, or any offensive military operations along the Serbian border, would not be tolerated and would result in a general Russian mobilization."

"But," Cistler interrupted, "that's almost the same statement the Russians issued when the Austrians marched into Bosnia in 1908. They didn't do a thing then. What makes you believe them now?"

"The difference, Dr. Cistler, is that in 1908 the Russians issued the statement publicly. This telegram was stamped 'Most Secret—Eyes Only.' In addition, in 1908 the Russians couldn't have acted in the Balkans because they were exhausted from their war with Japan and substantially weakened by the 1905 revolution.

"But now the situation is different. The Russian army has been revitalized. It is the most powerful in Europe. In sheer numbers it baffles the mind. Tankosic and I agreed that the assassination plan was worth the risk. I approved the plan, and as you know, Ciganovitch provided the young men with weapons."

"Wait a minute," Cistler said. "I don't understand. What of the Austrian ultimatum to Pastich? Why haven't the Russians put pressure on Vienna?"

"I will get to that, my friend. But if you are to get the whole picture, you must understand events chronologically."

Apis sat back in the chair, allowing himself a gold-capped grin of satisfaction.

"Let me ask another question," Cistler said softly. "Why are you telling me all this?"

"Your finger has been broken and your dog killed. You're not curious to know why?"

Suddenly Cistler remembered the question he most needed an answer to. "You haven't hurt Stega?"

"Stega?"

"My daughter, Stega!"

"To be perfectly honest, Dr. Cistler," Apis said with a slight smile, "I did not know you had a daughter. I take it Milan Ciganovitch threatened to hurt her?"

Cistler nodded.

"There is no cause for you to worry. As you know, Ciganovitch is in no condition to do anything to a woman." The bald and the bearded *komitadji* chuckled. "And unlike Ciganovitch, I do not hurt innocent Slavs. I leave that to the Austrians; they are experts at such things."

Cistler did not bother to hide the relief that flooded his old face.

"Anyway, Dr. Cistler, I had Ciganovitch supply your clients with weapons. I also put Ciganovitch in charge of the travel arrangements. This is where the story becomes curious. The day after your clients left Belgrade, I received a telegram from the captain of the border patrol in Loznica, explaining that he had just received orders from the prime minister's office to close the border to three young students. The captain, being a loyal member of the union, requested further instructions. I sent those instructions. He was to telegram Pastich that the three students had already crossed the border.

"I was astonished that Pastich knew about the attempt we were making. But the question that almost drove me out of my mind was, *How did he know?* There was no question that there was an informer. For two days I wrestled with the problem. To my knowledge there were only four men in Belgrade, beside the students, who knew about the assassination plans: myself, Tankosic, Ciganovitch, and the Russian military attaché, Artonov. I foolishly suspected the Russian."

Cistler continued to listen. His hands no longer trembled, and the knot of fear in his throat had disappeared.

"Of course, I found out later that the Russian was not the informer, but my suspicion of him completely blocked out the possibility that Ciganovitch was the traitor.

"I knew, or rather suspected, that Pastich would attempt to warn Vienna. Pastich, of course, could not afford to mention either the Union or me by name. So I didn't think his warning would be taken too seriously in Vienna. Austrians cannot lose face in front of Slavs. I did not think that Ferdinand would cancel his trip to Bosnia just because of Pastich's warning, but I still was not sure how Pastich knew about the assassination attempt in the first place.

"Before I could investigate further, I received several reports from my agents in the field. As well as chief officer in the Union, I am also chief of Serbian military intelligence. A telegram from Berlin came in, reporting a series of high-level meetings between the Kaiser and Moltke, and large-scale troop movements along the German-Belgian border. The telegram also reported tensions between Russia and Germany.

"I requested further information from my operatives in Vienna and St. Petersburg. A telegram from Vienna came first. It stated, as I had assumed, that Pastich's warning had been ignored. But it went on to report that there had been high-level meetings between Austrian and German military men.

"I tried to fit the pieces together, but I could make no sense out of it. At first I thought that perhaps the meetings were about the military maneuvers that Ferdinand was going to attend in Bosnia. Perhaps Ferdinand was mad enough to think he could personally lead an invasion of Serbia. But this theory was much too simple and was destroyed by what I already knew about the maneuvers. It was simply a tour of inspection, and it would be almost impossible for Austria to attack Serbia from the west. I put the idea out of my mind.

"On June 28, I informed several friends in Sarajevo that I wanted first-hand information as soon as it was available. At one-thirty, barely an hour after it had taken place, I learned that although they had blundered miserably, one of the young men had been successful and the Crown Prince was dead.

"But the news that had really shocked me was that all three *komitadji* had been captured alive.

"This was when I made a serious mistake. I panicked, and ordered Ciganovitch to Sarajevo to kill the three young men."

"Instead of that," Cistler broke in, "he merely broke my finger."

"Don't feel so bad," the bald *komitadji* who still stood by the door interrupted. "Ciganovitch ended up with a broken prick."

"He never used it properly anyway," the bearded *komitadji* added with a chuckle.

Apis glared the two men into silence. He did not tolerate jokes about serious affairs.

Cistler poured himself more *vinjak*. "For a man as busy as you are," the old man asked, "you seem to have a lot of time to spend talking to me."

"The court does not meet until ten in the morning. We have all night, Dr. Cistler—all night long."

"You may have all night," Cislter replied, "but I have a defense to prepare."

"You will be much better equipped to defend your clients after you finish listening to what I have to say." Apis paused and lit another cigarette, making a mental note of how much *vinjak* the old lawyer was consuming.

"You can imagine how concerned I was at hearing that the three young *komitadji* had been arrested. The security of the entire Union was at stake. I had made plans for the eventuality of an Austrian invasion but not for the possibility of civil war. And unfortunately, civil war might have erupted if the information became public that the union had supplied the weapons used to kill the Crown Prince of Austria.

"As I said before, sending Ciganovitch to Sarajevo was a mistake, but it was a full three weeks before I realized how large an error.

"Tankosic had personally supervised the training of the three young men, and he had an especially high regard for Princip's devotion and courage. He found it very puzzling that Princip had been arrested. You see my point, Dr. Cistler? If Princip was as devoted as Tankosic believed, he would have drunk the cyanide. I could arrive at only one conclusion: the cyanide had been tampered with. Ciganovitch was the only one who could have been responsible.

"Things began to fall into place. Ciganovitch was the informer. It would suit Pastich if the three students didn't die but lived to testify against the Union. Prime Minister Pastich can't have realized the consequences of this. Anyway, I wanted to execute Ciganovitch immediately, but Tankosic stopped me. He wanted to find out how much information Ciganovitch had passed on. It was then that I decided to come to Sarajevo myself."

"Why did you kill Moyen?" Cistler asked, and sipped at his *vinjak*.

"I didn't. Although I might have, had I known that Moyen was Ciganovitch's contact. As it was, Ciganovitch saved me the trouble. Before he died, Ciganovitch told me that Moyen had come to visit him in Sarajevo. Moyen told Ciganovitch that his name was going to be mentioned at the trial and warned him to get out of the Balkans as fast as he could. Ciganovitch must have realized that there was no place for him to hide, even outside the Balkans. He knocked Moyen unconscious and drove a woman's hat pin through his ear and into his brain. I understand from the newspapers that the police believe Moyen drowned. A pinhole in the eardrum is hard to find even for a doctor experienced in autopsies."

"But you still haven't told me why you're here," Cistler said. "Why have you come to see me?"

"One minute and then you'll understand," Apis replied softly. The lean, bullet-headed chief of the Union did not appear threatening. There was nothing in his manner or tone of voice that was menacing. "Before I left Belgrade, I sent Tankosic to St. Petersburg. Not only to arrange for Russian pressure to be put on Vienna, but also to find out what is really going on along the Russian-German border. It may only be saber rattling, but I suspect it may be something more important than that.

"You must understand, Dr. Cistler, that Serbia is prepared for an Austrian invasion only if Russia comes to our aid within the first seventy-two hours. If the Russians do not come to our aid, Serbia will fall. Tankosic will see to it that the czar does not waste any time protesting the invasion."

Apis lit another cigarette and grimaced as the harsh smoke burned his tongue. "You see, our military plan calls for us to lose Belgrade. Belgrade is too close to the Austrian border. We have drawn up a line of defense which the Serbian troops will retreat to. At that line the Serbian army will stand and fight. The Russians will launch an attack to the north and split the Austrian forces. The Serbian army will then launch a counterattack, and we will have the Austrians in a vise. When this happens the Slavs in

Bosnia will revolt, and Austria will be forced to sue for peace—a peace which will cost them Bosnia!"

Apis puffed on the cigarette and grinned at Cistler's incredulous expression. His gold-capped teeth sparkled in the lantern light. "This plan depends upon two things, Dr. Cistler. First, that the Russians come into the war within the first seventy-two hours. I am, of course, not talking about a general mobilization. Everyone knows that would take at least six weeks. Just a regional mobilization will be enough to crush the Austrian invasion.

"Secondly the plan depends on the Serbian army's being able to hold the line of defense until the Russians come to our aid. I am sure that the Serbian army will be able to hold this line, provided there are no internal disorders. Now you begin to see my point, Dr. Cistler. If there is the threat of civil war, the Serbian army will be split and the Austrians will crush us. I cannot allow that to happen. I cannot allow any of the information that has come into your possession to become public."

Apis looked calmly at Cistler and finally asked, "What would you do, if you were in my position?"

Cistler had not expected the question and appeared startled by it. What would he do? His gaze fell upon the two *komitadji* who leaned against the wall by the front door. Their machine pistols were still withdawn from their holsters, but they were no longer aimed at him. Cistler trembled. He thought he knew what Apis was going to do, but he said, "I don't know what I would do."

"Oh, but you do know, Dr. Cistler. I think if you thought I was as dangerous as you are now, you would have me shot. Wouldn't you?" No smile appeared on Apis's face. It was a serious question.

"I don't know what I would do," Cistler mumbled. "I do not take murder as lightly as you do."

"Of course you don't. You're a lawyer, not a *komitadji*. But allow me to explain further. There is a time element involved. The trial is set to begin tomorrow, the same day

Pastich must answer the Austrian ultimatum. Pastich and I disagree about most things, but he is a patriot and will not sell us to the Austrians. I have no doubt that his reply will be unsatisfactory. By this time next week, Austria and Serbia will be at war. Now understand this, once war is declared, there can be no threat of civil war in Serbia—all Serbs will stand together against a common enemy. But I am worried about the trial tomorrow, about what you or one of the defendants might say. So the solution to our problem is to postpone the trial until after the war has been declared. Don't you agree?"

Cistler thought for a moment and then warily nodded.

"Good. I see you now understand the problem. Let us look for solutions together."

"Listen," Cistler blurted, "I partially understood the problem before you arrived. I had already decided not to mention the Union at the trial." Cistler went on to describe the defense he planned based upon Article 25 of the Congress of Berlin. Apis waited politely for Cistler to finish before he chuckled.

"The prosecutor general would cut you to ribbons. You would be the laughingstock of the court. Not because what you have said is false, but because it is true. In the world today, if people do not hide from the truth, they laugh at it. As soon as the court stopped laughing, the prosecutor general would put Gabrez on the witness stand and confuse him into making very dangerous admissions. No, Dr. Cistler, the solution to our problem lies in postponing the trial."

"I could ask for a postponement."

"You already have, and it was denied. I sincerely doubt that the presiding judge has changed his mind."

Cistler's mind was alert. His fear had disappeared. When Apis had first entered his home, the old lawyer had had no doubt that the intruder's intention had been murder. But now Cistler was not quite so sure. Cistler was sure there was a way to postpone the trial. He just had to think of it.

"Correct me if I am wrong, Dr. Cistler," Apis said, "since

my knowledge of Austrian law is slight, but wouldn't it be grounds to delay the trial if there was no defense lawyer present?"

"Yes," Cistler replied quietly. "Under Austrian law the defendants must be represented by counsel. All I'd have to do is fail to appear. They couldn't begin the trial without me. I could become ill—"

Cistler broke off as he saw Apis nod to the two *komitadji* who stood by the door.

"I could pretend to be sick."

The bald and the bearded *komitadji* walked over to where Cistler sat and stood behind him.

"What are you going to do?" Cistler demanded, his voice quivering with renewed fear.

"We're going to help you pretend to be sick," Apis said softly, again flashing his thin, twisted smile at the old lawyer. "It is regrettable but necessary."

Cistler suddenly recognized that the entire conversation had been a prologue to this. The bald *komitadji* unwrapped a length of rope from about his waist.

Cistler understood that the Union leader intended to kill him. The old lawyer recognized now that it was the fact that he was going to die that had allowed Apis to reveal the Serbian war plan. Cistler's stomach burned with fear and anger.

"You're crazy!" Cistler shouted. "You are really mad!"

"Please do not shout, Dr. Cistler," the bald *komitadji* murmured. "We don't want to hurt you any more than is necessary."

"Necessary? None of this is necessary. The assassination wasn't necessary! The Union isn't necessary! That silly damn Austrian ultimatum isn't necessary! God have mercy on our twisted minds!"

Apis gestured toward the bearded *komitadji*, who stood on Cistler's right. The two men bound Cistler to the chair.

"Perhaps history will tell the truth about you in time, Dr. Cistler. History has a funny way of sorting out truth and lies. But perhaps it will be comforting for you to think of yourself as the first casualty in the great Slav war of unification."

Cistler opened his mouth to reply. He would have called Apis a damn fool, a coward, a disgrace to civilized man. But the old lawyer didn't have the chance. The bald *komitadji* stuck the neck of the *vinjak* bottle in the old lawyer's mouth.

Apis diverted his eyes. Despite his outward coolness, Apis was sorry about what had to be done. Under different circumstances, he might have found himself liking the old lawyer.

The bearded *komitadji* took a handful of Cistler's old gray hair and jerked his head back. The bald *komitadji* thrust the neck of the *vinjak* bottle farther down Cistler's throat. Choking sounds came from the old lawyer, and brown *vinjak* trickled out of his nostrils.

CHAPTER EIGHT

The Trial

The following morning went by slowly for Gavrilo Princip. He stood beside the narrow barred window of his cell and stared out over the courtyard. The sky was gray, and a steady rain fell.

Dr. Cistler had not yet come to Gavrilo's cell, but this did not really surprise the young prisoner. By this time Ciganovitch or some other *komitadji* had probably killed the old man.

A soft tapping came at his cell wall: "The guard just brought me trial clothes. A black suit. I will be the best dressed *komitadji* in Bosnia."

Gavrilo cast his eyes around the gray courtyard before replying to Nedelijko: "Perhaps they will bury you in it."

The wall between Gavrilo's and Nedelijko's cells was silent for several minutes. And again Gavrilo wondered about what the old lawyer had said. Would he really represent the Slav people? Gavrilo did not want that responsibility. All he had done was his duty. He had recognized the need of his people, and he had served them. That didn't make a man either a hero or a villain.

The soft tapping came again from the wall: "What will you say if they ask us where we got the weapons?"

Gavrilo replied: "We bought them in Belgrade from a veteran of the Serbian army. We do not remember his name."

The next tapping that came from Nedelijko's cell was hesitant and nervous: "I am frightened, Gavrilo. What will these Austrians do to us?"

Gavrilo allowed himself a small, sad smile before he tapped back his reply: "I too am frightened, Nedelijko. But it is our fear that makes us brave. Without fear we would be madmen. In the courtroom you must remember one thing. Remember how difficult it is to bury a Slav. The Austrians do not have coffins strong enough to hold true patriots. Our ghosts will walk through Vienna and roam through the palace, frightening the lords!"

§   §   §

At nine, an Austrian guard appeared and handed Gavrilo an ill-fitting black suit. Across the gray courtyard, Gavrilo could see the spectators begin to arrive. Gavrilo had not thought of himself as entertainment before. The thought made him shudder.

At quarter to ten, two guards appeared, opened Gavrilo's cell, and chained the young prisoner between them. Again Gavrilo wished that Cistler had given him the poison. The guards led him down the rough-cut stone passageways to that wing of the prison which served as the court.

As he entered the courtroom, Gavrilo again felt the eyes of the spectators upon him. Trifun and Nedelijko were already seated in the front row on the left. Dr. Cistler was nowhere in sight.

Gavrilo saw the court as an artist might, through eyes that were both intimate and distant, familiar and foreign.

He could see both curiosity and hatred in the expressions of the crowd, and he shared those feelings. He recognized that the courtroom was a symbol, but a symbol that would make sense only if one allowed oneself to believe in it. The portrait of the emperor that hung behind the judge's bench struck Gavrilo as a summation of this disjointed, nonsensical world.

The portrait was a caricature of pomposity. The old emperor, nearly bald, stood next to a bust of Hadrian, one hand braced against it. The other hand held the hilt of a jewel-studded ceremonial sword. Gavrilo felt a silent chuckle well up within him. Did no one else realize how absurdly fragile Austrian authority really was?

Perhaps Gavrilo might have actually laughed out loud, if he hadn't suddenly become aware of a second, different portrait. This painting hung on the wall of his own mind, but it was as grotesque and ludicrous as the one that hung in the courtroom. It, too, was a caricature. The self-portrait of a *komitadji*. A picture of himself as a martyred patriot, a hero to his people—as pompous and vain as the old emperor, as single-minded as the steady rain that tapped relentlessly against the courtroom windows.

But it was only my duty, Gavrilo repeated to himself. He believed in duty and would continue to believe in it until he died. Through months of starvation in Austrian prisons, Gavrilo would clutch at duty. It was the only thing that made the world sane. There would be moments of self-doubt. But they would only be momentary interruptions in his faith, and he would remind himself that he had done his duty, and the pain within his bones would become tolerable and the world would again make sense.

A court officer opened a door to the right of the judge's bench and ordered those present in court to rise. Three black-robed judges entered and took their seats.

The presiding judge waited for the spectators to quiet down and then gaveled the court into session. He called for the prosecutor general and the defense counsel to approach the bench. The prosecutor general rose and walked toward the presiding judge. The spectators were absolutely silent. Not even the sound of a pencil scratching against a reporter's pad. Still there was no sign of Dr. Cistler.

"Where's Dr. Cistler?" the presiding judge whispered angrily at the prosecutor, who shook his head in helplessness. The whisper wound its way around the courtroom. The same question was on everyone's lips. Where was Cistler?

One of the older court officers raised his eyebrows, as if suggesting that this was to be expected when Slavs were allowed to practice law. An Austrian reporter chuckled softly, thinking that perhaps the old man had forgotten about the case.

The prosecutor general leaned forward as if to whisper something to the Presiding Judge, but at that moment, a wild-looking old man burst through the rear doors of the court.

"If you're looking for me, I'm right here! This idiot won't let me in!"

All eyes in the court turned towards the apparition in the doorway. There stood Dr. Cistler in his shirt sleeves. His shirt was missing all its buttons and hung open to the waist. His gray hair was soaked from the rain and lay matted across his forehead. He was unshaven and smelled strongly of stale *vinjak*. The idiot Cistler had referred to was a short Austrian court officer who held him by the arm, preventing him from entering the courtroom.

"I'm here!" Cistler bellowed. His voice was slurred and drunken, and his balance was unsteady. He jerked his elbow loose from the court officer's grip and staggered a few steps farther up the center aisle. "Much to everyone's goddamn dismay, I have come to witness justice!"

The old lawyer gesticulated wildly. His old gray eyes flashed fury and rage, as if Jeremiah himself had entered the court.

The prosecutor general and the presiding judge exchanged puzzled glances.

"Are you ill, Dr. Cistler?" The presiding judge asked and the courtroom erupted into spontaneous laughter. The smell of stale alcohol trailed behind the old lawyer like a loyal pet. Cistler glared through the laughter at the presiding judge, and stumbled several steps up the aisle before he leaned on the back of a chair.

"I am not ill," Cistler barked. "I am drunk. Not just a little drunk. I'm roaring drunk, stinking drunk. If you really want to know how drunk, you'll have to ask Apis how much *vinjak* he poured down my throat."

Again the courtroom broke into laughter.

The presiding judge gestured to a court officer, who came up beside Cistler and took hold of the old man's arm.

"Get your foreign hands off of me." Cistler pulled away from the court officer and continued weaving his way up the aisle. The officer crinkled his nose at Cistler's smell and stared helplessly at the presiding judge.

"I am drunk!" Cistler cried again. There was the rage of vengeance in his voice. The courtroom stilled, and the laughter stopped. "You won't have to disbar me," the old lawyer bellowed at no one in particular. "I resign. I resign from the lunacy of justice. May God in heaven have mercy on all of you crazy bastards!"

Cistler made a sweeping gesture, lost his balance, and fell to his knees. Reluctantly, the officer who had been following Cistler caught the old man's elbow and helped him to his feet.

"You are in no condition to be in court!" the presiding judge snapped.

Cistler threw back his head and laughed. It was a wild, insane burst of laughter. Bitter and angry. Mocking the ears that heard it.

"Drunkenness is the only condition in which this court makes any sense," Cistler roared back at the judge. His eyes were burning with the fire of anger and alcohol. He had ceased to care about his reputation, about the future, about his own life. Only one thing mattered to the very drunk old lawyer, a vague memory of his old school motto: Truth is the wellspring of justice.

The presiding judge ordered the court officer to escort Dr. Cistler out of the courtroom. But the old lawyer pulled away from the officer.

"This court is illegal!" he shouted. "You have no right, no legal right, to exist. Article 25 of the Congress—" Two court officers caught hold of Cistler's arms and began dragging him toward the rear doors.

"I am drunk," Cistler roared as he approached the rear doors. "I am drunk and by this evening I'll have one hell of a hangover. But you crazy bastards are sober, and by this evening you'll have a war on your hands. Tell me what kind of goddamned sense *that* makes! God help us all!"

Gavrilo Princip watched the two court officers thrust Cistler through the doors and wondered if it wouldn't have been more merciful for Apis just to have killed the old man.

Epilogue

For historians of the Great War, this novel will probably read like fiction, which is a good thing, since that is what it is intended to be. Nevertheless, for those readers who are concerned about "what really happened," this epilogue is written.

Prime Minister Pastich, who was real, replied to the Austrian ultimatum at five-forty-seven on July 25, 1914. Pastich had not been in Belgrade when the ultimatum was received and had rushed back from the country to take charge of drafting a reply. His reply was conciliatory, accepting all the Austrian demands except one—that Austria be allowed to send delegates to Serbia to take part in a judicial inquiry against those implicated in the Crown Prince's murder.

Pastich was almost apologetic when he pointed out that Austrian participation in such a judicial inquiry would violate the Serbian constitution and the law of criminal procedure.

Curiously enough, Pastich's reply was handwritten, with many crossings out and insertions. This was because the single typewriter in the prime minister's residence had jammed earlier that afternoon. But messy presentation of Pastich's reply may have helped Berchtold make his decision to reject it.

On July 27, Berchtold went to visit Emperor Franz Joseph and talked the old man into signing a limited mobilization order. Austria broke off diplomatic relations with Serbia. On the following morning, Berchtold took the declaration of war to Emperor Franz Joseph. The emperor paused before he signed it and asked Berchtold if it was really necessary. Berchtold merely nodded, and the Emperor signed.

The declaration of war was telegraphed to Belgrade. Pastich received it just after one in the afternoon on July 28. On July 29, Russia ordered a general mobilization of troops, and two days later Germany declared war on Russia.

On August 3, Germany declared war on France and invaded Belgium. Great Britain, furious over the violation of Belgian neutrality, declared war on Germany. By August 4, most of the industrialized world was at war.

The historical characters presented in this novel have been re-created as faithfully as possible. The story of Crown Prince Ferdinand and his morganatic wife, Sophie, is drawn extensively from historical records. Their bodies were taken by train from Sarajevo to the coast, where they were loaded on a steamer bound for Trieste. At Trieste the imperial couple were put into iron caskets and taken by carriage to Vienna. The carriages, under direct order of Prince Montenuovo, were driven nonstop day and night, exchanging horses every ten miles. Nowhere along the route were the carriages allowed to stop.

The feud between Montenuovo and Ferdinand was not over simply because the crown prince had been assassinated. Montenuovo refused to allow the bodies to lie in state, and since it would be a joint funeral, Montenuovo also refused to allow Ferdinand to be buried with full military honors. No foreign royalty was invited, and most of Austria's royalty missed the funeral because it took place in such great haste.

The funeral took place in a small chapel in the Hofburg. At one end, before the altar, was a raised platform on which the coffins rested. Surrounding the platform was a forest of candlesticks, each burning unsteadily in the drafty winter palace. On the chapel walls were the banners and coats of arms of the different Hapsburg families.

Actually there wasn't one platform, but two. Ferdinand's casket was a good two feet higher than Sophie's. The lid of the Crown Prince's casket was decorated with his imperial crest, his general's cap, his sword, and his medals.

The only decorations on Sophie's casket were a pair of white gloves and a fan—the symbols of a lady in waiting, a rank she had never been able to escape. Even in death Sophie had not escaped humiliation.

Their three children did survive the Great War. By virtue of their father's morganatic oath, they were not considered Hapsburgs and were not exiled by the Austrian Republic in 1918. Later, Ferdinand's sons joined the struggle to keep Austria separate from Nazi Germany.

Ernst went to the Nazi propaganda office in Vienna and ripped down posters of Hitler.

When the first "VIP" transport left Vienna on April 1, 1938, the two brothers found themselves crowded into boxcars on their way to Dachau. At Dachau, Max and Ernst were treated no differently from their barracks mates: Jews, common criminals, and leftists. They witnessed floggings, saw men hung up by their wrists, were made to run in circles with cement blocks tied about their necks, and were starved until continued survival seemed no longer a matter of genuine concern.

During the winter of 1939, the "politicals," including Max and Ernst, were transported to Camp Flossenburg, near the Czech border. They were assigned work in a rock quarry and were housed in outdoor pens. In December dysentery broke out. After some days, the SS guards began to fear contagion and abandoned the camp. During this time both Max and Ernst served as aides to an Austrian inmate doctor.

Their duties consisted of burning corpses to prevent further infection.

In 1940 Max was released, but Ernst was sent on to Buchenwald. After three years Ernst, too, was released. Neither brother recovered his health. Ernst contracted a heart disease and died of a stroke in 1954. Max returned to Artstetten and lived another eight years. Both brothers are buried at Artstetten in a crypt next to the one occupied by their parents.

Their sister, Sophie, now Countess Nostitz, is still alive. She lives quietly in Salzburg.

General Conrad von Hotzendorf, who was quite real, got the war he wanted—a bigger one than even he had bargained for. Hotzendorf's fear of peace was exceeded only by his fear of defeat—a fear that was realized for the empire and for him personally.

Prince Montenuovo, who was also quite real, remained in the highest esteem of the emperor. Regarding the arrangements he made for the funeral of Ferdinand and Sophie, Emperor Franz Joseph sent him a congratulatory message that read in part, "most cordial gratitude and complete appreciation for your excellent and faithful service."

Governor Potiorek of Bosnia got his promotion and was given command of Austria's southern armies against Serbia and Montenegro. Potiorek proved to be a worse commander in the field than he was a host at home. The Serbians mangled his armies and drove him back across the Bosnian border twice before the end of 1914. He was soon replaced, which proved a relief not only to the Austrian army but also to Potiorek, who had lost all his self-confidence and wanted only to retire.

Emperor Franz Joseph died. In 1916 he was succeeded by Archduke Karl, and in 1918 the Austrian monarchy collapsed, and Emperor Karl was exiled.

Count Harrach, who was real, was counted among Ferdinand's few friends. He was not, however, killed in Sarajevo. On the fatal trip from Sarajevo's town hall to the hospital to visit von Merrizi, Harrach rode on the running board of Ferdinand's car, shielding the archduke from attack with his own body. Unfortunately for Ferdinand, Harrach chose the wrong side of the car.

And of the conspirators: Dragutin Dimitrievitch, who was real and was really known as Apis, did, in a span of fourteen years, carry out at least four successful assassinations and planned at least five others. In 1916, Apis sent an emissary to attempt the assassination of Greek King Constantine, and in the next year Apis was brought to trial for seeking contact with the enemy and organizing an assassination attempt against the life of the Serbian heir apparent, Prince Alexander. Although this last accusation has been repeatedly questioned by historians, it was on this charge that Apis was taken to Saloniki, given a perfunctory trial, and executed by a firing squad. According to an eyewitness, Apis died as he wished his own victims had, dry-eyed and smiling.

Ciganovitch, who was also real, did not die in Sarajevo, nor is there any evidence to suggest he was a homosexual. There is evidence, however, that he was a double agent working for the Pastich government. His name was mentioned during the Sarajevo trial, as was Tankosic's. As a result, both Ciganovitch and Tankosic were cited by name in the Austrian ultimatum of July 23, 1914, as men the Serbian government must arrest. Major Tankosic was arrested in Belgrade but was released after the declaration of war. He was killed in action during a Serbian retreat in 1915. Ciganovitch, however, was never arrested by the Serbian government. In fact, he served in Tankosic's regiment during the war. In 1917 Prime Minister Pastich furnished Ciganovitch with money and a false passport and sent him to the United States, where he waited out the war. The price Ciganovitch had to pay for his escape from the Balkans was the open betrayal of Apis. Ciganovitch was the government's star witness at Apis's trial in Saloniki.

In 1919 Milan Ciganovitch returned from the United

States to Serbia, where he received a grant of money and land from the government. He died in 1927, the only conspirator to die of natural causes outside prison.

As you will read in the history books, there were seven conspirators instead of three. Aside from Gavrilo Princip, Nedelijko Cabrinovitch, and Trifun Gabrez, there were Danilo Ilich, Cvetko Popovic, Mehmed Mehmedbasic, and Wasco Cubrilovic. For the sake of the novel, I reduced the conspiracy from seven to three for two reasons—first for simplicity's sake and second because, with the possible exception of Danilo Ilich, the other four conspirators did very little to aid the actual assassination. All four failed to fire their weapons, and none knew the full depth of the planning in Belgrade. It was Gavrilo, Nedelijko, and Trifun who planned the assassination, who received the weapons, and who smuggled them across the border into Bosnia.

Gavrilo, Nedelijko, and Trifun were each sentenced to the maximum the law would allow—twenty years' hard labor.

They were sent to Theresienstadt Prison in the northern part of Austria. The fortress at Theresienstadt would become, only twenty-five years later, an efficient Nazi death camp. By the winter of 1915, Gavrilo was not the only conspirator with consumption. On January 23, 1916, Nedelijko died of tuberculosis.

Trifun lasted a little longer, dying during the winter of 1916 of starvation.

Gavrilo lingered on. The climate in his damp cell proved fertile for the consumption in the marrow of his bones. His flesh rotted. His bones became weak and feeble. To hold his decaying arm in place, a doctor wired his elbow to the upper part of his shoulder. But this could only be a temporary measure, and soon the limb was amputated. Finally, on April 28, 1918, seven months before the end of the war and the birth of Yugoslavia, the nation of united Slavs, Gavrilo Princip died. He was twenty-three.

The Austrians, still not wanting to provide the Southern

Slavs with martyrs, buried the three young men secretly in a Roman Catholic graveyard. One of the soldiers on the burial detail, a Czech, made a map of the graveyard, showing the location of the three unmarked gra▾ ɔs.

In 1920, the graves were exhumed and the bones of the three students, along with the bones of Bogdan Zerajic, were taken to Sarajevo and were given heroes' burials.

Today, the bones of the students lie together beneath a large stone slab. The grave is overgrown and is hardly noticed any more. Even the inscription is difficult to read: "Happy is he who lives forever, for he has reason to be born."